"On the flame of Gracefeel!"
I held my spear, Pale Moon, in both hands and offered a prayer. The wyvern was fighting against the glowing wall, and the veins across its whole body were turning black, noxious air pouring from each and every one. The black miasma was encroaching on the sacred walls, breaking them down, and then—

William

Meneldor

Contents

Prologue	5
Chapter One	14
Chapter Two	51
Chapter Three	84
Chapter Four	121
Chapter Five	181
Final Chapter	229
Afterword	237
Bonus Interview	240

Illustrations: Kususaga Rin
Illustration and Typesetting Design: Kimura Design Lab

Under the sun's light,
a torch avails nothing.
Flamebearer,
where ought thy torch to be?

— Gracefeel's Question

THE FARAWAY PALADIN

Volume 2: The Archer of Beast Woods

Written by
Kanata Yanagino

Illustrated by
Kususaga Rin

THE FARAWAY PALADIN VOLUME 2: THE ARCHER OF BEAST WOODS
By Kanata Yanagino

Translated by James Rushton
Edited by Sasha McGlynn
Layout by Jennifer Elgabrowny
English Print Cover by Kelsey Denton

This book is a work of fiction. Names, characters, places, and incidents are the product of the author's imagination or are used fictitiously. Any resemblance to actual events, locales, or persons, living or dead, is coincidental.

Copyright © 2016 Kanata Yanagino
Illustrations by Kususaga Rin
Cover Illustration by Kususaga Rin

First published in Japan in 2016 by OVERLAP Inc., Tokyo.
Publication rights for this English edition arranged through OVERLAP Inc., Tokyo.

All rights reserved. In accordance with the U.S. Copyright Act of 1976, the scanning, uploading, and electronic sharing of any part of this book without the permission of the publisher is unlawful piracy and theft of the author's intellectual property.

Find more books like this one at www.j-novel.club!

Managing Director: Samuel Pinansky
Light Novel Line Manager: Chi Tran
Managing Editor: Jan Mitsuko Cash
Managing Translator: Kristi Fernandez
QA Manager: Hannah N. Carter
Marketing Manager: Stephanie Hii

ISBN: 978-1-7183-2391-9
Printed in Korea
First Printing: April 2022
10 9 8 7 6 5 4 3 2 1

Prologue

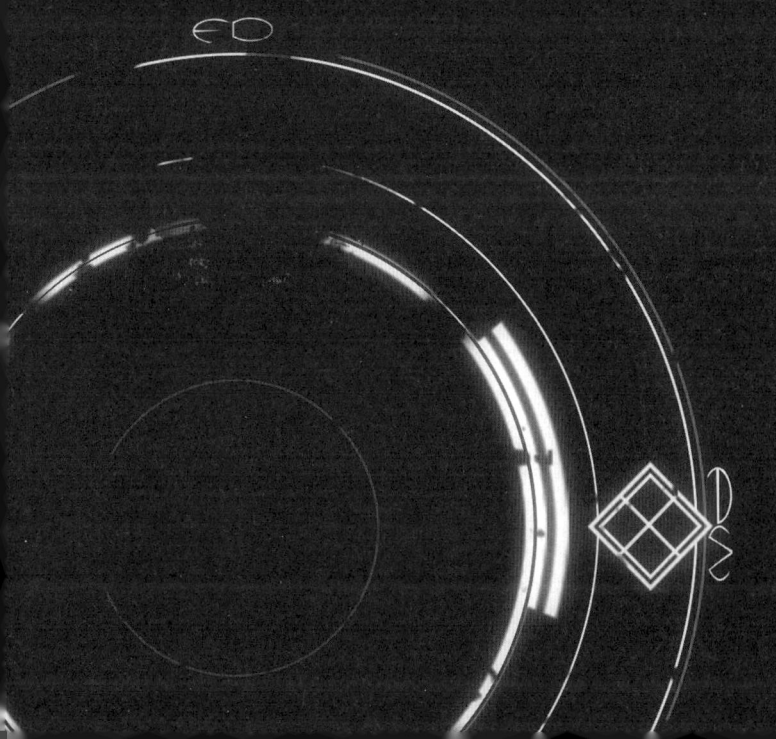

The overcast sky was thin enough to permit the western sun to filter through, but even with my head tilted toward it, I couldn't feel its warmth. I didn't think I needed to worry about frostbite, but the numbing chill of the air was hard to ignore.

This area's climate rarely had snow even when it was cold. When it did snow, there would be a thin layer on the ground at most. I'd known this back when I was in the temple. Even now it was "just" freezing, and there was no sign whatsoever that snow was coming.

I pulled my cloak tighter around me and concentrated on putting one foot in front of the other. I was walking on the dirt by the side of a cobblestone road. Walking *on* the road would actually have been dangerous. It had already deteriorated with age and was full of holes. I'd be likely to trip unless I was very careful.

"Ugh… Too cold." My breath came out as a white mist.

Setting out in winter had, I thought, been a bad move from a common-sense perspective.

I, William G. Maryblood, had left the temple only a few days after that final battle with the god of undeath where I fought to defend my parents' souls. That final battle had been on the day of the winter solstice. That is to say, the middle of winter.

To be honest, even I thought it hadn't been a very wise thing to do, but after making graves for Mary and Blood and giving them a funeral, if I'd spent the winter at that cozy temple waiting for spring,

Prologue

I'd have wanted to stay forever. I'd protect their graves and persuade Gus to let me live my life as the protector of the seal that had long kept the demons' High King imprisoned in that city. It was an attractive, almost irresistible idea, even though I knew it was wrong. However, the act of holing myself up and being spoiled by the gentle tolerance of my family would have been just the same as my previous life. If I stopped moving, if I didn't take action, I could tell that this idea would grow and grow inside me. So I couldn't hesitate. I had to believe in myself and step forward.

That said, I was making very sure I wasn't going to collapse and die by the roadside in the cold weather. If worst came to worst, I was even considering turning around and heading back to the temple for the time being. Gus would probably laugh at me after the overly dramatic way I left, but there was no need to feel bad about turning back. I could just think of it as reconnaissance—checking the condition of the roads and the places that could be used for camping out—and set out again in the spring. Even that would be a much better use of time than just sitting inside and doing nothing. So I took little breaks every once in a while, set up camp when night fell, and all the time in between I walked, just walked, with my gear on my back, enduring the cold.

I'd had several encounters with demons already. That city of the dead was where the High King was sealed, and some of them had probably been keeping watch over it. It wasn't surprising that they were coming to attack me. A human had come out of that city, so they'd obviously want to capture me and make me tell them what I knew. But small fry like them were no match for me. I'd been trained by Blood, Mary, and Gus.

I had several surprise attacks launched against me by strange and misshapen demons that were a blend of animal and human, but I sensed them coming, preempted them, and with the aid of my spear—Pale Moon—I systematically turned them to dust. It was my first time fighting against demons that hadn't been turned undead, but they didn't give me any real problems. I dispatched them swiftly and without hesitation, just as Blood and Gus had taught me to do. I'd fought with an immortal god; no-name demons weren't going to get the better of me now. As for the city of the dead, Gus had told me he'd be strengthening its defenses with a grand magic called Maze Fog, so there was probably no need to worry about it.

My seemingly endless trek occasionally took me past some ruined stone buildings of various sizes. They had probably once been post stations or resting places along the highway. Many of them had either collapsed or been burned or destroyed, the victims of an old war. But there were still some left that retained much of their original structure and promised to make that night's camp somewhat less of a hassle.

Looking at how there had been facilities like this available, I thought that Mary, Gus, and Blood must have lived in a pretty advanced civilization while they were alive. The ancient Roman Empire came to mind from memories of my past life.

"Which would currently put me at the fall of ancient Rome... no, after that. Except we were invaded by demons and not by barbarians..."

From what I could picture based on my previous world's history, it didn't seem likely that things were very good. I used to like history and stuff, enough that I didn't just swallow all the talk about Rome being civilized and the Middle Ages being some kind of "Dark Ages," but even so...

Prologue

"It's been a couple centuries since then, and people still haven't come back here... That can't be a good sign... can it?"

I was talking to myself again. This was what walking on your own for so long did to you, apparently. To keep from being bored I'd also been singing to myself, but even with two worlds' worth of songs to draw from, I was fast running out of material. I'd already gotten sick of the landscape around here too, but I looked around again just for the sake of it.

To the right and a reasonable distance from the main road, there was a pretty impressive river that must have been a few hundred meters wide. The area near it was an expanse of sparse shrubland. I could imagine that when the weather got warmer, those shrubs would grow taller, making it a lot more difficult to see across. The reason there were no big trees along the river was probably that they kept getting flooded out whenever the river swelled, so they weren't able to grow uninterrupted.

Looking beyond the river, there was another expanse, this one of forest. Trees were covering the whole area. It was the same to my left: almost all trees. It was a completely virgin forest, dark and quiet, and pervaded by an atmosphere that felt... I don't know, *forbidding*, like it demanded my respect. If I wandered carelessly into it, I would be constantly tripped up and forced to slow down, and if I lost my sense of direction inside, there would literally be no coming back. So I was avoiding it for now, only going in when I needed to search for firewood for camp, and even then only as far as I had to. I was lucky to have this road right next to a source of water; there was no reason to make things hard for myself. I just needed to follow the path.

I walked a while longer, and the sun started to set. The road was leading me up a hill, and I couldn't tell what the situation was like beyond. I traipsed up it in silence.

When at last the scenery came into view, it took my breath away.

"Wow..."

The ruins of a vast stone city were lit up by the glow of the setting sun. Streets of countless houses spread outwards in a circular fashion from both banks of the large river. Judging by how there were still traces of supports, a large bridge seemed to have once connected the two sides of the city. I could see facilities like a river port and warehouses. This would probably have been quite a prosperous place where traders gathered with their goods.

But now, all of it was horribly destroyed and reduced to ruins.

The wall surrounding the city was pitifully broken in numerous places, and the blackening still visible on the houses suggested they had been burned down, probably shot by flaming arrows. I could also see deep, bowl-shaped craters in various places. It must have been a pretty big spell they used to cause that. And finally, water from the river had flooded in through the destroyed structures, and the town was half submerged.

Prosperity and ruin. The greatness of human accomplishment and the heartlessness of conflict. The flow of time and the impermanence of all things. This sight made all of it more real.

I stood on the hill for a while taking it in and then, after tracing the road ahead of me with my eyes...

"Aghhh..."

Downstream, the large river forked into several branches—perhaps the destruction of the city or a weir had changed its flow—and one of those branches had completely swallowed up the road I was meant to be following.

I put my hand to my forehead and sighed deeply. "The terrain's changed..."

Prologue

Well, of course a river's not going to still be the same after two hundred years. Yup. Nothing I could do about that.

...Now what?

I spent that evening in the ruined city, offering the prayer of Divine Torch so the souls wandering there could pass on. The lost souls followed its flame like fireflies and returned to the night sky. Together with the shadows of the destroyed city wavering in the light of the campfire, they produced a very fantastic scene.

I got up early the following morning and prayed to the god of the flame. I scooped up some water and used a Word to purify it before I drank. Then I used benediction to create holy bread and ate it with some of my supply of meat jerky.

I puzzled over what to do about the road for a little while, but there weren't actually any real choices to be made. I had nothing to help me cross the river, so I just decided to follow its outermost branch downstream.

The ground started to become sludgy with mud; it probably had something to do with the river splitting into lots of tiny branches. The forest around me was feeling increasingly oppressive.

It would be a mistake to venture much farther from the river than where I could still hear it flowing. I decided that if I was unlucky enough to get lost in the forest, I would forgo any other plans and just focus on finding the river and heading upstream. I'd be able to return to the temple that way at the very worst.

How many days had it been now since I left the temple? The fact that I hadn't talked to anyone for days was leaving me feeling very lonely and empty. I prayed as I walked, offering this loneliness, this emptiness, in dedication to my god.

Everything was so quiet.

I was already starting to run out of the meat jerky and other preserved food I'd brought with me. Needless to say, there was a limit to the amount of food I could carry. If this were an ordinary journey, I'm sure I would have just replenished my stocks as needed by buying food from a store or a house as circumstances dictated. But the first goal of this journey was to find a dwelling like that, so resupplying on the way clearly wasn't going to be possible. I was getting to experience firsthand why mountaineers who took on unexplored mountains were so insistent on their food being lightweight and high in calories.

Noon had passed some time ago. It looked like it was going to be another day without discovering any signs of people. If I hadn't learned to produce holy bread with benediction like Mary, the very act of leaving the temple and seeking human habitation might have been physically impossible to begin with, due to the radius of how far I could travel. I felt another wave of appreciation for the god of the flame, and an obligation to express it. For a little while, I immersed myself in prayer.

Suddenly, I heard something. A loud rustling. Something rushing through the forest thickets at a furious speed.

Now, I was fully alert. I flung off the leather sheathing Pale Moon's blade and held the spear at the ready. I was just beginning to wonder if it was another demon attack when a large boar came charging out at me.

Not only was it a bit bigger than an ordinary boar, something seemed to have made it very agitated. Its eyes were bloodshot and it was foaming at the mouth. Its sharp, curved tusks came up to about my thighs.

Prologue

While my brain was uselessly reminding me that getting stabbed in the femoral artery was no laughing matter, my muscles, trained by Blood, were moving on their own. I sidestepped the hog's attack and jabbed my spear in close to where its front legs met its body and it had its most vital organs: its heart and lungs. I felt the blade pierce its skin, and as soon as I knew the blade had gone in deep enough, I yanked it back out to prevent it from being ripped out of my hands. The hog's momentum carried it straight forward, and it crashed headlong into a tree. It staggered about for a while, then spewed blood, collapsed, and stopped breathing.

It looked like I'd gotten a good stab through its major organs. But I knew never to underestimate the toughness of wild animals. You could approach them thinking they were dead, only for them to suddenly go into a frenzy. It was possible to end up seriously injured that way.

I watched it for a moment, and as I started to consider using Pale Moon to stab it one last time from a distance to make sure it was definitely dead, I noticed something. Stuck in the side of the hog opposite to where I'd stabbed it, there was a white-feathered arrow.

"What—"

Before I had time to figure it out, I heard the sound of underbrush rustling again behind me. I turned. Between the trees, shadowed by branches, was the figure of a person.

Chapter One

The stranger was wearing a cloak with a hood that made it difficult to see their eyes, and in their hand they held a uniquely decorated bow. An arrow with white feathers had already been nocked on the string. The stranger hadn't drawn the bowstring back yet, but they seemed to have an alertness about them that told me they could have that done in an instant if they felt like it. Their cloak and outer garb were in hues of soil and grass, and they were wearing tall leather boots and leather gloves. A short machete was hanging from their waist, and they had several other knives as well. This person was probably a hunter.

Dead silence.

Me versus presumed hunter. Neither of us spoke or moved.

The tension thickened with every passing moment.

Not good, I thought. I should have been appreciating the emotion of my first meeting with another living person right now, but I couldn't even afford to do that. This was seriously not good.

First contact had accidentally been established between two complete and total strangers in the middle of the woods. My previous life's knowledge alone could have told me this was an extremely dangerous situation. After all, this was a forest far from civilization. There was no judicial system or law enforcement here. In other words, if violence suddenly broke out, I couldn't hope to receive the slightest bit of assistance. It was a place like that where we had run into each other, both of us strangers, and both of us armed.

Now... what would be the right course of action here?

Should I smile and ask for a handshake or something? I put myself in his shoes: if an armed man I'd suddenly run into grinned at me and held out his hand... could I take that hand?

Maybe I was supposed to let go of my weapon to show I was harmless? What if they already intended on fighting me? And what if they suspected a trap? What about the possibility that when I let go of my weapon, that movement could be misinterpreted as the first sign of an attack?

Use benediction to show I'm a devout follower of a god? No, that would still leave the possibility of me being a priest of an evil god, trying to hide my true nature. What's more, I had to question whether they'd really just stand and watch while I started to use a skill right in front of them.

That's right—*I had no way of proving I wasn't a threat*. And even worse, I didn't belong to a community. Therefore, I couldn't even provide the name of someone who could vouch for me. That meant I had no way to prove my character. In my previous world, cultural anthropologists had warned of the dangers of accidental first contact with unknown people. Tension and wariness ran high in this kind of situation, and it was possible for that to develop directly into a lethal fight.

My heart rate was creeping upwards. The hunter was still deciding how to handle this situation, but I could tell that they were as tense and on their guard as I was; the sharp stare being cast over my equipment from the depths of their hood was proof. They were being pressed to make a decision between fight or flight.

The hunter dropped their hips a tiny amount. The tingling sensation on my skin grew stronger.

Chapter One

This was bad. Just really bad. At this rate, we were going to end up fighting to kill each other.

As I desperately searched for the right words and turned my eyes to what the person was carrying, I suddenly realized: the bow the presumed hunter was carrying—I'd seen that style of bow before, in Gus's natural history lectures. Yes, that was—So I should—

Panicking internally and moving very slowly so as not to trigger an attack from my opponent, I placed my right palm on the left side of my chest, and pronouncing every word as clearly and carefully as possible, I spoke—

"*The stars shine on the hour of our meeting.*"

The hooded person before me seemed surprised. "Old Elvish…?" they said with a tremor of shock in their voice. It was a beautiful voice as clear as a bell. "You have a connection to the elves?"

"No. But I thought you might."

I had a memory of that type of bow. According to Gus's lectures on natural history, Rhea Silvia, the free-spirited goddess of water and greenery, had as her minions a race of beautiful and long-lived people descending from the greater fae that had been created long ago by the Progenitor. They were a race called the elves, and it was to them that this bow belonged. So I thought that using an Elvish greeting might help to loosen a little of the tension.

"Keh!" the hunter spat out disdainfully. "Well, you're not wrong."

I'd guessed right. The hunter's voice had softened a little, but this time it was my turn to be surprised: despite having quite a musical voice, their tone sounded pretty rough. I'd heard that the elves' long lives made them a patient and very graceful race…

"Eh. Whatever." The hunter relaxed their posture and pulled off their hood.

Chapter One

The first thing that caught my eye was the silver hair. Furrowed brows, sharp eyes of jade, a slender nose, elegant chin line, and tight, thin lips. From beneath the hood emerged the face of a boy with a somehow feminine beauty.

His ears weren't the long, pointed ears I might have expected, but were short, about the same size as a human's, and only a little more pointy. If I remembered my lessons correctly, that was characteristic of a half-elf, a child of mixed race born between elves and humans—

"Better question," he said, cutting across my thoughts. "You do that?" He pointed at the hog lying on the ground and then at the blade of my spear, wet with blood.

"Yes, that was me."

He frowned. "That's an old way of speaking…"

I was confused for a moment, but after thinking about it, I realized that about two hundred years had passed since Blood and Mary's time. That was more than enough time for a language to change, even if this world did have races like the elves that lived much longer lives than humans. I must have sounded old-fashioned. Maybe even archaic. In terms of English from my last world, I might have sounded like I was speaking using words like "thou" instead of "you." I'd have to listen to how current people spoke and fix my speech to match so I wouldn't make people wary of me.

"Sorry. It's kind of a habit."

"Weird, but whatever. So this thing," said the silver-haired half-elf, turning the topic back to the hog. "This was mine." He pointed to the arrow sticking out of it.

The arrow's feathers were white, the same as the other arrows in his quiver. The fact that there hadn't been much time between me killing the hog and him turning up also indicated that he probably wasn't lying.

"You butted in and killed it," he said bluntly.

The reason he was practically accusing me of stealing his kill was probably because he was wary of exactly that happening to him. He wanted to stop me before I got the chance.

The urge to say sorry was almost instinctual—a habit from my past life—but I avoided it. "Yes. It came charging at me, so I was forced to do it to defend myself. But—" This was, in fact, a matter for discussion. It was time for negotiation tactics. "I *did* finish it off, so I assume I have at least that much right to it."

I was hoping that this might lead to me finding a village of some kind—though whether that would be an elven one or a human one, I had no idea.

The negotiations went on in depth for a little while.

The silver-haired half-elf was quite the skilled negotiator; I, on the other hand, had no real-world experience in negotiating and was pretty much at his mercy. He appeared to be in the same age bracket as me, but elves—and indeed, half-elves who shared some of the elven blood—were said to live longer, so for all I knew he could have been considerably older than I was. Despite this, I somehow managed to hold my ground, and we eventually settled on a deal where I'd get the shoulder on the side I'd stabbed in exchange for helping to butcher the hog.

Butchering a wild hog takes a good deal of work.

Chapter One

To start with, we had to carry it to a river, bleed it out, then clean it down together. Its fur was covered in mud. It had probably been wallowing in it somewhere.

"Ahhh, the feckin' thing's in bits," Silver-hair said, looking at the head of the arrow he'd pulled out of the wild boar. It had broken to pieces. It must have hit a bone.

I watched him detach the arrowhead and carefully stash it away in his pocket. It looked as though metal items were pretty valuable in this area at the moment. "We've gotta dig out the fragments," he said. "If someone bites into one of those after this thing is meat, they're gonna have a bad time."

We made use of a flat area of rock by the river to carefully take out the fragments of the arrowhead, then started work on butchering the hog. I'd developed some level of skill at this thanks to Blood, but Silver-hair was even more efficient than I was. The subcutaneous fat was delicious on wild hogs, so the test of your knife skill in this situation was how close to the skin you could cut. And he was terrifyingly precise and fast as well.

"Now then." He stuck his knife in under the hog's jawbone and cut all the way around its neck. He looked to have reached the neck bone, so I held the head and twisted it around to dislocate it.

"Heh. You know your stuff." He threw me a grin, so I smiled back. Then, with a few little movements of the knife, he cut through the flesh and sinew and separated the head entirely.

I laid the hog's carcass on its back and held it in position, and he started cutting down its belly all the way from its throat to its back end, being careful to only cut the skin. Cutting in deeply would cause damage to the internal organs, which would result in... um, what's a nice way of putting it... the contents of its intestines, bladder, and reproductive organs spilling over everything and making a huge mess. With this approach, there would be no need to worry.

When he was done with that, he made cuts in a number of places with a hatchet, and then together we forced the ribs apart. We cut around the anus, cut open the chest cavity, cut down the diaphragm, peeled off the membrane down to the backbone...

"Out you come..." He grasped the hog's trachea and esophagus and pulled them toward the back end. All its guts came out at once in a single mass. He was efficient at this.

At this point, it looked quite a lot more like "meat," the kind I'd seen frozen and hung up in movies and on TV in my previous life. I faced the hog's head we'd removed and put my hands together in prayer.

I'm sorry. And thank you. We won't waste what we've taken.

"You're a real believer, aren't you?" he said playfully, gently shrugging his shoulders. "Mmkay, as agreed, one shoulder for you." He skillfully inserted his machete into a joint of the meat which was once a boar and sliced off just its front shoulder. "And that does it for portioning."

"Yep."

With a blood-soaked hatchet and a short machete in our hands, we exchanged smiles in recognition of each other's hard work. "Guess we better eat the liver though. It goes bad real fast," he said.

"Ah, I've got a pan."

Fresh liver is delicious.

We'd been working in the cold, winter river, so my hands were already frozen stiff. While Silver-hair was away collecting driftwood, I gathered together some dry twigs and quickly set fire to them with a whispered *Flammo Ignis*. I thought I'd better keep it a secret that I could use magic for now. It wasn't that I thought he couldn't be trusted... although that was possible. I just didn't know enough about modern society. Magic may have been accepted in Gus's time, but I didn't know how society regarded it today.

Chapter One

"Brrr... Gods, it's cold." I took off my boots and warmed my hands and feet beside the fire.

After a while, Silver-hair came back. "Freezing," he said, tossing some driftwood into the fire. Then he took up position beside me. We grinned at each other for some reason.

"Okay, here's what we've been waiting for," I said.

"Ya."

I held the pan over the flame and put in some hog's fat. Once it had amply coated the bottom of the pan, I put in the strips of liver which I'd already cut up, then shaved off some rock salt and sprinkled it over. A sizzling sound accompanied the gorgeous smell of cooking meat.

I closed my eyes and put my hands together. "Mater our Earth-Mother, gods of good virtue, bless this food, which by thy merciful love we are about to receive, and let it sustain us in body and mind."

"Damn, you really are hard-core religious." The silver-haired half-elf was looking at me incredulously. It seemed he wasn't the type to have much belief in these things.

But thinking about it logically, I was the one with memories of a previous life. Wouldn't it have made more sense for me to be the one impatiently waiting to eat, and him to be religious? Despite being in the middle of prayer, I was amused by how backwards that felt.

"For the grace of the gods, we are truly thankful."

"Awesome. Let's eat."

He may have been impatient, but he was at least polite enough not to ignore my prayer and start eating before me.

After I finished praying, we each took a knife that we'd washed and cleaned, jabbed it into a piece of cooked liver in the pan, and lifted it out. Steam was rising from it. I stuffed it into my mouth.

It was hot. And so delicious. The strong flavor of liver with just a pinch of added salt filled my mouth. Gods, it was good. I caught myself wishing for a cold beer.

Even the wrinkles on Silver-hair's forehead had loosened. Meals eaten after hard work really are delicious.

Before I realized it, the sun had almost set.

"Huh? You want to know... the way? What?"

When I asked him the way after we'd finished eating, he looked at me strangely, just as I'd expected.

That was when I knew I'd been right to leave asking this until the end. The question was a little dangerous. It invited queries that would be difficult to answer. Such as—

"Seriously, where'd you even come from? I've never seen you around here."

"Well, that's... hard to explain. I'm not sure what to say."

If I were one hundred percent honest with him and said, "I was brought up by undead in a ruined city, fought the god of undeath, and set out on a journey," he would find that story so crazy that I had absolutely no confidence that I could get him to believe it. Not having a way to prove who you were made things very difficult, no matter the society. Humans have no way of proving themselves harmless on their own; they can only ask other people to vouch for them. In my previous world that came from social systems like the family register and ID cards, but in this world it seemed to come from your relatives and local community. My not having those was equivalent to declaring to the world that I might be a dangerous person. But a sorcerer who uses Words can hardly afford to lie... so for the time being, I decided to be somewhat vague so I wouldn't have to lie outright.

Chapter One

The elves, who were minions of the god of fae, Rhea Silvia, were said to have a strong affinity with other fae minions. Evidently this half-elf who had inherited elven blood was no exception.

I remembered once reading in one of Gus's books that the essence of elementalism was being sensitive to, empathetic with, and accepting of the nebulous and fickle. It was yet another branch of the mystical, separate from "magic"—the power of Words, with its focus on theory, knowledge, memory, and repetition—and from "benediction," which offered protection and divine grace for acting with religious faith and discipline.

"Bye," he said simply, and plodded away with the hog on his back.

It had been the only conversation I'd had with another person in almost ten days. Maybe that was why I felt a strange urge to not just let him go. Before I knew it, I was calling to him as he left.

"I'm Will! William G. Maryblood! You?"

There was a pause before he responded. "Menel. Meneldor. I doubt we'll be seeing each other again though," he answered, walking away. "Try not to die on the road."

With the butchered hog on his back, he ambled off, the ground around him illuminated by the shining fairy's light. I watched him go without attempting to tail him.

Wary of creatures that might be attracted to the smell of blood, I moved a good distance from where we'd butchered the boar. I kindled another fire and used rope to tie my sheet of canvas between some trees to make a rudimentary tent. I inscribed Signs that would serve as warning alarms in various places and incanted Words with the power to ward off insects and things of a demonic nature. Finally, I laid down my blanket and went to bed. The pork shoulder I got would be tomorrow's breakfast.

I'd held a conversation with a real, living person. It had actually gone surprisingly well. I'd been worrying for nothing.

Menel. Meneldor. I seemed to remember that it meant "a very fast-flying eagle" in Elvish. He had been a bit rude, but I'd had fun talking to him.

He'd said we'd probably never meet again. As I drifted off to sleep, I hoped that someday we would.

In the dead of night, I heard a voice.

"O flame."

In the fog between slumber and wakefulness...

"O flame of mine."

...was a young woman with black hair and a hood that obscured her eyes.

"As you travel these faraway lands—"

Ever reticent and expressionless, she spoke her wish:

"Prithee, bring light to the darkness."

And then, like strikes of lightning, numerous visions lit up the inside of my head, burning themselves into my mind.

Weapons. Screaming. Chaos. Blood. Blood. Bodies. Bodies. Bodies. And—silver hair.

I inhaled sharply.

"*Lumen!!*"

As I imbued light into Pale Moon's blade, I hurriedly readied my equipment and dashed into the night forest.

I kept moving, my path lit by magic. That I had no faster way was maddening. The revelations had blatantly been forecasting a tragedy, and Menel was going to be victim to it.

Chapter One

I clenched my teeth.

I'd been suspecting it, but now it was confirmed: the age I was living in was seriously dangerous. Someone you met today could be a corpse tomorrow. Crazy...

I looked around me. There was nothing but dark forest. The winter meant that the grass wasn't too overgrown, at least, but I doubted I'd be able to reach Menel's village in this blackness just by pressing on blindly. I did have the option of tracking his footprints, but if I was that thorough with my search, I didn't know if I'd make it in time. Not to mention that Menel might well have covered his tracks. He was wary of me, after all, and he was a professional hunter. If he was remotely serious about hiding his tracks from me, I wouldn't be able to do anything about it.

I incanted a number of Words in quick succession. These were Words of Searching, to use for detecting things.

"That way!"

It was a simple magic that only estimated general direction, but it was better than nothing.

I got ready to be very reckless.

Holding my shield up, I powered through the forest thickets, leaped down a steep slope, and incanted Feather Fall to soften the landing. I pushed onward, making heavy use of a variety of techniques that anyone used to normal forest walking would definitely frown at if they saw me.

The fact that there was a settlement meant that there should be a pretty open space somewhere. Stopping from time to time to get a general sense of direction with the Words of Searching, I kept on running.

All of a sudden—there it was. I could see open land outside the forest. There were fields with rows of furrows, and beyond them, through the darkness of night, I could just about make out the outlines of a dozen or so houses surrounded by a wooden fence. It looked like nothing was amiss.

"I'm... not too late?"

No... There was a chance, a reasonably good chance, that the tragedy had already occurred. I didn't know the cause of what I'd seen in that revelation. It could be a demon, a goblin, an undead creature, a beast... If I approached carelessly, it was possible that I'd take a hit before I was ready.

I incanted several Words and killed the light dwelling in Pale Moon's blade. First things first: scouting. I decided to keep my ears open and approach with caution. Keeping my body low to the ground, I exited the forest and approached the fields. Then, I heard talking.

"Thought I saw something shining in the forest..."

"Sure you weren't seeing things?"

There were two lanterns, and they were getting closer. Holding the lights were two men, one middle-aged and one an adolescent, each wearing a fur smock over a faded tunic and carrying a club in his hand. My first thought was that they might be on village night patrol. At least, they didn't seem on edge as they would have if a disaster had occurred.

Then things weren't as I'd seen them in that revelation yet, after all. Thank the gods.

"Hm?"

As I was beginning to relax, the older of the two men noticed my shape caught in his lantern light. I smiled awkwardly at him and decided to walk over. I figured that if I named myself as an acquaintance of Menel's, they wouldn't immediately get rough with me. They looked at me and had barely opened their mouths to speak when I stepped forward hard and lunged out with my spear.

Chapter One

"Wha—?!"

"Hyeeek!"

There was an echo of clashing metal. I stepped forward again and swung my spear to the side without breaking flow. There was another metallic clash.

"Get back!" I stood in front of the two to protect them, blocking whatever it was that was flying at us with my shield.

The attacker! If they were using a projectile weapon, then they weren't a beast. That left demons, goblins, and the undead. I quickly glanced at what had fallen, hoping I'd be able to pin down the identity of my opponent.

It was *an arrow with white feathers.*

My mind froze. That very instant, there was a sudden noise. The twang of a bowstring! I raised my shield and deflected the arrow flying my way.

Arrows coming from the front are essentially points. It's very difficult to knock them away with a spear. While shielding the most vulnerable areas of my body, I expanded my conjured light and looked in their direction.

At the end of my line of sight… frowning with a serious look on his face… was a silver-haired half-elf with an arrow nocked on the bow in his hand.

Behind him stood about ten more men in slightly dirty clothes, armed with basic clubs and spears. There was no doubt.

"Menel…"

Menel's settlement? A disaster was going to befall him? I had to rush in and save him? How foolish had I been…

Menel—Meneldor wasn't going to be a victim of the tragedy I'd witnessed.

He was the *perpetrator.*

My brain couldn't keep up. Why was Menel... We'd shared laughs and smiles together, hadn't we...?

"Go. Secure the village," Menel ordered. "I'll deal with him."

The men behind him started to scatter.

"Wai—" I tried to move to stop them when another arrow flew my way. If I dodged it, its course would take it right into the two behind me. I deflected it with my shield.

"I said not to follow me... Seriously, brother..." Some kind of emotion flashed in Menel's eyes, but it disappeared in an instant. "Die."

The feat I saw in the next moment was incredible. He fired three arrows—aimed at my face, arm, and leg—in a single, fluid, uninterrupted motion.

My mind was still a muddle, but my body—trained by Blood—reacted to Menel's amazing attack with precision. While using my shield to knock away the arrows coming at my arm and face, I pulled my leg back and turned my body sideways, dodging the final arrow.

"Ah... ah..." The wordless gasps of the two behind me began to turn into screams. They had finally started to understand the situation. "Everyone! Wake up! Wake up!"

"We're under attack! Bring weapons! Hide the women and children!"

"Tch!" The screams seeming to put him under pressure, Menel fired more arrows at me. Every one of them was brutally accurate. I was certain that if I hadn't had a shield, I'd already have several arrows sprouting out of my body. And to think I'd considered not bringing it at all; as it turned out, this thing was saving my life.

As I advanced while keeping up my defense, Menel retreated, keeping the same distance between us.

Chapter One

If this was his ideal separation, then... I'd close that distance!

"*Acceleratio!*" An explosion of speed—

"'*Gnomes, gnomes, slip underfoot!*'" Menel shouted at almost the same time. The ground suddenly wriggled all over, trying to take my legs out from under me.

In all likelihood this was Slip, a spell that made use of gnomes, the earth elementals. I was still accelerating; if my foot got caught, my momentum would likely cause a fracture.

I could see Menel grinning with satisfaction. He'd used that elemental power at the absolutely perfect moment, and I had no immediate strategy for dealing with this kind of thing. And since I had no strategy—

"SSEHHH—HNG!" I slammed my foot down with all my strength. There was a thunderous *boom*. The ground shook powerfully, and the gnomes stopped their work as if frightened into stillness.

"*What?!*" Menel gaped at me. So did the men trying to attack the village. Even those who had come out with weapons, intending to fight back, were staring at me with eyes wide open.

They were all evidently unaware—that if you got ripped, you could solve pretty much everything by force!

"Fig!" Menel backed off further, cursing.

After shooting arrows at me in quick succession, he slung his bow over his shoulder and started throwing knives. They came at me in an arc—maybe he had a special way of throwing them, or maybe the knives themselves had some trick to their design—curving toward me from the left and right. The ones that were safe to avoid, I dodged by turning my body; those that weren't, I deflected with my shield. I pressed even closer. Shields really were convenient. I was glad I'd brought one.

Menel looked like he had finally resigned himself to face me. He held his hatchet ready to strike, and then—

"'Salamander! Scorch him!'"

From behind, Fire Breath bellowed toward me out of the flames of the middle-aged man's lantern. Without turning around, I stuck out my spear and thrust it into the flames, dispersing them. I'd pretty much seen that coming.

"No way." Menel looked stupefied.

His feint was positively straightforward compared to the god of undeath's lack of scruples and the tricks Gus and Blood had pulled on me when they got serious.

As Menel stood there, I closed the distance.

"You're feckin' strong..." he said with a bitter smile on his face.

I rammed the handle of my spear into his solar plexus.

I heard the air being forced out of his lungs, and he fell to his knees. His diaphragm was spasming and he couldn't control his breathing. He wouldn't be able to move properly for a while. In the meantime, I incanted the Word of Web-making to restrain him.

I looked toward the village. There was no battle; everyone had just been watching our fight in amazement. I counted myself very lucky.

I decided to capture the rest of the raiders before anyone got hurt.

The outcome: nobody died.

After striking down Menel, I managed to neutralize the rest of his ten-strong band of raiders with relative ease by using the Words of Sleep and Paralysis. Somehow or another, a terrible raid had been avoided, and although there were a few people injured, I had no trouble healing them with my benediction.

Chapter One

Because of this, I received a great deal of thanks from the people of the village as "a passing kindhearted holy warrior"—but by the time the sun had started to rise on the village square at its outskirts, my face was showing nothing but displeasure.

In the center of the square was something like a small shrine, where a pile of irregularly shaped stones had been stacked. It was a shrine dedicated to the good gods. I could imagine that it had been created by piling up stones that villagers had unearthed while cultivating the fields and didn't know what else to do with. In that sense, it was probably also a monument to their agricultural efforts.

If the custom here was the same as what Gus had taught me, important discussions were often held before the gods in small settlements like this, sometimes while making oaths to them. Even in my previous world, there were many regions that held assemblies and important votes before their gods. In this world, however, where the gods could exert their influence upon reality, this custom carried even greater significance.

At this very moment, in this square with its shrine, the men of the village were holding a debate concerning how to deal with the village's assailants, who had been paralyzed and tied up.

"For the hundredth time—"

"Hang the ruddy buggers! End of discussion!"

"Listen to what I say to you!"

"First off—Hey! I said, first off—"

"They just suddenly came and attacked us!"

"Look, that ain't what's important here!"

What a mess. In fact, it looked like everyone was just shouting at each other.

This was awful.

For a moment, I wondered why they were behaving like this—and then I suddenly realized something about the villagers. They all had different skin tones, each one of them had a different accent, and in their agitation, some of them were angrily shouting out coarse vocabulary I hadn't heard from any of the others.

As I took notice of this with surprise, a middle-aged man approached me.

"My 'umble apologies, sir, for the disgraceful display. Thankee kindly for the 'elp, I'm much obliged." He bowed his head to me. I realized that this was the same man I had met earlier, one of the two who had come under Menel's first attack. "Name's John, sir."

"Ah, you're welcome. Umm... My name is William. Uhh... So..." Ignoring the people yelling at each other for the time being, I tried to get a better picture of things through John.

Just as I'd heard from Menel yesterday, I was currently in Beast Woods, Southmark. The woods were deep and expansive, with ferocious creatures and even more dangerous "beasts" running rampant. As a result, John explained, the influence of the Fertile Kingdom that ruled this area did not extend here.

"I will say that we 'ave a lot of characters of, shall we say, int'restin' 'ist'ries..."

Criminals, runaway serfs, those who had fled here from fallen nations, would-be adventurers still trying to make their way by ruin-hunting—all kinds of people who, for one reason or another, couldn't live in the city had naturally gathered together and formed this village. Apparently, there were a number of such settlements dotted about these woods.

Naturally, the settlers' places of origin, their norms, and their perceptions of law all varied wildly. No wonder they were like this when they tried to hold a meeting. I sympathized with their difficult situation, but at the same time—

Chapter One

"I wonder what will happen to them." I glanced at Menel. He had been bound by the Words of Web-making and Paralysis and left to lie on the ground; I couldn't see his expression from where I was standing.

If you formed a group and raided a village in an area beyond the reach of the law, then failed and got captured... I had to admit what would happen to you was kind of predictable.

Menel would be killed at the hands of the mob and left to hang... or something along those lines, I guessed.

That left a bad taste in my mouth. I could sense that I was acting soft—a carryover from my past life—but there was still something making this a little difficult for me to accept.

As selfish a reason as it was, the idea that people I'd captured were going to die—that I would, in essence, cause the deaths of others—wasn't something I wanted to be confronted with, nor did I want brutal mob justice to be one of the first things I got to see upon entering civilization. Furthermore, even if he was a bandit, I didn't feel good about the prospect of watching someone I knew, someone I'd had a conversation with, die in front of me in a state of paralyzed confusion.

I mean, after leaving the city, I figured the first place I'd come across would be an outskirt area with poor law and order, so I'd been prepared for things to get a little rough, but I never expected it to go this bad this fast.

Fighting off bandits is a classic adventure-story trope, but now that I'd run into them in real life, I realized how hard they were to deal with. You couldn't just send them on their way and expect no trouble later. As I was wondering whether there was anything I could do—

"'Fraid I don't know what's gonna 'appen to them, either."

"You don't know?" I tilted my head. In a situation like this, I'd been expecting that whatever solution they settled on would probably involve killing the raiders.

"They're familiar faces, see. Our neighbors, if you will, from th' nex' village over. Ah, I say neighbors, but they ain't immediately adjacen' to us. There's a day's walk between us through the woods and 'cross a brook."

"Huh?"

The neighboring village raided them? In the middle of winter? Without any warning?

"They weren' well off, none of us are, but they 'ad enough provisions, 's far's I know... I'd've said they were right nice people for residents o' these woods, and I though' we'd been getting along quite well 'til now."

Hmm. That did sound mysterious.

"Wha's more, tha' silver-'aired elf, 'e 'as a good reputation 'round this neighborhood as a renowned wand'ring 'unter. 'E's 'elped us many times in eliminating dangerous beasts. Sev'ral of us here owe our lives to 'im. I don' understand it."

I was starting to see where John's doubts were coming from and had just nodded in agreement when I noticed a shift in all the shouting at the meeting.

"Very good, very good," an old man said, clapping his hands loudly. "I'm sure you're all getting tired of talking. Why don't we all have a drink of water?"

It did look like everyone had yelled themselves hoarse at this point. The old man must have been waiting for that perfect moment to join the meeting.

He was short, with hair that had turned almost completely white, and he used a cane. He seemed friendly, but he had a look in his eyes that told me he was a man to keep a close watch on.

Chapter One

The small scar near his left eyebrow was very distinctive. It looked like an old blade wound.

"Tha' old gentleman is Tom," John told me helpfully. "'E's the village elder."

While the water jug was being passed around, Tom began to speak. "All right. You don't have to stop drinking, but I'd like it if you would listen to what I have to say for a moment. First of all, just to check: the ones laid out here are mostly from the next village, yes? And then there's the silver-haired hunter."

The elder's speech had a smooth flow to it that seemed to draw me in. Because he'd timed this just when the villagers were tired of talking and were now drinking and taking a breather, all those men who had shouted so much were making no attempts to interrupt the elder's words. *He's clever*, I thought.

"John, I believe you saw these people rush into our village last night, armed with weapons. Is that correct?"

Everyone's eyes turned to John, who was sitting some distance away from the rest of the others at the meeting.

"I did indeed, Elder," he replied calmly, nodding. "And I was saved by this 'oly warrior."

"Mm. Please, allow me to also express my thanks."

"There's no need," I said. "It's, uh… It was all thanks to the guidance of the god of the flame."

"Then I must express my gratitude to that god as well," Tom replied. Turning to the shrine, he gave an informal bow of worship and smiled. His expression reminded me just a little of Gus.

He briefly shot me a meaningful glance, and while I was still trying to figure out what exactly it meant, he continued. "Well, let's see. For the time being, can we assume that while we're here discussing this, you will protect us in the event that something happens?"

"Hmmm..."

It sounded as though Tom wanted this conversation to head toward getting an explanation from the bandits. He wanted to get to the point where he could say that it'd be safe to release their paralysis because I'd be around for protection if they started getting violent again. I thought for a moment and replied, "On the flame of Gracefeel, I will protect everyone here."

The reason I kept the object of that sentence vague was just in case I found out this village had a good reason to come under attack. Depending on the circumstances, I might also have to protect the assailants.

"Then we'll be safe even if they turn on us again," Tom said, smiling lightly. He seemed to have picked up on my intentions. "Everyone, I am thinking we should start by getting them up and asking them some questions. What do you all say?"

One of the villagers who had been chugging down water finished his drink with an audible sigh of satisfaction. "Elder," he said, "it ain't a good idea to give people you're gonna be hangin' a chance to chat. You start feelin' sorry for 'em and then it ain't so easy to do the deed. Stuff like this is best done quick."

I could see a few people agreeing.

The people this far out were probably reasonably used to rough things like this. The fact that they half knew their attackers probably had a lot to do with it as well.

"Surely you must agree it's dangerous to remain ignorant of the facts? Besides, it wouldn't be good to make the holy warrior who helped us out think we've got something to hide." Tom seemed to have gotten the villagers onto his side. He turned to look at me.

I nodded back.

Menel may have had a blunt personality, but he hadn't looked like a person who enjoyed killing people and stealing their goods to me.

Chapter One

And although I'd entertained the possibility, it didn't seem like the people of this village knew any reason why they deserved to be attacked, either.

What on earth had happened here? What was the reason that these people had attacked their neighbors?

While pondering that mystery, I went from person to person and undid the Words.

◆

After I went around unbinding the people from the neighboring village and asking them to explain themselves, a situation jumped out at us that was even more dreadful than before.

"Demons. Our village was done in by demons…"

"Many people died."

"They brought beasts the likes of which I'd never seen…"

To summarize what they told us: Their village, which was about a day from here, had apparently been devastated by an attack from demons and the beasts they brought with them. Around half the villagers had been killed, several buildings had been burned to the ground, and those lucky enough to have escaped with their lives had nowhere to go. With women, children, and the injured to protect, they were left to simply await death in the bitterness of winter, without food, walls, a roof, or a single possession.

That was the situation they were in when—

"I was the one who suggested looting," Menel said in a low tone, his head down. "They wouldn't have stood a chance of beating demons backed up by beasts. I suggested that instead of just lying down and dying, they go loot somewhere nearby, fill their bellies, and go somewhere else. Anywhere else."

Apparently, Menel had happened to pass by that village while tracking the wild boar and had quickly gathered their situation. Then he'd hunted down the boar to satisfy their immediate needs and returned with the meat as they stood freezing in the forest. That was when he had suggested looting, and rallied the men together to carry out a night raid.

From their point of view, this village likely couldn't afford to take in many refugees, and even if they attempted to ask for their help, they could see the rejection coming. If the village was concerned about them becoming thieves, they might even be attacked. In which case, they might as well become thieves in the first place, attack before the village understood the situation, take the goods, and get away from the demons.

In a place where the kingdom's power didn't reach, it certainly was a logical decision to make in a crisis. But then, Menel—

"You didn't live in that village, right?" I asked. "Why did you go so far out of your way for them?"

"Marple, the old lady from the village," he said briefly. "She did a lot for me."

"What happened to Marple?" Tom asked, frowning.

"They said she died."

"...I see." He nodded quietly.

"I was the one who suggested it. Hang me. I led the others astray. Let them go. Please."

The discussion was thrown into disorder. Screams and shouts began to be traded back and forth: some crying, "Like hell we can do that, hang 'em all," others saying they should find some way to offer protection to old acquaintances, while others insisted they couldn't possibly provide for them.

John and Tom wore grim expressions.

"Elder..."

Chapter One

"Mm."

They were in a situation where village-destroying demons were right nearby, but before that discussion could get underway, they first had to pass judgment on these people, who were both their neighbors and originally victims themselves. It must have been frustrating.

"We have a debt to the hunter, and I sympathize with the plight of our neighbors... However," he said painfully, "they must hang."

Even if the villagers released them, they would still have no place to go and would probably plan another raid. Which meant that now that they'd attacked, the village had no choice but to kill them, both for their own protection and to save face.

Even if unavoidable circumstances had led the raiders to this, the villagers would still kill them for safety; they had neither the methods nor the resources to save them. The attackers, too, knew that even if they had asked for help, no mercy or tolerance would have been afforded them, and that was why they'd had no choice but to opt for violent methods from the beginning.

Being rational meant being cruel. This was the exact concern my parents had voiced about the outside world. The state of things out here was indeed dark.

Many people would have called this a hopeless situation. They would have said that was the kind of violence and cruelty often found in remote places, and no good could come of getting tangled up in it.

I had neither a reason to intervene in this incident nor a duty to get involved to begin with. I could just pretend I hadn't seen a thing, and keep on heading to the town up north. I was sure I could find some way to fit in if I found an urban area that was slightly more civilized. There was no point in getting caught up in every bit of trouble I came across.

I knew that would be the wise decision.

However.

My mom had told me that she wanted me to do good, to love people without being afraid of loss. My dad had told me to always move forward and have confidence in the outcome, to not let my worries hold me back. And their words were still there in my heart.

And so I decided to say *screw it* to being wise, and take a tiny but daring step forward.

"Excuse me!"

For the sake of the words my parents had left me, for the sake of keeping the oath I'd made to my god, I was going to try to overturn the "hopeless situation" before me.

◆

I raised my voice as loud as possible, and to my relief, everyone turned my way. Enunciation was important to using the magic of Words effectively. I was using the training Gus had given me to its fullest.

Spreading my arms wide exaggeratedly to focus their attention, I chose my first words carefully—

"Can this be solved with money?!"

The villagers' eyes looked as if they might pop out of their heads. I pressed on, trying to stay one step ahead of their comprehension.

"Compensation. Atonement money. Do you have a custom like that here?"

According to Gus, it was a custom in many regions that when some kind of wrong had been committed, the matter could be settled with a payment of silver or livestock instead of blood. The knowledge I had from my previous life supported that claim. Such customs had been

Chapter One

followed in regions all over the world, from Germanic to Celtic, Russian, and Scandinavian. I read somewhere that it still existed in some modern-day Islamic areas, where you could choose between qisas or diya—retaliation or compensation.

At this rate, blood would be shed. If I could solve that with money, then that was what I was going to do. I could imagine what Gus would say: *"How wonderful money is—it can even buy blood and retribution!"*

"Ho-Hold up, hold up! Sure, we do that, but who the hell is gonna pay?"

"These guys ain't got no more than the clothes on their backs!"

I got a response. What's more, it hadn't been "Atonement money?! How dare you!" but rather a practical question of who would pay. If they'd rejected the idea flat out, things would have gotten complicated, so I very gratefully snapped at the opportunity they'd given me.

Inside my head, the mental machinery that Gus had equipped me with was being set in motion.

"*I* will pay!"

Murmurs again spread throughout the crowd.

"Settle down, everyone." Tom calmed the villagers, then asked me, "Why is that, holy warrior?"

"It is because demons are my mortal foes and caused my parents' deaths." While I exaggerated a little to make myself sound more convincing, it wasn't a lie. It was true that Mary and Blood had died because they had stood against the demon forces. "And I am a priest bestowed with my god's protection. I have sworn an oath to my god, the god of the flame, to drive away evil and bring salvation to those in sorrow. If evil demons have done harm to these people, then these people shall have my aid."

45

I declared my position as I stood and gestured dramatically. These speaking tricks had also come from Gus.

"Furthermore, the demons cannot be left alone to occupy that village. I will head there to fight them. That being the case, the man over there—" I pointed at Meneldor. He was looking at me, dumbfounded. "He is a talented hunter who knows the woods, is he not? I would like to hire him to track down the demons. I will pay handsomely."

The buzz of chatter arose from the villagers once more. If they could reclaim their demon-besieged village, there would be no need to fight each other. The outstanding grudge could be settled with atonement money, and they could call it even. Everybody wins, with the sole exception of one benevolent holy warrior known to nobody, who would suffer a reasonably large loss.

They talked things out amongst themselves, and it wasn't long before they came to the same understanding. The fact that I had tossed a few gold and silver coins in front of them had also given them an effective push.

"Are you certain abou' all this, sir?" John asked me. "This arrangement's all upside's far's I can see, but there's nothing in it for your good self—"

I smiled back at him. "If you gain from this situation, then it will have been the gods blessing you all for your good natures," I said while praying to my god for a tiny miracle. "Gracefeel, god of the flame, ruler of souls and samsara, is watching over your lives with eyes of mercy."

As I spoke those words, the miracle I wished for appeared. A tiny flame rose up before the village square's shrine dedicated to the virtuous gods. A low gasp came from the onlookers, who chanted words of gratitude and offered their own prayers.

Chapter One

I helped people in a crisis while spilling as little blood as possible. And though I might have overdone the presentation a little, I reminded them that you exist, as well. I suffered a bit of a financial loss, but as your hands, as your blade—maybe the way I overcame that situation wasn't too bad?

After I whispered this in my mind, I got the feeling that somewhere, my god had given me a little smile.

◆

I talked it over with everyone, and we had a representative from each village take part in a sworn ceremony to settle their bad blood.

As soon as that was done, I set about protecting the survivors of the demon-attacked village who had been physically unable to participate in the raid, such as women, the elderly, and children. They were huddled together around a campfire in the forest, shivering from the cold. They were frightened of me at first, but after I got Menel to explain the situation, they quickly understood.

Many of them were injured or starting to catch colds, so I healed them using the blessings Close Wounds and Cure Illness. Then, I got the first village to shelter them temporarily, with the promise that it would only be until I retook the village that had been attacked.

They took them in with open arms, though I was pretty sure there wasn't an ounce of goodwill in why they did so. Yes, we'd struck a deal, but they were probably also considering the value of holding them as hostages against the men, who they'd also been forced to take in for the time being. That said, protection was protection, and I was glad for it.

I imagined what would happen if I died trying to take back the village. It was possible they'd become unable to support the people they'd sheltered and be forced to kill them. As I prayed by the shrine, I thought about how I had to win at all costs.

Meneldor approached me. "What's your endgame?"

"Hm? What I said it was. I'm not hiding anything." I couldn't ignore the spread of the demons, and I wanted to keep everyone from killing one another. All I had done was take the measures necessary in order to make that happen.

"Oh, right, I'm working for you already. I guess it's easier to ask for forgiveness than permission."

Oops. That wasn't how it was meant to go. I felt like it was important to get Menel's approval. "Can I hire you to reclaim the village and track down the demons?"

He frowned. "Uh, brother? I incited pillaging and murder. Are you sure you don't need to pass judgment on me, O holy warrior?"

"I've already closed the book on that by paying them compensation. And you didn't do it by choice, right? You couldn't abandon the village—the village that helped you—in its hour of need."

I could have just said that a sin was a sin. All of them, Menel included, had technically had the option of lying down and dying without harming anyone, and if they had been able to choose that option, that may have been very noble.

But choosing to steal from another instead of accepting death wasn't despicable; it was natural. Even more so if they had people like women and children they felt an obligation to protect.

"I'd prefer not to pass judgment on a normal person making a normal decision if I can help it..."

He tutted. "Ever thought I might hold a grudge and stab you in the back?"

Chapter One

"If I die, it's the villagers who suffer." At least until I took back the village from the demons. I couldn't imagine that the silver-haired hunter in front of me was incapable of weighing the gains against the losses.

Menel finally looked away. "You're an easy mark. Someone's gonna rob you blind someday soon, and that'll be the end of you."

"Maybe, yeah." I couldn't help smiling. That was a future I could imagine. I reminded myself that I couldn't keep on taking from Gus's gift; I had to earn money somewhere to make back the amount I'd used.

"Keh. Whatever, brother. I'll work for you. I need the money for them, anyway."

"Yeah. Thanks for your help."

Menel's lips curved cynically, and he nodded. "On that subject, what are we doing then, *master*?"

"Moving on in, I guess? We can't afford to waste time..."

That was followed by silence and a faultfinding stare.

I... I did have a plan... of sorts... But maybe I should have expected he'd be against this. Maybe I had been a bit thoughtless...

"Eh, you're right." Surprisingly, he nodded. "We *had* better move fast. I mean, *there's a good chance the guys in the village have become undead.*"

I fell silent. I'd forgotten.

Just as this world was filled with the protection of the virtuous gods, it was also filled with the *benevolent* protection (depending on your perspective) of the god of undeath, Stagnate.

It was extremely rare for the god of undeath to call out directly to talented heroes, form a contract with them, and create high-level undead, as had happened with Mary and Blood. However, due to the pervasive nature of the gods' protection, it was nothing special for a person who died with lingering regrets to rise again as one of the undead, and it could happen for any number of reasons, including enmity, confusion, or simply death coming too suddenly to realize or accept.

"There's no need to give the guys back in the village an eyeful of their undead parents, siblings, and children. We should probably finish 'em off quick if we can."

I nodded in agreement. "I have to return them to samsara before they start wandering and become lost."

I only needed to locate them, and I could return them to samsara with the god of the flame's benediction. But I couldn't do anything about lost souls that I had no way of finding. I had to act before that happened.

"But do we have a chance against the demons in the village?" Menel asked. "If there's a whole pack of them, and they've got beasts as well..."

"Yeah."

Well... Yeah, I thought. *I don't think that part's going to be a problem, Menel.* After all, I'd been mowing down undead demons day after day under that city of the dead, so by now—

"I'm used to it."

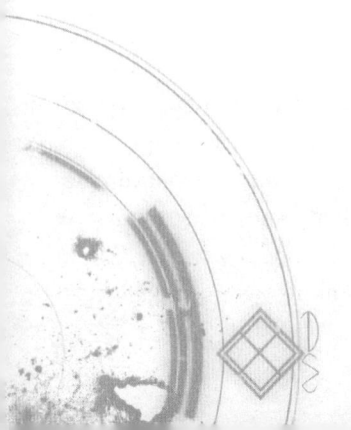

Chapter Two

The following morning, after spending the night under their hospitality, I was seen off by Tom, John, and the other villagers, and I left to take the other village back from the demons.

Guided by Menel, I made my way northeast. After a reasonable distance, I met a branch of the wide river, took some stepping stones across it, and moved on through the forest. Treading on dead leaves and clambering over the mossy trunks of fallen trees, I followed after Menel with an appropriate level of caution.

I'd gotten surprisingly used to following his trail. These woods had such bad visibility I was close to losing my bearings, but Menel pressed forward without hesitation. From time to time, he called to the fairies, and the thickets and bushes moved themselves out of his way.

Blood once told me to never get in a fight with an elf in a forest, and now I understood clearly why: the odds were good that you wouldn't even get a fight; you'd just be toyed with and killed.

Taking periodic breaks, we advanced through the forest quite quickly.

"We'll camp here," the half-elf said.

The sun had started to set. We'd been told that it was about a day to the neighboring village, so our destination was probably very close.

Chapter Two

"*'People of green, grant me a night's shelter. A bed of grass and roof of trees, and tolerance for a sudden guest.'*" He incanted a spell to call the fairies, and the trees around us bent into a dome. Soft grass grew at our feet, and bushes crowded together on the outside to protect us.

"Wh-Whoa, incredible!" It was worthy of being called a tent of trees. As elementalist techniques went, that had to be pretty difficult, didn't it?

"It's not that impressive. Go to sleep."

"Don't we need someone on watch?"

"We'll leave that to the fairies dwelling in the trees. If anything happens, they'll make a fuss and wake us up."

The amount of effort I'd had to go through to camp up until now seemed ridiculous.

Menel was a skilled hunter and expert elementalist. As an enemy he was frightening, but as an ally, he was a great asset. Now if only he'd open up to me a little more…

"Hmph." There he went again.

"Did I do something wrong?"

"I'm what you call ill-bred, I guess. I don't like guys like you who look like they had a cushy upbringing. I'll repay my debts, and I'll do my job properly, but that's as far as it goes."

So unapproachable, I thought.

"We'll be at the village tomorrow morning. I'm guiding you and that's all. I don't plan on helping you beat up demons."

"Yeah, I know."

Menel had a sullen look on his face. We'd had the fortune to meet, and although we'd crossed swords, I wanted us to get along. But I wasn't having an easy time of it.

A while after we both went silent, Menel was lazily gazing in the direction we'd be heading tomorrow. After seeing the pained look in his eyes, I couldn't bring myself to intrude and ask about the relationship he'd had with the people of that village.

We lay there in silence on the soft bed of grass, and I slowly fell asleep. The magical awning of greenery felt very comforting.

◆

The following morning, a thick fog filled the frigid air; maybe it was because we were next to a river. The way that milk-white mist drifted slowly between the trees felt as if I had wandered into a place not of this world.

As I walked onwards following Menel's lead, the foundations of an ancient stone wall came into view.

"A ruin?"

"Yeah. Nearby."

Due to factors like the availability of water and transport, the places most suitable for establishing a settlement weren't that much different now than they'd been in the past. And if there was an ancient ruin nearby, it could be taken apart and its stones repurposed. It was an intelligent way of building a village.

Archaeologists from my previous world would probably have deplored dismantling a ruin, but fortunately (or perhaps unfortunately), there was no one in this period of history who would bemoan the loss.

We steadily approached the village, keeping ourselves hidden behind the ruin's old stone walls and crumbling buildings. I could hear several creatures moving.

"They're about," Menel said quietly.

Chapter Two

I nodded.

"I'll scout. Wait there," he said and moved forward with completely silent footsteps. He had perfected this to a level that would put most experienced scouts to shame.

Blood had taught me the technicals of scouting to a certain extent, but judging by this, yeah, Menel was probably better than I was. As a rule, the trained are better than the untrained in any field. That was just obvious.

Spear in hand, I waited in the shadow of one of the ruin's walls. After a short while, Menel returned.

"They're doing some weird ritual in the remains of the temple just outside the village."

"What's the temple like? What kind of demons are they?"

"The temple's something like this." Menel started drawing the layout on the ground with a stick. "There's no ceiling anymore, and the walls have collapsed in a bunch of places. They've taken up position in the middle here performing their ritual. Two Commanders, faces like lizards. What were they called again…?"

"Vraskuses? With scales and a spiked tail?"

"Yeah, that sounds right."

I'd fought a vraskus back when I first obtained Pale Moon, the spear I was holding. So, there were two of those, and—

"What else?"

"A few Soldiers roaming outside the temple. I managed to spot one beast inside, but there might have been more."

"Any details on the beast?"

"Its face looked kind of like a person's. It was as big as a horse, but with a lion-like body and bat-like wings."

"That's a manticore."

Beasts with dangerous spiked tails. I'd heard from Blood that they were "a little dangerous"—Blood's "a little" sometimes being my "reasonably" or "considerably"—so I'd have to brace myself.

Menel was looking at me with a bemused expression.

"What?" I asked.

"You know a hell of a lot about this."

"I've been taught a lot of stuff."

Gus put a lot of effort into his natural history lectures, and Blood loved to tell stories about when he was alive. They had both told me that when going against a monster, it was important to have prior knowledge about their weaknesses and methods of attack. Unknown foes were the most terrifying.

"Well, okay," I said. "I'm glad that's all we're dealing with."

"That's *all*?"

I had some experience fighting demons, but none against those ranked General or higher. If I'd had to fight those, I'd have been worried about the risk. But if they were just two Commanders accompanied by Soldiers with a beast in tow, there were plenty of ways I could make it work, with the advantage of knowing the situation beforehand.

"Let's crush them."

◆

They were the remains of an aged little temple. The ceiling had fallen in, and the space inside was around the size of the classrooms I'd known in my previous world.

Lined up at the rear of the building were statues of the gods, among them the god of lightning, Volt, and the Earth-Mother, Mater. Their faces had been scraped off. It was probably the work of the demons.

Chapter Two

It took a lot of effort to destroy a statue; scraping off their faces instead to make them "nobodies" was something I'd come across in the history of my past world as well.

Praises to the gods, which should surely have been present on the wall, had also been scratched off. In their place were many Words written in a large, eerie script. Those Words, written in blackened blood, were praise for Dyrhygma, the god of dimensions worshipped by the demons. Stretched out and squashing the flowers below Dyrhygma's crest, which featured an arm grasping the eternal cycle, was the manticore that Menel had mentioned.

Farther forward, at the center of the temple, on the uneven stone floor with grass growing from its cracks, there was a pile of human bodies.

With the corpses, the beast, and the crest before them, the two demons—a wild mixture of human and crocodile—chanted Words blaspheming the virtuous gods in harsh, sonorous voices. I could tell it was some kind of ritual, but I didn't know exactly what kind. That wasn't surprising, given that even Gus's knowledge didn't cover the intricate details of these kinds of dark ceremonies. For now, all I knew was that I couldn't let this continue.

Hiding the sound of my footsteps, I crept forward, readied my spear, and simply thrust it into one of the vraskuses' necks. Just like that, the creature collapsed and turned to dust.

"■■■?!" Taken by surprise, the other vraskus screamed out something in demonjabber, drew its curved sword, and swung it around.

Its reaction to the surprise attack was faster than I expected. The large movement I had to make to avoid its blade broke the effect of the Word I had cast upon myself: the Word of Invisibility. It played tricks on others' visual perception of the user, making it extremely effective when ambushing enemies that relied on sight.

I'd used this magic to escape being seen by the Soldiers outside and break right into the middle of the ritual site. I didn't want to get into a situation where I had to contend with two fully prepared vraskuses and a manticore while I was tied up with Soldiers. That really would have been dangerous. Instead, I was using the method that Gus and Blood had taught me: surprise, initiative, and *division*.

"*Cadere Araneum.*" As the manticore was about to advance, I hit it with a web to restrict its movements and entered close-quarter combat with the vraskus.

I deflected the horizontal sweep of its sword with my shield and stabbed repeatedly with my spear. Taking into account the vraskus's tough scales, rubbery skin, and thick muscles, I aimed for its joints, efficiently inflicting wound after wound.

At this stage, the Soldiers outside seemed to have noticed my intrusion as well.

"*Currere Oleum.*"

I layered grease near the temple's entrance to buy myself some time. As the vraskus's tail came at me from a blind spot, I sliced it off with the blade of my spear without even looking, and with the return swing I drew it across its throat. Number two turned to dust.

Not a moment later, the manticore ripped through the web and roared.

"*Acceleratio!*"

I was there in a single bound and drove the spear's blade into its neck.

The manticore, sounding like it was choking, swiped angrily with its arms, trying to resist. I increased my pressure, forcing the blade in and pinning the beast to the wall of the temple. A strike from its wildly flailing claws dragged across my mithril mail. Still pinned, it tried to swing its spiked tail at me.

Chapter Two

Taking aim at its body, I spoke the Word "*Vastare*" and blasted a vortex of destruction directly into it. The roar of the blast combined with the bellow of the beast as its insides were turned to pulp. Finally, both faded until there was silence.

A big, showy magic attack like that came with risks, so I hadn't much wanted to use it, but the manticore had been putting up too much of a fight. Trying to finish it off with only a spear would have taken too long.

"And that just leaves..."

Remaining vigilant, I drew the spear back and held it couched. There were only a few left. They may have only been Soldiers, but I had to keep my wits about me until I finished this. Yet as I stood there so ready to fight, there was no sign at all of any enemies rushing in.

Confused, I stepped outside to see the Soldiers turning to dust and scattering. White arrows were sticking out of their chests and necks.

"Oh!" Perfect execution as ever, but— "I thought you weren't going to get involved?" I asked.

"You had it in the bag anyway. Just saving time." Menel appeared from the shadows, took a look around, and furrowed his brow. "Pretty sure you can't just march in and beat guys like that solo... normally..."

"Yeah. The conditions were just right." If I'd charged in and tried to fight this many enemies head-on, a very close and desperate battle would have been unavoidable. Observe the opponent first, surprise them, and exterminate them without allowing them to make use of their strengths. All this was part of a warrior's battle tactics.

"No, even with that, that kind of strength isn't normal. You doing anything special?"

"Uh... Eating a whole lot of holy bread?" Mary had prayed for a loaf to give me with every meal, so there was a chance it had changed my constitution. The god of undeath had said something about that, too.

"Eating bread doesn't do this, brother."

"I guess not." Menel was right. You couldn't build muscle just by eating a lot of bread without doing any training.

"Whatever, enough on the bread. Temple's clear. You think it's safe to assume that you stamped out the bulk of them?"

"We'll go around the village, clear out any left over, and take it from there, I guess."

Whether we were going to bury the bodies or search the area to see if there were any more survivors, it would be difficult in a place where enemies could still be lurking. I thought we were probably okay now—I couldn't sense any more demons—but we'd need to go around the village once to play it safe.

I prayed for the bodies piled up in the temple, and then the two of us headed toward the village.

In any event, we had won. Winning the battle had been our greatest initial source of worry, so while there were still plenty of reasons to be apprehensive, I felt quite relieved, and I got the impression that the same was true for Menel.

"I hope there's at least someone who's still all right," Menel said, looking anxious.

"Yeah."

But just at that moment, we heard a feeble and childlike voice.

"Men...el..."

Menel's expression froze.

◆

Chapter Two

I looked in the direction of the voice. There was some kind of small hut, perhaps a shed, and something was crawling out of it toward us.

"Menel..."

It was the corpse of a boy, burnt black and its bones half exposed. Only the top of its body was left; everything below the waist had been either severed or burned off.

"It was demons, they, umm, attacked the village." The corpse looked up at Menel with empty sockets. Menel was still frozen in place.

"I was hiding just like you told me to... I didn't do anything dangerous..." It crawled closer, dragging itself forward on its elbows. *"It was hot, but I put up with it and didn't make any noise... 'Cause..."*

Menel was shaking. Both his hands and jaw were tightly clenched.

"I knew you'd come." The corpse smiled; it was a blood-curdling and gruesome sight, and yet it felt warm. *"And you did. Thank you."*

With a frightfully happy look on its face, the corpse extended a hand to Menel. Menel tried to take it, but he hesitated for just a second. I couldn't tell if it was because of his revulsion toward the corpse, distrust of the undead, regret at not having made it in time, or guilty conscience. Whatever the case, the corpse sensed his rejection, and its face filled with despair.

"Huh...? Wait... Why? Am I..."

I knew there wasn't a moment to lose. I fell to my knees, picked up the blackened corpse—and hugged the boy tightly.

"H-Hey!" Menel looked at me, disconcerted.

It's okay, Menel, I thought. *Embracing the undead isn't anything to be afraid of.*

"You did a great job," I said. "We're very proud of you."

"**Huh? Who are you, mister?**" Still in my arms, the boy tilted his head. Flakes of charred skin fell off.

"I'm Menel's friend. I'm sorry about Menel. He's just a little tired. He isn't quite with it. Please forgive him."

"**Okay.**" The boy nodded.

"Good boy. Come on, Menel." I held up the boy's arm for Menel to take.

This time, he didn't hesitate. He squeezed the boy's badly charred hand. "I'm sorry I wasn't here sooner." His voice was trembling.

"**It's okay.**"

"You must be tired out. Go to sleep."

"**Good idea... I feel really... sleepy...**"

"Dream well."

"**'Kay...**"

Even as he trembled, Menel didn't look away.

"Gracefeel, god of the flame. Repose and guidance."

It was the blessing Divine Torch. As the boy closed his eyes in peaceful sleep, the flame rose softly into the air and took his soul, along with those of so many others drifting nearby, with it toward the heavens.

Menel watched until it could no longer be seen, and then, after a while, he spoke.

"Hey, uh…"

"What is it?"

"I'm sorry."

"For what?"

There was silence as Menel chose his words. "I was looking down on you and you didn't deserve it. I thought you were some muscleheaded rich kid who fluked the gods' protection and disappeared up his own ass. Just a do-gooder without a clue." He sighed. "So… I'm sorry."

Chapter Two

"It's no big deal." I gave him a smile.

Despite the deep anguish on his face, he gave me a slight smile back.

◆

The two of us walked around the village together.

Menel never hesitated again after what had happened. He held the hands of the undead who still had their intelligence and reason, and bid them words of farewell. Those who did not—those who had been taken over by hatred and madness—I purified using the power of the protection of the goddess of flux.

"Gracefeel, god of the flame. Repose and guidance."

Divine Torch was an effective technique to use against the undead, but it wasn't all-powerful. If the undead themselves resisted the technique, whether it would have an effect became a contest between the strength of the user's protection and the attachment of the undead. For instance, if a high-level undead on par with Gus, Blood, or Mary seriously tried to resist, it was dubious whether I would be able to guide their souls with my prayers. If I could become as advanced a user of benediction as Mary then it might be possible, of course.

Anyway, for that reason I was slightly concerned that there might be some people in this village who were beyond my abilities, but luckily no one here had become that powerful an undead.

The spectral body slipped out of the crazed woman who was standing in front of me, brandishing a cleaver. Bewildered, her spirit took a look around her and soon understood the situation. I placed my hand over my heart and said as if making a vow, "Leave the rest to me." The woman smiled, nodded, and one more soul returned to the eternal cycle.

"Umm." I checked around me. It was hard to tell because of the fog, but I thought we'd more or less finished going around the obvious places. "Menel, are there any more houses?"

"One more... Follow me." Menel walked ahead, stepping on the bare, well-trodden earth.

The house, located deep in the village, had been completely burned to the ground. It looked like it had once been quite a large building, with maybe three or four rooms. The other houses had just one or two large rooms plus a shed and pen at best.

Menel gazed at that house for a while. He took a deep breath in and slowly released it. Then, tightly squeezing his hand into a fist, he called out. "Yo! You here, Marple?"

"Oh?" A specter appeared, slipping through a soot-covered pillar. "It's you, Menel." She was an old woman who looked like she had lived quite a number of years. But her back wasn't bent, and she still looked full of vim and vigor.

I briefly thought of Gus—and the instant I did, I realized something, and a chill ran through me. This was bad. The ghost of this old woman called Marple was probably close to fully materialized. Where the other ghosts were indistinct and lacking in clarity, the old woman's body was as well-defined as Gus's. I couldn't say anything about her combat ability, but I got the feeling, somehow, that her soul was going to be tenacious. If she was confused or distraught and resisted my blessing, it was possible that sending her off might be beyond my abilities. And that would mean that I might have to use a weapon that worked on specters—a weapon like Pale Moon or Overeater—to cut up the old woman's ghost in front of Menel...

"Heheh. You needn't worry so much, young man."

Chapter Two

She'd seen through my moment's hesitation…
Then, she smiled. "I'm not senile yet."
The light of wit certainly dwelled in her eyes.

◆

"Good to hear. Looks like you still had some unfinished business and got left behind. Don't worry though. Look, this guy's a genuine, principled high priest. Met him by chance." Menel started talking to the old woman's ghost. He was being awfully chatty. "He can send lost souls like you back to be reincarnated, heal the wounded—he's a whiz at all that stuff. So us two'll do something about the village. Go on, thank him and get going already."

I was a principled high priest? He was really playing me up.

"Or is there something else? Some message you wanted to give someone? I'll tell them for you, so you—"

"Menel." With a single word, the old woman ended his verbal barrage. Then, she sighed. "You've been misbehaving again."

I didn't miss the twitch in Menel's shoulders. "N-Not really… Where's this coming from? You sure you aren't going dotty?"

"I can read you like a book."

"Oh yeah? How?" Menel feigned ignorance, but it wasn't working. Marple continued with conviction.

"You're a terrible liar, dear. And a difficult child. But deep down, you're a scrupulously honest person with integrity."

Menel looked like he was trying to say something back, but the words wouldn't come out. The old woman simply smiled. They kind of looked like family. One living, and one undead. The days I'd spent in a family of four floated back into my mind.

"Killing and stealing... Someone like you isn't cut out for all that nasty business."

Menel had no reply.

"And it's high time you admitted it. Stop living through clout. Give up this way of life of always fighting with others." Her words showed no restraint, cutting Menel's lifestyle to the ground and discarding it as casually as a butcher tossing unwanted parts.

"Shut up..." Menel's voice, by contrast, was shaking. "Shut up! Stop talking to me like you've got all the answers! What was I supposed to do then?!" He was yelling, on the verge of tears. "You died, the rest of the village was starving and freezing! What the hell else could I have done?! My strength is the only thing I can count on! Or are you saying I should have prayed to God?! When has God, when has *any* fig god ever helped me?!"

Menel tried to grab the old woman's ghost, but his hand swiped the air.

"Pig shit... This is... Pig shit!" Menel dropped to his knees and buried his head in them.

All I could do was watch.

"I've had enough... Let me go with you..." As fog swirled about the devastated village, the sorrowful tones of the half-elf's beautiful voice echoed around. "The life of a half's too long for me..."

Those who inherited elven blood lived several hundred years. His life wouldn't end so easily. Even after losing the people and places important to him, he would continue to exist. What words did I possibly have to offer him? I had no idea.

"Listen to me, Menel. Meneldor." Marple raised her voice, her tone serious. Menel looked up. "God has given you one more chance." She smiled slowly. "One last time. Wash your hands of this wretched way of life."

Chapter Two

Her smile was full of love. I was even reminded of the Echo of the Earth-Mother Mater I had once seen. She might not be able to swing a sword or use magic, but I was sure that this person had something far more amazing and precious than anything I possessed—such was the power of that smile.

"You may hate God, but God will always love you. Whether you realize it or not, God is always shining on you, unremitting, untiring." Through the silence of the perished village, the voice of the perished woman carried clearly, whispered like a young child telling her friend where she'd hidden away her treasures. "Now, it's all down to you. All you need to do is see the light." She smiled. "Give it a go, and I promise you it'll all work out."

Menel was covering his face and weeping silently, his shoulders shaking.

Then... the woman turned to me.

◆

"Now, Father, may I have a word?"

"Of course."

"Could I ask you to take care of this silly boy? He isn't a bad person at his core. Would you... well... get along with him?"

It was the last wish of a person departing this world. I nodded firmly. Marple gave a satisfied nod of her own.

"Oh, yes... About the demons with beasts who attacked the village—it seems it wasn't a case of lone demons wandering here by chance. They have a leader and a base where he lives deep in the woods, and he sends out underlings to various places from there. I don't know the exact details, but it sounded like they had some truly evil things planned involving taming beasts and attacking people."

"Don't tell me you can speak demonjabber?" Not even Gus knew much about that language. Maybe some research had been done on it sometime in the past two hundred years?

"Well... That's a long story from long ago."

What kind of past did this woman have?

"Judging by the direction they were sending out their familiars and so on, I'd suspect their base is in the direction of the Rust Mountains, the fallen capital of the dwarves."

I looked west. Beyond the fog, I could faintly see a reddish-brown mountain range in the distance. That had to be it.

"Did you not want the burden?"

"On the contrary, you've been very helpful."

"Good," Marple said with a smile. "I was feeling guilty that I couldn't thank you in some way. If it helped you, Father, then I'm glad."

"Um, your unfinished business, might it have been..."

The old woman roared with laughter. "Of course it was! As if I could take that to the grave! Someone had to know!" She laughed for a while. "So, that's all. I hope you don't mind, but I won't be needing your guidance. God, you see, is already waiting for me."

I saw a faint flame beside the old woman. *Ah... You're here*, I thought.

"With that said, I'll be on my way," Marple said, and smiled.

The situation in the outside world wasn't good, just as my parents had feared. But there were people here. It wasn't all bad.

"Menel, keep your chin up. This world is full of things that can't be undone. You mustn't brood over them and let them hold you back. Stand up, face forward, and do what needs to be done."

"Fig. So you're just gonna say your piece and go," Menel said bitterly.

Chapter Two

Marple laughed. "Look in a mirror, dear. We both like to do things our own way. Gracious, what a boy." She smiled, crow's feet forming at the corners of her eyes, and put her incorporeal arms around Menel, rubbing his back with hands that couldn't touch.

"All right," she said calmly. "The rest, I trust to you."

"Okay." I placed my hand over the left side of my chest, and returned a vow. "You can leave it to me."

She smiled.

And another soul returned to samsara.

◆

After Marple went back to the cycle of reincarnation, Menel was in a daze for a while.

Once he regained his composure, we had a discussion and decided to begin dealing with the bodies of the villagers.

I repurified the remains of the temple with magic and blessings, and made it into a sacred area that creatures and beasts couldn't approach. For each of the villagers' bodies, I put my hands together and prayed for them, cleansed them with magic, lifted them onto my back, and lined them up at the ruined temple. Pray, cleanse, lift, carry. Pray, cleanse, lift, carry. Pray, cleanse, lift, carry.

I repeated this over and over. No matter how grotesque the body, I gave them all equal treatment.

As I worked, I thought about the state of the outside world. It was looking pretty bleak right now. How many battles had I gotten into already in the small number of days since I had left the city of the dead? Dangerous beings like demons and beasts were widespread and hadn't even been driven out of areas where people were still living their lives.

And when people suffered from these attacks, the result—either due to extreme poverty or the failure to organize a buffer of emergency supplies in advance—was the continual creation of starving bandits. Because of the cold rationality created from everyone having nothing to spare, there was no mercy or allowance made for others, nor was there any semblance of law or order.

Violence was rampant, and survival of the strongest ruled above all. This was the case for at least the entire region known as Beast Woods, if not an even wider area. Even just the brief glimpse I'd had of it was pretty darn awful.

Of course, I could have shamelessly said, "That is their culture, their society, and their choice. It's not my place as an outsider to interfere," and passed through while assuming the attitude of a neutral observer.

My hometown was the city of the dead, not these woods. I was only a passerby, and had no obligation to do anything with regard to this area. The societal problems of an entire region weren't going to be fixed overnight by the efforts of just one person, so I had the option of just dealing with the immediate problem in front of me and only getting as involved as my oath required.

From the look of things so far, I seemed to qualify as a pretty strong warrior even in the outside world, and I also had my powers of magic, my god's protection, and a good amount of wealth. If I wanted to live in peace somewhere inconspicuous, I could probably accomplish that surprisingly easily. I just had to find some city that wouldn't make too much of a fuss about my origin, blend in, and I was sure it would work out.

However...

"As you travel these faraway lands—"

"Prithee, bring light to the darkness."

Chapter Two

If that was my god's wish, then I had to lend her an ear. I owed her a debt too great to ever repay.

That said—

"What should I do...?"

The heart of the problem wasn't the demons or beasts. It was the compounded societal issues of poverty and disorder that surrounded them. I could defeat the demons and beasts with a sword or a spear, but societal problems couldn't be cut down with a demonblade. As I thought about what to do, I prayed, purified, lifted, and carried, over and over.

◆

A few days later, the villagers returned to the besieged village. It was scorched all over, and many of the buildings had collapsed. When they saw the state of it with fresh eyes, they looked to be in shock.

Together, we scraped together the remaining farm tools, dug some holes, and held a simple funeral service to mourn the dead.

Everyone took turns piling a little bit of earth on top of the bodies lying in the graves. To make it feel like a legitimate funeral, I spoke some passages from scripture I had once been taught by Gus and Mary as I watched the villagers work. However, I wasn't following any prescribed form; I was really only borrowing from what others had told me to make it "sound right." It looked like I'd need to make contact with a priest belonging to a proper organization somewhere and learn from them.

After the funeral had started to wrap up, I decided to raise a question.

"So, umm... What are you all going to do now?"

There looked to be enough surviving houses that if the survivors all lived together it would work out; however, many of the fields had been rendered useless. If they couldn't eat and the only route available to them was going to be pillaging, then I was thinking I might be forced to give them money and have them spread out to neighboring villages...

"Hahaha! Well, you just watch." The villagers laughed off my serious expression. They beckoned me over to a barn, where they started digging up the dirt. Straw bags and pots filled with grain came out one after the other.

"Ohh..." I said.

"You see, robberies and burnings ain't anything special around these parts."

"Yes," another villager said. "If you can get back, you can get by. That's *if*, mind you."

"You're very generous, but we ain't planning on taking advantage of you, Father. We can cope, don't you worry."

Some people who had disappeared into the woods surrounding the village also started to come back with food and other supplies. God knows where they'd hidden those. It looked like these people had no intention of allowing themselves to be beaten so easily. Maybe the people here were cursed to become desperate muggers time and time again, but it was that very aspect that had also fostered the villagers' toughness and strength of character.

"Well, this is a great relief." At the very least, it looked like I'd been more than a bit of a busybody to think I needed to watch over the whole affair from beginning to end. It was just that the demons and the beasts together had been a little too much for just one settlement to handle on this one occasion. They could handle themselves without me, in their own way.

Chapter Two

In which case, what I should have been thinking about wasn't how to completely take care of them throughout the whole process, but merely how to contribute. And that was a good question...

Fires were being stoked, and I heard the lively voices of the women starting their cooking. Evidently there was going to be a bit of a feast tonight, to celebrate their homecoming and to mourn those who had died.

"Father, we owe you a debt of gratitude for giving us back our village."

"We'd be more than happy for you to join us."

"I'd be glad to," I said, nodding—and then suddenly, I noticed. "Huh?"

At some point, Menel had disappeared.

◆

I told the people preparing for the feast where I was going, and went to search for Menel. He seemed to have left his stuff here, so it was unlikely that he'd gone far.

I couldn't see fairies, but sorcerer's theory stated that all things in the world were made from the Words. Reading the difficult-to-interpret Words and Signs that represented the trees and soil, I walked through the woods, somehow managing to follow his trail.

I took in the smell of the dry winter forest. Some of the trees around me were bare like weather-beaten skeletons, while others were deep verdant evergreens. The sky was glowing red in the west; the sun was well on its way to setting. Cold wind was whistling through the trees. It was beginning to get pretty dark.

"*Lumen.*" I made Pale Moon's blade glow softly.

It wasn't a good idea to act carelessly. There had only just been an attack by demons and beasts. They could jump at me from anywhere. I had no intention of dropping my guard.

Remaining alert to my surroundings, I walked step by step through the woods, and as I did so, I thought about Menel.

Is he okay? I wondered. Parting with Marple must have hit him pretty hard. Putting myself in his position, I thought it was probably like if I had lost Blood or Mary in a sudden incident.

Expressing it that way gave me a new appreciation for how hard this had to be for him. I couldn't imagine that someone like me, who Menel had only met a few days ago, would be able to do anything for him in a time like that. Perhaps what he really needed was some time alone to think things over, and what I was doing was just unwanted meddling. But even so...

— *Could I ask you to take care of this silly boy?*

I had certainly been asked, so I probably had a duty to at least keep an eye on him. If he said I wasn't wanted, then I would just have to turn around and leave dejected. After all, until just a few days ago, I'd been a sheltered boy who had never seen another living human in his life. I had zero experience points in social interaction, so when I'd set out into the world, I'd been prepared from the beginning for everything to go south.

As I walked along confidently thinking that if I made a fool of myself I could simply cringe about it later, I arrived at a bit of an upwards slope. I could see what was left of perhaps a stone wall running across it.

A phosphorescent fairy danced lightly across my vision. I followed the momentary blinking with my eyes, and when I looked up I saw, almost entirely hidden by trees, the remains of a small and timeworn building that might have been an ancient watchtower.

Chapter Two

Built on a small hill which could be used as a vantage point, the structure had since collapsed, leaving only the base behind, around which fairies were blinking like fireflies. As if they were concerned about someone, they were whispering to each other while stealing glances inside.

There was no doubt in my mind—he had to be there.

I carefully made my way up the slope, paying extra attention to my feet and the loose mossy stones. Once I reached the top, I circled around the partially collapsed stone wall, and my field of vision widened.

"Ah."

As I looked down from the hill, I saw the city built from stone below me. The countless houses along the streets spreading outward from the river had aged, crumbled, and been taken over by forest, and now stood only as a reminder of the city's former prosperity. The color of the sunset, changing every moment, gently illuminated them all.

"Hey, Will."

There he was, sitting with one knee up, against the base of an evergreen tree that had spread its roots between the stones of the broken watchtower. A sorrowful look in his jade eyes, his fair skin was lit by the sunset, and his slightly pointed ears peeked out from his flowing, silver hair. The fairies' phosphorescence occasionally danced around him.

"Menel."

Even when he was feeling down, he was picture-perfect. *Attractive people have it good*, I randomly thought.

◆

"Can I sit here?"

"Knock yourself out."

I sat down beside him. "This is a nice view."

"Yeah, from the outside."

I gave him a puzzled look.

"That ruin's a den of undead. It's devoured countless adventurers. No one's ever come back from there alive."

Is that so. "Then I'd better go in there later and return them all to the cycle of rebirth."

"What? Were you even listening?"

"Yeah, you said it's a dangerous place. So I have to do something about it."

Menel shook his head and put his hand to his forehead as if he were trying to cope with a headache. "Of course you'd say that. I forgot who I was dealing with." He let out a massive sigh. "Being with you throws me off my groove. I thought I was, y'know, more cool and collected than this."

"*Cool?*"

"Yes, cool! Fig!"

"Hahaah..." I treated him to a deliberately mocking laugh. He growled in frustration.

I was surprised at how much fun it was to tease him—or more, to watch his reactions.

I was having quite a lot of... discoveries, I guess, talking with Menel. I first thought he was a pretty nice guy; then he tried to kill me without any hesitation at all. That had been something. Then I thought he was stubborn and difficult, but he was actually genuine, with a funny side as well.

This probably wasn't limited to Menel. Humans in general are pretty multifaceted. They have harsh, inconsiderate sides, and they have charming sides that put a smile on your face.

Chapter Two

There's a lot to see, as long as you're willing to look for it. Maybe confronting these kinds of things was what building a relationship with another person was all about.

As these thoughts went through my head, Menel and I teased each other. The last time I'd had this kind of fun with someone my age might have been when I was a kid in my previous life.

After we'd gone at that for a while, I asked him, "So, what kind of person was Marple?"

◆

Menel shrugged his shoulders. "She was a weird old lady. You could probably tell."

The sun was beginning to dip down below the horizon. The world turned from red to purple, and on to the color of night.

"I was born in Grassland to the north, in the Great Forest of Erin where the elves live. My mother… She had a very curious personality when she was young, and ran away from the forest. Then, after a few years, she came back pregnant with some guy's kid. She died an early death, apparently. As for me, I was growing faster than everyone else around me, and I couldn't get along with them, anyway. The whole deal with my mother was still dragging on… They were calling me a stain on their home… In the end, I thought I'd just run away from the forest, and… yeah. That's how it goes with mongrel halfs like me."

Pretty heavy, and he'd only just gotten started.

"Of course, the world of people wasn't a paradise either. It wasn't until after I left that I found out that for all its problems, I'd had it easy in the Forest of Erin. Fortunately, I knew how to handle a bow and a knife, and most importantly, I could see fairies." A fairy stopped on the tip of Menel's extended finger, frolicked there, and then left again. "I was strong enough to kill the hell out of whatever or whoever came to prey on me. If not for that, I'd be in some back alley whoring myself out right about now."

"You do have a pretty face…"

"Don't *agree*, goddammit."

"I just thought you'd have been pretty popular with guys who are into that."

"Feck off."

What did he want me to do? Lie? That said, I didn't have a sexual inclination toward those of my gender, so my thoughts didn't go any further than *he's got a pretty face*.

"Anyway, the point is, for a bunch of reasons, I became an adventurer. Southmark still had a lot of ruins, so I made use of the Fertile Kingdom's open policy and crossed over here." Menel had a distant look in his eyes. "Then, one of the people I'd banded together with betrayed us and poisoned us. I was this close to getting killed."

I had no words. How vicious…

"It was greed that did it, I bet. The spoils from the ruins were too good. Luckily, I barely touched the poisoned food, so it didn't get me that bad. I somehow managed to kill the fecker, but still…"

So this was the standard in this region of the world. It was so savage, and the difference in the way things went here compared with my past life was staggering. I could imagine Blood and those like him having a riot out here, though.

"All the other guys I knew back then were dead on the ground, foam around their mouths, and the poison and my wounds were making my head all fuzzy. I have no idea how I bumbled my way to the village in that state, but I did, and that was where I went down, just outside there. And Marple took me in. If it wasn't for that old lady… Of course, back then she wasn't quite so old."

Chapter Two

Menel continued to speak, that faraway look still in his eyes. "She really was a strange old woman. She took me in, some sketchy and surly guy lying half dead on the ground, and she gave me food to eat and a place to sleep. She even lectured me on living a proper life. There were a ton of people like that, different circumstances but similar stories—they'd all ended up settling in that village after being picked up by her."

"Who *was* she?"

"Beats me." Menel shook his head. "She said she was an 'uneducated country bumpkin' or some crap. Please. Anyway, she's dead now, and the truth's gone with her. Happens a lot on this continent."

I remembered a saying from my previous world: "Everyone has a story." And unfortunately, a single human being cannot pore through them all.

"So, she took me in, and she may have been a preachy old bat, but I owed her one. I couldn't stomach settling down in the village and playing the part of a farmer, but... I did go around to the nearby villages, doing my best impression of a hunter. 'Cause hunting dangerous animals was something I could do."

Menel talked nostalgically, as if he were cherishing a broken treasure. "Beast Woods has a ton of nasty creatures in it. People were finding me pretty useful. I'd found a place where I belonged."

And then—

"Without any warning, it was gone."

The village, attacked by demons; the nice old woman, Marple; the children in the barn—all of that was gone.

"So I decided I wasn't gonna be someone who gets stuff taken from him. I was gonna be a taker, and protect what I still had left. Which failed spectacularly, thanks to you." The silver-haired hunter breathed a long sigh. "That's what this place is like. You've gotta be like that if you want to survive out here."

He sounded like he'd given up, like a tired old man. "Living longer than other people in a place like this... It's painful, you know? Just hopelessly painful." His words held no intensity, just exhaustion and the sense that something inside him had been worn down to nothing.

"Sometimes I wish I was dead."

◆

I didn't know what to say to Menel after his emotional outpour. It reminded me of my previous life and the time when the god of undeath's words had thrown me into a pit of despair.

I wondered how I could comfort him. I wondered how I could encourage him. I didn't know. I couldn't do as Mary, Blood, and Gus had. I couldn't think of anything.

This was something I'd become painfully aware of when I met the ghost of the old woman Marple. There were certainly gods in this world, and if you received their protection, you would become able to heal wounds and cure illnesses. It was almost a little superpower, like the ones you found in comic books. But it wasn't as if it gave you more life experience. It didn't give you the ability to say the kinds of words that could resound in someone's heart, words that could help someone through hard times.

I could heal the body, but not the heart. That was something that, in the end, a person had to take charge of themselves. And as the silence dragged on, I was unable to say anything. What was I *supposed* to say? I wished someone would tell me. What was I supposed to do in times like this? I had no experience with this in my previous life, and I didn't have much in this one, either. If Blood, Mary, or Gus were here, they might have been able to come up with

Chapter Two

something. But for everything I had learned, I couldn't produce the right words, not even a single sentence, to save my life.

"U-Um... I, I guess, you... uh..." I mumbled something, but it didn't help. Gods... I felt like I really had regressed to how I used to be. But Menel was in a really bad place right now. I had to say *something*.

But while I was racking my brain, Menel exhaled sharply. "Right," he said, stretching his arms above his head to loosen up his stiff body. "Sucks, but gotta move on!"

Huh?

Menel looked at me and tilted his head. "Hm? What's up? You done making stupid faces?"

"What? Huh...?" I was confused.

No, wait, hold up. He had just been so depressed, and now he... wha?

"Haha, he's losing it. Y'know, the normal you and the you that does the priest thing are like two totally different people."

"*Pleeeeeeease* shut up."

"Too bad, 'cause you're pretty cool when you're full-on priest."

"I wasn't—I was just—uhh..."

After taunting me a little, he bounced lightly to his feet and looked at me with serious eyes. "Will... William. Priest of the god of the flame. I'm grateful to you. For stopping me before it was too late, and for saving the guys in the village. So—" He put his hand on his chest, gracefully descended to one knee, and bowed his head before me. "With you as my mediator, I ask the protection of the god of the flame."

This was the standard phrase used when changing your guardian deity and oath. Startled by the sincerity in his voice, I hurriedly stood to face him.

"Will you do this for me?" he asked.

"I shall be your mediator and bring you together with my god." I responded with the standard, age-old reply I'd once been taught by Mary. I placed my hand gently on Menel's head and prayed to my goddess as he knelt. "I pray for you to the god of the flame. May Gracefeel love you, shine on you, and be with you on your journeys."

In the darkness, I felt a faint flame glow warmly in the air behind me.

"Then to my guardian deity, I make this oath." Menel raised his eyes and looked up at the flame. "I will atone for my sins and live a positive life, looking forward." It was a powerful declaration. "Please light the way before me with your flame."

That had also been Marple's wish for him, to the very end.

"Menel..."

"Life's hard a lot of the time. Sometimes it beats me so badly I want to just lie there and die. But I'm not gonna stay down." He shrugged and put on a brave smile. "I'm gonna get up somehow, and just like Marple said, I'm gonna keep looking forward and do what needs to be done."

My previous life ended without me ever being able to recover from my despair, and it had taken a pep talk from Mary for me to manage it in this life too. But Menel had mustered the strength to stand back up all on his own. He had found a way to resolve his internal struggle, changed his attitude, and sought out how to behave to make up for his past behavior—and he had done all this by himself.

He'd had Marple's words to help him, and he was probably putting up a brave front as well... but even so, I couldn't have done what he had. How arrogant was I, to think that he needed my words? He was strong. Stronger than me. Stronger than I'd ever thought.

Chapter Two

If only I'd had this kind of strength in my past life; maybe something could have been different then. When I thought about this, my chest tightened with a feeling of regret that I couldn't shake. "Menel, you're awesome, really," I said with admiration. "I truly respect you."

"What, feck off," he said, rising to his feet and giving one of my shoulders a playful shove. "You're the awesome one. How do you *get* that good at fighting?"

"It's not me that's awesome. It was my teachers."

"Can't imagine what your childhood was like for the life of me. Eh, whatever, I'm not gonna pry," he said, walking past me. "Let's get back already. Food's probably close to being done by now."

"Oh yeah. You're right. We'll make them worry if we're away much longer." I followed after him, and we headed back to the village together.

The feast of homecoming and mourning was just beginning. Though it was small for a "feast," they wouldn't stop offering me drinks. Menel tried to keep a low profile in the corner, so I dragged him out and made him get involved. He resisted, and we ended up getting in a weird scuffle.

It was a night of competition, of tomfoolery, and of moments spent quietly, listening to the fondly remembered stories of those who had passed away.

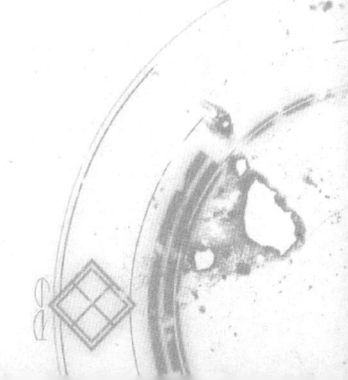

Chapter Three

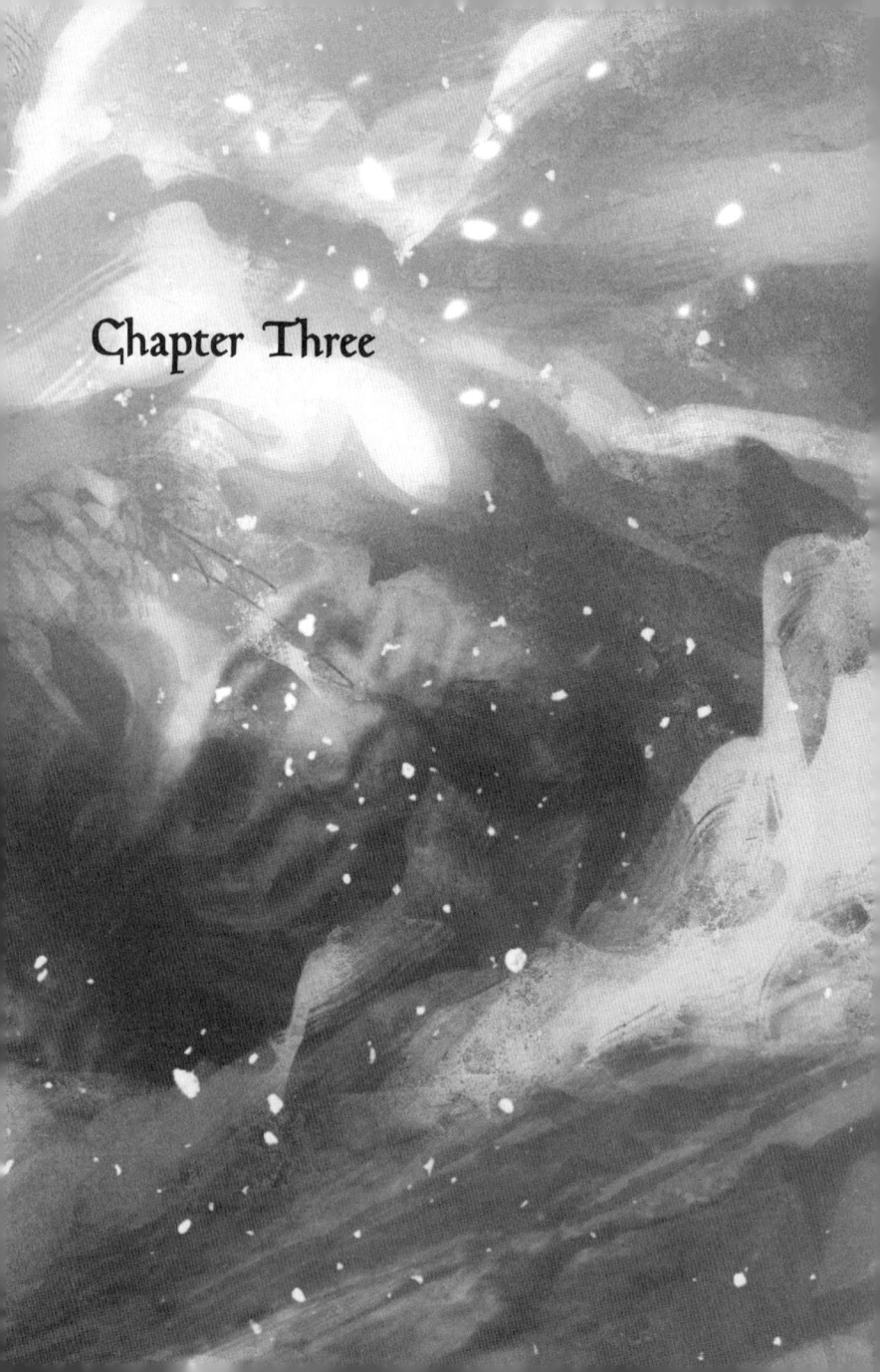

"All our livestock's been wiped out, and a whole lot of tools that'll be impossible to replace have been smashed."

"Wow..."

There were still a lot of problems for the villagers even after taking back their village from the hands of the demons. Many of their draft animals and tools had been lost. The villagers had serious expressions on their faces as they discussed the problem from all angles.

"We're gon' needa stock up at Whitesails..."

"But what do we do about the money?"

"We need help also."

An unfamiliar word came up in their conversation, so I asked Menel. "What's Whitesails?"

Menel looked at me like he was looking at an alien. Was "Whitesails" the name of a place that you couldn't help learning if you spent any amount of time living here?

"What is the deal with you, seriously?" he asked. "Were you living under a rock?" Then he gave me a brief summary of the history of this region.

Apparently, Blood and Mary's era was now referred to as the Union Age, in which all kinds of races had formed a large confederation. With the exception of regions like this one at the border, it had been a peaceful golden age without much conflict.

However, the influx of demons that followed caused the Great Collapse, and the Union fell apart. Southmark was lost under the flood of demons. The Hundred Heroes—that referred to Blood and the others who had helped him—killed the demons' king, but all the same, mankind was forced to abandon this continent for a while.

Crossing the channel and the inland sea called Middle-sea, mankind retreated to Grassland in the north. But as a result of the Great Collapse, the central government of Grassland lost its ability to govern, and the continent fractured into smaller regions that vied for power. There was no quick end to the infighting among all those military factions, and while it continued, no division saw good reason to interfere with the darkness in Southmark, farthest of all places and teeming with undead, demons, and goblins.

After the Fertile Kingdom unified the southwestern part of Grassland, that changed a little. Over the last few decades, they had been expanding and rebuilding with a vision to retake Southmark, and Whitesails was the port city that was currently the heart of the settlement effort coming from the north.

No wonder Menel had given me that look of utter disbelief for not knowing it.

Anyway, Whitesails, which was the port at the north side of Southmark and the base for their settlement project, was apparently crammed full of immigration ships and trade vessels. And with so many of those going in and out, it was natural that suspicious folk, those with things to hide, and people forced to leave their homelands would also turn up.

Proper immigration procedures were as good as nonexistent in this era, so of course, there was no way to shut those kinds of people out. Some dived headfirst into the organized criminal underbelly in Whitesails, while others slipped away, made homes, and planted

Chapter Three

fields on the very edges of the borderlands, where the influence of those in power didn't reach. Independent settlements such as those were scattered around Beast Woods.

"Those sorts of people aside, a lot of adventurers come here as well. Though you could ask just how different the two really are..."

An "adventurer," he told me, was someone who earned their daily bread by trolling the ruins from the Union Age and taking on mercenary-type jobs. Adventurers weren't members of a single, unified organization; they were drifters, existing in almost any large town, who took jobs at special-purpose taverns and carried them out for a fee. Most were people down on their luck and unable to make a proper living, but that was why they saw the Union Age ruins as the key to fulfilling their dreams.

"In the unlikely event you find a pot of gold coins or something—*boom*, you're rich. Your whole life turns around, just like that. People who dream of hitting the big one call themselves adventurers and flock out here. Though, it's not just them, to be fair. There are also people hoping to become heroes, people like you who had revelations from their god—all sorts."

So you couldn't generalize them as just people living in poverty. It seemed to be a pretty complicated occupation.

"You've got your own reasons too, right?" he asked. "You're having revelations and helping people out, so you're probably also trying to spread your faith or something too, I guess? I mean, the southern continent used to have a deeply rooted faith in Gracefeel."

"Hmm... Can you tell me more about that?"

I asked him a few questions, and learned that the god of the flame had apparently once formed the basis for people's religious faith here in Southmark.

However, the flood of demons caused by the Great Collapse two hundred years ago made a mess of Southmark, and as a result, Gracefeel's followers scattered. Some were just barely able to flee to Grassland in the north and keep her name alive. But unlike the major gods, whose worshippers were numerous and not isolated to particular areas, Gracefeel's faithful seemed to have waned considerably.

Demons and beasts were running rampant. There were many villages where the people could barely afford to get by, and sometimes became desperate enough to become thieves. Faith was dwindling to the point of disappearing completely. Things were awful in a lot of ways. And knowing that the mission I'd been given by my god was to do something about it somehow made me feel even worse.

Blood, Mary, Gus? Outside is a really scary place, I lamented inside my mind. Then I slowly breathed in and out again.

To be honest, this was blatantly too much of a burden for me, and I'd really have liked someone else to do it, but I had sworn an oath to my god and decided to live a proper life. In the name of my faith, I decided to do as much as I could. "First things first. This village."

"About that. You've done enough already, so I'm sorry for asking this, but the people here don't have any money. If possible, they'd like to borr—"

"Menel, let's go explore some ruins! We'll split whatever we find!"

"What?" Menel's mouth dropped open.

◆

"I can't believe you're this good at ruin-hunting as well..."

"I'm used to it."

Chapter Three

Menel and I conquered the ruins that neighbored the village, and saw off the spirits of the wandering undead there at the same time.

I'd been thrown into the city of the dead's underground quarter and had some seriously hard training at the hands of Gus and Blood, so I was relatively good at this kind of thing. Menel's past experience as an adventurer had clearly helped him too; he was very quick on his feet.

By collecting money and magical items from the ruins, Menel got the amount he needed to rebuild the village, and I succeeded in replenishing the various supplies I'd consumed. I'd been told that there were a lot of untouched ruins around here, so it seemed that I'd be able to amass the funds I was going to need on my own, at least for the time being.

"Seriously, who *are* you..." Menel wondered aloud.

"You weren't going to pry, right?"

"Yeah, and I'm sticking to that, but... hell."

I was on a journey north with Menel. Our destination was the same—Whitesails, the most prosperous city in Southmark—but our reasons for going were different.

Menel's was simple: he needed to go there to buy the draft animals and various tools that Marple's village needed.

As for me, I had many reasons. I wanted to help Menel, I wanted to learn about the activities of the demons in Beast Woods, and I wanted to get more information on the continents and countries of this world. Doing something about the demons' suspicious behavior, spreading faith in the god of the flame, helping villages—all of these required first heading to a city where people and things gathered.

We were walking through Beast Woods. The view surrounding the trail barely changed, and the heavily wooded forest let little light through. Fortunately, with it being late winter, the bushes and undergrowth weren't that thick—but even so, we had spent so long walking that it was starting to feel like we were just going around in circles. I'd seen nothing but this same kind of scenery for several days now.

Today too, we had been walking about half the day, and as the sun was starting to shine through from high in the sky, I could hold it in no longer. "We *are* making progress... right?"

"Of course we are," Menel said. "Starting to get you down?"

"Kind of."

"Well... Can't say I blame you. I can't wait to get out to a village somewhere, or at least to a nice, open plain. The ears of winter wheat should be waving in the wind at this time of year. Should be pretty beautiful."

"Oh, that sounds really nice," I said, getting a little excited as I imagined the view.

Then, a long, loud, and piercing shriek filled the air, and a second voice with it. "H-Help! Anyone!"

Menel and I glanced at each other, and immediately ran in the direction of the voice.

◆

There was a deafening bellow.

It came from a gigantic ape with dark-brown hair. The ape was easily over two meters tall, and I estimated its weight at close to three hundred kilograms.

Chapter Three

It was *big*. Its arms were thick, as were its legs. Its torso, its neck, its lips, its eyes—all were large and bulging. It reminded me of the depictions I'd read in martial arts stories in my previous life.

There was another high-pitched shriek. Two people were frantically running in our direction and away from the ape. One was a scrawny man with a pack on his back who looked to be a hawker. The other, carrying a stringed instrument of some kind on her back, was a little girl—no—

"A halfling, huh," Menel muttered.

She was definitely very short, and a pretty fast runner for her size. Her ears were pointed like leaves, and her hair was red and curly. I'd learned about halflings from Gus—they were a vagabond tribe of cheerful little people who enjoyed singing, dancing, and eating... Hmm, now wasn't the time to be thinking about this.

The two of them ran madly toward us. The short girl caught up with the man and his goods and began to pass him. "What are you doing?!" she cried. "Dump it! Dump it, you dingbat!"

The hawker looked ghastly pale and was sweating profusely as he tried to run. "But—" he started.

"Nuts to your but! Oh, why me?!"

Before they could bicker any further, the giant ape charged them, and with two simultaneous yelps they darted away in opposite directions. Taking advantage of her small body, the girl rolled into an area heavily obstructed by branches.

It looked like she was going to be able to get away.

But she looked at the hawker, and saw that now he was the one being chased. Her eyes went hard with determination. Shouting, "Hey! Over here!" she picked up a tree branch and threw it at the ape. Evidently, she was hoping to draw its attention to her.

I stepped between the short girl and the ape instead.

"Look a—ah?! Wh-Who—W-Wai—Watch out!"

When the giant ape saw that I had barged in front, it stopped its charge. Its large eyeballs rolled in their sockets toward me, and it stared. Then, its enormous mouth opened wide as it roared and threatened me with its long, thick canines. Its rage made the air tremble.

I stared unblinkingly into its eyes.

It roared again, pounding on its chest with the palms of its hands. The sound was incredible, like it was beating a set of enormous drums.

I stared unblinkingly into its eyes.

In my peripheral vision, Menel seemed to be helping the hawker to his feet, but I wasn't going to take my eyes off the ape. I kept on staring. The ape was looking back at me while emitting a very low growl. Blood had told me that in an encounter with a wild animal, you lose the moment you look away.

Come on then. Wanna wrestle? I'm game.

I continued staring intensely, letting the ape know that I was more than willing to fight. Its growl grew steadily fainter, and it began to back off. Finally, the staring contest was ended by the ape breaking its gaze, and it turned around and headed back into the depths of the woods.

I breathed out.

I didn't have to fight. *What a relief*, I thought, and turned around.

"Are you all right?" I said, and the halfling girl came flying at me.

"What was that?! What was *that*, that was crazy crazy crazy! Hey tell me tell me, who are you, an adventurer?! Giant apes don't stop just 'cause you *look* at them, that's just wow, I mean *wow*!"

Her eyes were sparkling with curiosity.

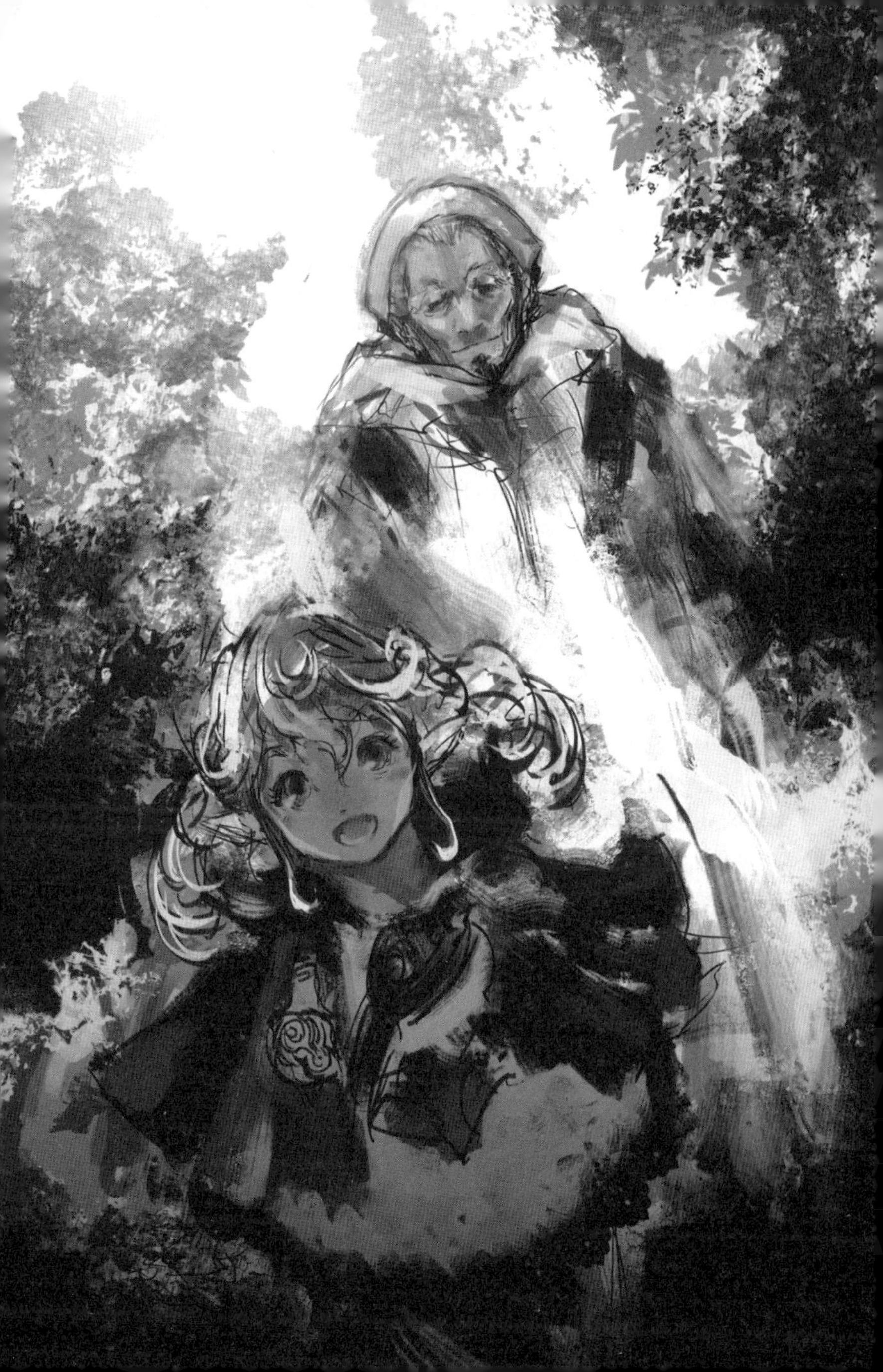

"I'm Robina! Robina Goodfellow! I'm a troubadour, I sing, I dance, I go where the wind takes me, you can call me Bee! And this dweeb is a hawker, he's Antonio! But I call him Tonio! The ships of the trading company he was working for all sank one after another and it folded, so now he passes himself off as a hawker on country roads at the border!"

Robina had red, curly hair and a childlike physique. A halfling girl—could I call her a girl? A "young woman," perhaps? She looked small, but she probably had a longer lifespan than humans, so I wasn't really sure of her age. What I did know: she talked *a lot*. I'd never met anyone like her before.

"Hahaha... I don't believe there's anything left for me to say. Hello, my name is Antonio. Please feel free to call me simply Tonio. As Robina says, I'm a lowly hawker of goods. I was on my way back to where I'm based in Whitesails, when... well, dear me, that was a close shave. Thank you truly."

Antonio was a bearded man somewhere in his late thirties. He looked peaceable and friendly, but a little fatigued, lacking any get-up-and-go... Yeah, no offense to him, but I could see where Robina was coming from with her "dweeb" comment.

"I'm Meneldor. I used to be an adventurer, but now I'm a hunter around here. I was just going to town to buy some stuff. And this is—" Menel looked at me.

Self-introductions were never my strong point—not in my previous world, and not in this one. I always got nervous at times like this. "William. William G. Maryblood. I'm an adventurer, and a priest to the god of the flame, Gracefeel." I made sure to smile. "Call me Will." Yeah, that was probably passable.

Chapter Three

"Wow that's a real noble's name, wait did you say Gracefeel?! Gracefeel's that one right, from the south! The god that has basically no priests anymore! Whoaaa, what a discovery you are! And you're not just a priest you're also a skilled warrior? I mean you must be, who else just stands in the way of a giant ape?! So are you or what?!"

"That's about right," Menel said on my behalf. "He looks a little slow, but he's ridiculously good. I mean, I've been walking with him, and there's hardly been a single beast attacking us."

"You mean even the beasts know how much stronger he is and they *avoid* him?! Whoaa, that's amazing!"

Hm? "There's normally more beasts than this?" I asked.

"I would say so... That is why it's called Beast Woods." Even Antonio was looking at me as if I had something wrong with me.

"What about you two, you alone?" Menel asked, looking around. "Didn't you have any bodyguards? They get killed or something?"

"Well, the thing about that, you see... I'm ashamed to admit that when we ran across the giant ape, they all ran off..."

"And they made such a foofaraw over it that the ape got worked up and then look what happened! Giant apes *never* attack people normally!" Robina sounded very frustrated. "They just look scary, they're actually really nice!"

When Menel heard this, he burst out laughing. "So they showed up totally unprepared, ripped you off the up-front payment, and ran for it! You need to work on your eye for people, brother, if you're gonna be a merchant!" Cackling, he slapped Antonio on the shoulder several times sympathetically. Antonio looked embarrassed and timid.

It seemed like this was something every adventurer went through once or twice. That was a bit of a shock... More importantly though, that meant that these two had lost their protection.

"What are you going to do now?" I asked. "If you like—"

"We can tag along if you want," Menel chimed in. "You can pay us back later." His eyes were very loudly saying, *You leave the negotiating to me!* so I was forced to keep my mouth shut.

"Hmm. And how would you like us to do that?"

"I'm looking to buy some draft animals from Whitesails. I've been helping this guy out with some ruin-hunting, and we made out pretty well from it, so I want to use the money to take the strain off the people back at the village."

"Ah, I see! Yes, I wouldn't mind helping you with that, of course. I have connections with a merchant I can introduce you to."

"That's a big help. Sorry for butting in. This guy can be a bit... His world knowledge has a few holes."

"Oh, so I was right with the noble birth thing? He does kinda give you that feeling, doesn't he?! Sheltered maybe, or like, naive..."

"L-Look, there's no point saying where I came from. You probably wouldn't believe me, and anyway, it's not something I can go spreading around..."

"So you're an adventurer from a noble house who's gotta keep his past a secret 'cause of *noble business*?! I get it! And not only that, a priest to a forgotten god! Wahaaa! How magical! This is poet-brain superfood!"

Wait... what? It seemed like no matter what we said, it only deepened her misunderstanding...

◆

Chapter Three

What followed that was several more days of walking along the trail through the unchanging late-winter scenery of Beast Woods.

Robina and Antonio quickly became Bee and Tonio. Tonio was gentle-mannered and skilled at closing the distance between himself and others; as for Bee, she held nothing back, to the point where I found it doubtful whether the concept of boundaries existed in her head to begin with.

Every time we got to a village, she would whoop out something like, "Woohoo! Here I am, baybee!" with a rowdy and cheerful laugh, and make sure everyone there had a wild time. After she'd sung, danced, livened up the place, and had plenty of tips thrown at her, Tonio would then open up shop. By then, everyone would be in a good mood, and their purse strings nice and loose.

They were a pretty effective combination. Even Menel was impressed by the way they did business. According to him, there were good hawkers and bad hawkers, just like everything else. They weren't all like Tonio; there were also a lot of aggressive sellers and others that were not much different from petty thieves. Which probably meant it was true that Tonio had originally come from a reputable company.

Tonio now had me with him, and he was putting this new element to fantastic use as well. Bee gathered people together, then I asked whether there were any sick or injured among them, gave them treatment, and we transitioned from a celebration of their recovery into a party. Apparently, the parties were getting into full swing even faster now because of this new approach.

"Okay," I said. "Show me your affliction."

I cast the miracles of Cure Illness and Close Wounds on everyone I could.

Just as the essence of magic was creation from chaos using the Words, the essence of benediction was rewriting reality using the influence and benevolence of the gods, the higher beings of this world. It really was faintly terrifying how people were healed as if nothing had ever happened to them in the first place, almost like erasing a part of a pencil sketch and effortlessly redrawing it. The greatness of the gods could never be matched by human magic.

Benediction was inflexible—you had to become the servant of a specific deity, each of which had a specific focus—so it was not a superset of magic, and there was some separation between the two fields. But every time I re-examined benediction, I was reminded of what an incredible power it was.

This power was one I was borrowing from Gracefeel. I had to be careful not to fall into the trap of thinking it was my own power. If I ever did, I was sure that nothing good would come of it.

"E-Excuse me," said the housewife I'd treated for burn scars on her arms, "how much should I give you in return for this?"

"Oh, that's not necessary. I'm only in training at the moment, and your thanks should go to the god of the flame, not to me. If you still feel like you owe something, please buy an item from Tonio." The woman bowed to me several times, then went over to where Tonio had laid out his wares. Menel was giving me a reproachful look for describing myself as "in training."

I wasn't pulling a fast one on her... I really was in training...

And like that, we walked from village to village treating people, playing songs, and selling things and buying them as we headed north over ten days.

I couldn't say just how far we'd traveled; the forest paths were constantly twisting, and we'd taken quite a lot of detours to stop by villages that Tonio knew. My senses told me we'd walked quite far, but it wasn't easy for a person on the ground to convert that into a straight-line distance.

In any case, today was another day in the gloomy forest.

Chapter Three

After an age spent doing nothing but walking, there was a huge, sudden cheer at the head of our group from Bee. As I ran to her to see what was up, my surroundings got brighter and brighter, and then my view cleared.

There were no trees to the left or right, and there was no gloom or darkness.

When I looked up, light was pouring down from the sun, which had started to tilt into the western sky. A clear blue sky of an imminent spring was spread out overhead. I lowered my eyes; the road gently meandered toward the horizon, and on both sides was a series of partitioned fields, creating a patchwork of beautiful, natural colors. A gust of wind blew, and the young, green wheat swayed.

Even though it wasn't cold, I got goosebumps.

"WHEAT ROAD! YAHOOOO!"

Bee danced around, then grabbed Tonio by both hands and spun around in circles.

Menel gazed at the wheat swaying in the wind, deep in thought.

The sheer expansiveness of the plain left me speechless for a while as well—then Bee grabbed my hands, and I too was dancing in circles. I laughed in spite of myself, and started goofing off with her.

However, because we spent so much time fooling around, the sun started to set well before we could make it to the nearest village. Visiting late at night and getting mistaken for robbers would just be stupid, and we happened to have come across a little shrine, so we decided to set up camp there.

"Heheh, I'm in a good mood today!" Bee said. "Why don't I perform for you all? Free of charge!" She took out a small three-stringed instrument shaped a bit like a pear (it was apparently called a rebec), and placed a bow against the strings with an overdramatic flourish.

"Ooh!" Menel said. "Generous of you."

She laughed proudly. "Oh right, have to pick something. Of the recent songs… 'Reystov the Penetrator' is overplayed right now, but then the 'Berkeley Tale of Valor' is such old hat…" She hummed in thought for a moment. "Right, I know! I can do one of the epics of the Three Heroes from the famous Killing of the High King. The Wandering Sage, the War Ogre, and the Beloved Daughter! Sound good?"

I thought my heart was going to stop.

"Oh, that's a good idea," Tonio said.

"Seems a fair choice," said Menel.

"Come to think of it, I haven't performed this one for a li'l while. Um, 'sup Will?"

"U-Uh, nothing, it's nothing! Please, go on! I'd love to hear it!"

"Oho! Nice, nice, that's just what I like to hear! Okay, let's get started!"

The bowstrings started to sing. It was a sad tone that made the air tremble, bringing back memories of distant homelands. My heart was pounding.

"Time marcheth on; nay, mayhap we are the travelers." Bee's voice, usually full of cheer, now took on a deep and mournful quality, the words carrying clearly through the night air. "The veritably strong, even the ingenious sage and holy maiden—they too perish alike with the turns of the moon, 'til nary a thing save for ash and a name endures…"

The sounds of the strings echoed through the air.

They had survived.

"Wherefore let the melody play strong, praying meanwhile that their deeds be everlasting, their heroic names echo down the ages."

Chapter Three

The sound of her voice was creating an indescribable sense of excitement inside me.

They had survived.

"Tonight I speak of the Killing of the Wyvern, but one of the many deeds of the Three Heroes..." Bee smiled at me. "Everyone, if I may have your silence and attention."

They had survived! Their names, even now, still survived!

◆

In the small, dusty, and poorly lit shrine, the rebec's melody echoed out with the crackling of the campfire.

After her prologue, Bee spoke masterfully about the heroes that would feature in the story. I was in a trance, almost as if I was floating on air. I felt such pride, such happiness... I had such fond memories of those days.

"The first, a child born in the south, in a remote settlement of savages. As he raised his first cry, a star fell from Leo, so it is told. The child grew and grew strong, and departed for parts unknown with his demonblade tempered by a shooting star. Known as the Lion, Star Sword, the Hired Blade, the Gods' Gift to Warfare... this man was Blood, the War Ogre. His path was the course of a raging blood storm, and his shouts of victory boomed forth like the roars of a lion."

My heart was dancing. *Damn you, Blood, you didn't speak about yourself at all.* So that was the history behind that sword...

"In the islands of Middle-sea was an infant with a gift: a natural affinity with Words. Bandits attacked his homeland; thereupon he confounded them with fog, and repelled them. The wise men of the time invited that child prodigy to their place of education. He leaped up the ranks thereof, two at a time. Yet soon he stood down from his position, and spake his immortal words: 'There is no truth in academia.' The Wild Wanderer, the Unrecognized Great Mind, the Torrent, the Culture Connoisseur—these are the names of Gus, the Wandering Sage. His true name unknown to the world, who knows now the depths of his mind and heart?"

No one knew the name Augustus? Come to think of it, Gus had said that some sorcerers, being users of the Words, thought that names were Words of power themselves, and so concealed their own and went by only a nickname or an initial. I guessed that the reason he'd so readily told me his real name was that he'd stopped being cautious about it after he died.

"Whence hailed the woman? Perchance a shamanic noblewoman of our own land; perchance the princess of a land afar. Or it may have been that a constellation of fresh-verdure spirits coalesced and formed her sparkling eyes of emerald, and the resplendency of the heavens solidified and became her flowing, golden hair. Whencesoever she arose, how can we doubt that in such a divine form dwelt the soul of a goddess? The Saint of the South, the Unmercenary Maiden Martyr, the Bringer of Blessings, the Dainty Flower... Mary, known also as Mater's Daughter. Her white and merciful hands, to which even fierce beasts bowed their heads, were the brilliant light that pierced through the darkness."

It seemed that Mary's history was unknown, and she was speculated as being of noble birth. I had to agree that her dignified style brought that kind of thing to mind, but if Mary had said to me, "Oh, it's nothing like that. I was born in a poor little hamlet!" I'd easily have been able to see that too.

Chapter Three

After all, Mary loved puttering around in the garden, sowing flower seeds. And once spring came, even the garden beside that temple would burgeon with blossoms…

"Long past now are those bygone days…"

Their voices, their faces, their words—they filled the inside of my mind, and I felt tears starting to come to my eyes.

"Ahh, memories and feelings as numerous as the stars: if thou hast no way home, I can but play thee loud, and carry thee on the blowing winds…"

The tale began.

◆

Blood had apparently once been a wandering sword for hire. The Union Age was mostly a time of peace, but even then, there had been a lot of fighting in outlying areas like this, against goblins, beasts, and other humans. Blood was one of those ruffians full of fight, earning his money by risking his life sticking his neck into all kinds of conflicts.

Come to think of it, I remembered him once giving me a suspiciously detailed lecture on the secrets to staying out of trouble when selling your sword skills. That must have referred to this.

And one day, a certain incident led Blood to meet Gus, and they resolved that problem together. The barbaric swordsman learned of the way of the wise man, and learned to rein in his wild nature and add the sharpness of intelligence to his blade—or so Bee's story went. But if they were the same back then as when I had known them, I could see Gus as the admittedly intelligent loose cannon, and Blood as the one with a surprising amount of common sense who followed after him, astounded by but used to the wizard's antics.

Their free-roaming journey continued, and one day, Mary entered the picture. Where that happened and what brought them together were apparently shrouded in mystery, but it was known that Mary established herself within the party as a surprising source of strength and decisiveness—yeah, I could imagine that—and the three, their abilities and personalities now balanced, built up a name for themselves as heroes of the hinterlands.

With that introduction out of the way, Bee began her recital of the story proper, saying that it was just one of their many deeds. It had occurred near some remote villages, and there had been a monster in the nearby mountains: a wyvern.

Wyverns were winged demidragons capable of flight, although if I remembered Gus's lectures correctly, it was the subject of academic debate whether to categorize them as demidragons or beasts. Although wyverns breathed fire like dragons, they had no front legs and were smaller, weaker, and more simpleminded.

Even so, they were still a significant threat. Hunting a wyvern required a reasonably sized, trained team to attack its nest. It was extremely difficult to secure a victory on flat land against a wyvern when it had absolute control over the sky.

It was also said that some rare wyverns could speak the language of dragons. These wyverns served the dragons, and lizardmen exalted them. As for the wyvern in these mountains, it was one like a beast: it had low intelligence and was unable to talk.

From time to time, when the wyvern got hungry, it would attack the villages, destroy the barns, and carry off the beasts of burden.

The people of the villages discussed the problem together, and decided to offer up one person a year as a sacrifice for the wyvern.

Chapter Three

In remote regions such as these, work animals' lives were often more valuable than people's.

The one chosen that year was a beautiful half-elf girl from a nearby village. She had been born to human parents, with her elven side coming from earlier ancestors. Naturally, the father suspected the mother of being unfaithful, and there were considerable arguments between them.

As she grew up, the girl herself became a source of discord due to her beauty. Some fought over her, while others looked at her with jealousy and envy and treated her as an outcast. The resulting strife led people to keep their distance, and from there, it was inevitable that she would be the one chosen to be sacrificed.

I once heard from my parents that it was hard for a half-elf to gain equal treatment living among humans, or even elves. Half-elves were beautiful, skilled, and lived long lives, yet not to the same extent as elves. Their only options were to stand in their natural place at the top of society, be placed at the bottom, or distance themselves entirely and live as hermits. Too exceptional to be a human and too quickly maturing to be an elf, it was hard for them to be treated as equals in either society. Menel's past had unfortunately followed the same pattern.

When Mary, Blood, and Gus dropped by the village and heard the situation, they had differing opinions. As the story went, Mary was strongly in favor of rescuing her, Blood asked if Mary planned on raising her as well and where the hell the money was going to come from, and Gus remained silent in contemplation.

It felt to me as though the actual conversation had probably been similar, but slightly different. The personalities the characters had in the story felt slightly off, particularly where Gus and Blood were concerned, and especially with respect to Gus's fixation on money.

In any case, what ended up happening was that Blood gathered the villagers together and told them, "We can kill the wyvern.

Is there anyone who can pay? Would you like to pay money to have the wyvern killed?"

A stir ran through the crowd of villagers, and their only response was silence. As things stood, the villages were functioning. What would happen if this failed and the wyvern was only injured and became enraged? And supposing they succeeded, adventurers who could kill a wyvern would command an enormous sum in reward money. Did they really want to go so far to save the sacrifices?

Amid the silence, Blood clucked his tongue and headed back to their lodging, leaving Mary with the words, "See that? That's reality."

But that night, the three were visited by a poor farm boy. The boy, who by the looks of it hadn't been taught any manners, gruffly held out several coins for them to take: copper coins coated in verdigris, and silver coins with worn-down edges and blackened faces. He didn't speak, but these were clearly the boy's entire savings.

Blood said, "You want us to fight a wyvern for this pittance?"

But Gus snatched the coins from the boy's hand, took a good, long look at the dirty currency, which didn't even have a hint of a shine, and said, "Ohh, yes, this is good money. Look at how it sparkles."

I was sure that was word for word what he said because I could visualize the scene as clear as day.

"Don't you agree, Mary?"

"Oh, I couldn't agree more, Gus. We've been given something very special."

"Mm. And I think, in light of the fact that we have received something of such value…"

"We'll have to do our job, won't we?" Mary smiled warmly, softly.

Blood scratched his head in frustration. "Goddamned softies. Working for nothing," he muttered.

Chapter Three

Then, the boy stepped up to Blood and proclaimed, "If it's not enough, I'll pay with myself. You saw them. No one here'd have the guts to come after me if you took me away. Sell me to a slave dealer or whatever you want."

"You ain't worth jack," Blood said, returning him a hard stare.

The boy didn't look away.

Blood broke into a broad smile. "Heh. So you do have guts. Guess even runts can be warriors." He cast his eyes over the boy. "I'm a warrior too. And when one of us warriors swallows his pride and asks for help, we oughta support each other. So... what the hell." He ruffled the boy's hair, a smile tugging at the corner of his mouth. "Let's get it done."

"Yes."

"Mm."

And so the three took on the wyvern.

◆

The wyvern soared. It flew fast against the wind, acting as if the sky was all its own. It was thinking that today was about the day for its food to get placed on the field at the base of the mountain. It was simpleminded, but it had enough intelligence to roughly follow the passage of time.

There was a simple altar in the field, and by it stood the sacrifice, wearing a veil and with her head lowered toward the ground. The creature swooped down, intent on devouring her.

At that moment, the wyvern was knocked back by an expanding wall of light. Rich, golden hair flowed from behind the sacrifice's veil.

It was Mary.

Without allowing the wyvern a second to recover, Gus appeared from behind the altar and cast the Word of Knotting.

The wyvern immediately attempted to withdraw from this unexpected situation, but it had no freedom to resist. In an instant, its wings were magically bound, and it plummeted to earth.

The sound it made as it hit the ground was booming, but the wyvern's body was tough. It drew a deep breath, preparing to defend itself against its sudden adversaries. Blood raised a war cry and charged, his sword firmly gripped in both hands, ready to strike.

The wyvern breathed fire.

Behind Blood, Mary was praying. Her blessing protected him and scattered the flames. Gus's fingers drew the Word of Knotting again and again, forbidding the monster flight. The sky denied to it, the wyvern bared its fangs and thrust its head at its attackers. A single swing of Blood's two-handed sword sent it flying from the rest of its body.

In that instant, did the wyvern's head realize what had happened to it? Three little "meals"—that was all there had been. And those little meals had *killed it*. Of course, its consciousness probably faded in a second or less as jets of blood spouted and soaked the earth.

The following day, the villagers came to check on the sacrificial altar and discovered the decapitated corpse of the wyvern, stripped of every part that could be exchanged for cash.

After that, Mary, Gus, and Blood took the poor boy and the half-elf girl with them and headed for a city. There was no place in the village for those two anymore.

Blood asked them what they were going to do, and the boy replied he'd come up with something. Hearing this, Blood gave the boy a dagger to keep with him. It was a magical dagger engraved with Words.

Chapter Three

"Old Gus engraved Words on it. It'll do more for you than most amulets. Every warrior's gotta have a shortsword or a dagger. Can't show off without one."

"Please take this too," Mary said, handing the girl a bag. "Take care of your bodies, and of each other. I'm sure you have lots of hard times ahead of you, but please, don't forget how important it is to persevere."

They looked inside the bag. It was full of silver and copper coins.

They both turned it down as fast as they could. This was more than the reward the boy had paid the three to do the job! The girl protested too—they couldn't accept something like this. But Gus shrugged and said, "Hmph. Whoever said I was giving it to you? This is an investment. I'm lending it, nothing more."

The two tilted their heads to the side in confusion. Lending it?

"Here is what we want from you," Gus said. "Live hard, increase your wealth, make a name for yourselves. Spread your names far and wide, so wherever they go, they are accompanied by thunderous applause. And when your names reach our ears, that is when we or a delegate we dispatch will come to collect what we lent you, plus interest."

Then Gus said he would tell them his real name, which they would use as a code word, and to remember it well. And so the boy and the girl learned the name of the Wandering Sage, the name unknown by anyone in this world.

The boy and the girl took each other by the hand and headed to the city together, and the Three Heroes took the main road in search of new adventures. And so, under a blue sky, the tale of the Three Heroes' Killing of the Wyvern came to an end.

"And there's a bit of a rumor that comes with this story…" Bee grinned mischievously. "Count Dagger of the Fertile Kingdom…

They say his proper surname was Wizardsdagger." The strings reverberated, the note and the story both lingering pleasantly. "Even today, at the count's mansion, an old half-elf lady is waiting for the Sage's delegate."

Then...

"The Sage passed away, but she still believes that one day, a delegate who knows his true name will come."

Their names...

"And she will return the dagger, the money she was lent, and the interest, as well as the amount that was entrusted to her husband."

Their names were still echoing.

"And she will say her thanks for what was done for her."

Over two hundred years later, and they were still echoing, right up to the present.

"And that's the end of my story. A story of great heroes that echoes down the ages, even today... Huh? Will? Will, are you crying?"

As she tilted her head and peered into my face, I panicked. My face was bright red, and my eyes were blurry with tears. I was only moments from a complete breakdown. "C-Crying?! No, I'm not crying!"

"Ohh yes you are! Your eyes are red!" Bee gave a satisfied laugh. "My awesome storytelling touched you, didn't it?"

"N-No, no it didn't!"

"Hehehe, fess up fess up!"

We teased and ribbed each other a lot that evening. As we joked together, I felt that something warm had flared to life inside my chest.

Blood, Mary, Gus.

There are so many people in this world besides me who still remember you.

There were so many.

And I could have cried for joy.

Chapter Three

♦

The following day, I was outside the shrine before the first light of dawn, practicing thrusting my spear and pulling it back. The fact that I had been on night watch duty since late last night had something to do with it, and I was just a little excited as well.

I'd now heard about the Fertile Kingdom. It was a country that had expanded from Grassland down here to Southmark. Count Dagger was nobility, and the expansion of the Fertile Kingdom to Southmark was a new development of the past few decades, so the half-elf woman in the story was probably back on the other continent. Which meant that if I crossed the sea, I could find someone I could talk to about Blood, Mary, and Gus.

I had a lot of things to deal with right now, so I couldn't just drop everything, but one day I wanted to cross the sea and pay her a visit. Thrusting the spear forward again with a grunt, I thought about how I wanted to feel like I'd earned the right to say with pride, *I was a member of their family.*

Mixing in some footwork, I jabbed out with my spear again, sharply. And sharper again.

In the language of battle techniques, "sharpness" didn't refer to simple speed. It referred to the swiftness of the switch between stillness and action.

Stillness…
Explosive motion.
Stillness…
Explosive motion.
Sharper. Sharper. Sharper still—
"Lo. I see you're hard at work already."

The voice broke me out of my concentration. How many of those practice thrusts had I done? I was pretty short of breath, so it had probably been at least a hundred.

"Tonio."

The one who had come out of the aged shrine was the man with the beard and mild smile. I went to put away my spear.

"Oh, no, I didn't mean to interrupt. Please continue."

"Ah, thanks…"

That said, I'd allowed myself to get way too absorbed in practice. I still had walking to do today, so it would do me no good to exhaust myself by pushing my body to its limits. I had to do some cooling down exercises anyway, so I decided to just practice my form. Tonio sat down on a nearby stump and watched me.

"I must say, you are strong, Will."

"Am I? You think so?"

"Well, I'm not sure how much this is worth, coming from someone who was cheated by a group of fraudulent adventurers…" Tonio laughed as if to conceal his embarrassment.

I listened while practicing my form with slow, gentle movements. Knock away the opponent's weapon, lower myself, upwards thrust…

"But I can at least tell that your movements are very polished. And more than that, if I may give my opinion as a merchant…"

"What is it?"

"I believe that spear to be a dwarven masterpiece, and you look perfectly natural with it. Someone who's a perfect match for a gem like that must be a gem themselves." He shrugged. "However, there is something I don't understand."

"Something you don't understand?"

Chapter Three

"Yes," he said. I suddenly noticed that behind his gentle gaze were the keen eyes of a merchant carefully evaluating a product. "What is it that you *truly seek*?"

◆

I paused and tilted my head to the side. "Truly seek? Hmm, well, what I want is for the god of the flame—"

"Those are your desires as a priest. Well, perhaps once one is a saintly priest, it becomes a way of life, but all the same... Do you not have any individual desires?"

"Why are you asking?"

"Because I am a merchant." Tonio laughed. "That which abounds far away, I sell close by, and that which abounds close by, I sell far away. That is what it means to be a merchant. Our business is in moving products, granting people's wishes, and ensuring their satisfaction in exchange for an appropriate price."

He spoke openly and honestly, but his tone was serious. It dawned on me that this was the creed which he lived his life by.

"And yet... I cannot picture how you could be satisfied," Tonio continued. "You are a bit of a mystery. You have muscular arms and plenty of pluck. Based on the way you heal difficult wounds and illnesses, you have earned the gods' blessings. I sense etiquette and erudition in the way you act, and you seem to have built up a financial cushion as well. And yet, you are sensitive enough to shed tears at a famous story as if you have barely experienced life at all. I have never seen a person quite like you before. It seems to me that 'nobility' is not quite accurate. You are like the holy knights that one hears about in stories."

Tonio smiled with his whole face. "So for my own edification, I thought I would ask you directly while I have the opportunity. What is it that you, as an individual, are looking for? Or are you indeed a representative of God through and through?"

I had to think about the answer. What *did* I want from the outside world—from this world? In fact, to begin with...

"Tonio, I, um... prior to now, I was living in a small and happy place, with people who... well, they were the ones who raised me, they were my teachers, and I also thought of them as my family. But just before I was due to set off on my own and become independent, I suddenly lost those people and was forced to leave. In their place, I gained the protection of the god of the flame."

Those events with the god of undeath—it seemed unreal, but they had only happened a few weeks ago.

"I still know so little about the world—about anything, really—so I'm basically just mindlessly following the mission my god sets for me, I think."

I didn't know anything about this place, so how was I meant to know what I wanted here? I thought that I probably needed first to learn about this world, this world that Blood and Mary and Gus had fought to protect, and I told him that. "So, the first thing I want to do is learn about the world. I think I'll discover what I want as I encounter things and learn about them."

As I said it, an image came into my head of Blood, Mary, and Gus laughing, and I pictured their exploits together.

I looked down a little, embarrassed. "Also, I... I'd like to make some friends... I guess."

That was something I hadn't been able to obtain in my previous world. A gang of friends like Mary and Gus had been to Blood. Those three had been my parents and teachers, but this was

Chapter Three

something they hadn't been able to give me, something I needed to go out into the world and obtain for myself.

"Is Menel not a friend?" Tonio asked.

Put on the spot, I gave a single laugh while I thought of an answer. "I think we get along pretty well, but he won't look at me as a friend, you know? And everyone else puts me on a pedestal, calling me 'sir' or 'Father' or something..." I couldn't get used to that, and I felt uncomfortable being respected so much when I was so ignorant about so many things. If Menel said we were friends, I had a feeling it would make me pretty happy.

"Yeah," I said. "Friends would be nice..."

Voicing it brought home the reality. I was saying I wanted friends because even at the age of fifteen (according to the solstice system), I didn't have a single one. That was pretty darn bad, I had to admit. So much so that it was a little bit funny. People really don't change much.

"I see." Having heard my answer, Tonio smiled cheerfully. "Then perhaps I will put myself forward for the third place position."

"Huh?"

"I fear incurring the wrath of Menel and Robina if I beat them to the punch."

Seeing me tilt my head in confusion, Tonio laughed loudly and rose from the stump. The sun had risen without me noticing. "All right. Let's collect some water and start preparing breakfast."

Tonio was good at cooking. For breakfast, he made bread by mixing flour with water, kneading it into dough, winding it around a stick, then heating it over the campfire. It was simple, but eaten steaming hot with cheese, some lightly grilled bacon dripping with grease, and a little salt sprinkled on top, the result was delicious.

According to Bee, Tonio's skill at cooking was the reason she was accompanying him. Apparently she was a halfling who really enjoyed eating.

As for me, I had learned how to cook, generally speaking, but the ingredients available to me in that city of the dead were extremely limited, so there wasn't much I knew how to make. And Menel, in contrast to his pretty exterior, was the kind of guy who didn't care about taste so long as he had something to eat, and it showed in his cooking. Tonio's presence had enriched our daily meals considerably.

We ate the holy bread I was bestowed each morning after my prayer as a snack while on the road. Meals were eaten two or sometimes three times a day in this world. Physical laborers in particular usually had a midday meal, and right now, we were in the middle of a journey. Walking all day took a lot of energy. I wanted a midday meal if I could get one, but on the other hand, I didn't want to stop walking. Tonio had been the one to suggest that we should light a fire for breakfast and leave the holy bread for lunchtime, and it had sounded like a perfectly good plan to me.

"You ask me when I'll be back home / I wish I knew that great unknown."

Bee often sang as we walked.

"The heavens open on a stagnant pond / We both fall silent as the rain beats on."

She didn't much care whether it fit the mood.

"If we don't know when, we'll say 'someday' / That someday, we'll embrace again / And laugh about today."

Oh. I thought it was going to be a depressing song about lovers, but it flowed beautifully into a hope-filled ending. Clever.

"Hehe." Bee sounded proud. "It's a pretty nice one, isn't it?"

"The final verse felt like a ray of light piercing through the clouds."

Chapter Three

"Yeah, exactly!" Bee said, equally entranced by the lyrics. "That's what's so great about it."

She really did like songs and poetry.

Chatting like that, we passed through several villages, which became more flourishing the further north we went.

Occasionally, we even came across places big enough to call a town, with probably over a thousand people living in them. In places like that, Tonio would quickly buy and sell and gather information, and then we'd move on. He looked like he'd mastered this process. I thought again about just how good of a merchant he probably was.

"Oh, right, I meant to ask you," said Menel. "How's Whitesails doing right now?"

I suddenly realized that he, too, had been cooped up in a remote village, so it must have been some time since he visited the port.

"The Fertile Kingdom is in a transition period at the moment with its new king," Tonio said.

"Wait, you mean Egbert II has…?"

"Yeah," said Bee. "His posthumous name's 'Egbert the Bold,' they're saying. He was a pretty good king, I thought…"

"So he's dead…" Menel closed his eyes. Somehow, I felt the dignified character of an aged half-elf in him.

According to Tonio and Bee, the Fertile Kingdom had recently suffered the passing of its king, and a new king had succeeded him.

The one who had enriched the kingdom thus far and shown an eagerness to expand into the southern regions was King Egbert II, also known as Egbert the Bold. After his death, he was succeeded by his son and heir, Prince Owen. From listening to them talk, I got the impression that King Egbert II had been a pretty brilliant man, and at the same time, the kind of person to want to run the show all on his own.

Although King Egbert II ran the kingdom excellently and led it to prosperity, the local feudal lords were not the least bit happy at having their rights and interests gradually eroded by the domineering tactics of the king and the aristocrats who were advising him. However, because he was actually producing results, they were unable to openly criticize him.

It was at a time like this that Egbert II's love of alcohol came back to haunt him. His death came suddenly and was attributed to a stroke or something similar. He may have surrounded himself with priests offering strong divine protection, but there was apparently nothing they could do in a case like this where he was there one moment and gone the next.

King Owen, who inherited the throne, was in the prime of his life, but he was said to be a pretty undistinguished person. He wasn't a degenerate or a wayward thinker, but he was neither as talented nor as wise as his father. In terms of the report cards I got from school in my past life, he would have gotten a run of Bs and Cs, but no As, even when including extra points for having the right attitude.

In terms of his personality, he didn't possess his father's decisiveness either, and the feudal lords that the previous king had kept under his thumb seized on the opportunity to assert themselves. They insisted that expanding to the south was a bad idea after all. King Owen replied that it was good, and that they should continue it. To which the lords complained about "our expenses" this, "our forces" that, "our defenses are suffering," and on and on, ad infinitum.

"Isn't that... pretty bad?"

"It is. It seems that the political situation over on the continent is a little chaotic. Fortunately, however, Southmark has not been greatly affected thus far. That would be due to His Highness's younger

Chapter Three

brother being dispatched here. His Excellency is an extremely gifted individual."

The king's brother, Ethelbald Rex Fertile, was a youthful man in his thirties. He was the son of Egbert II and his second wife, and didn't share the same mother as King Owen; however, it was said that he took after his father, excelling equally in the arts of the sword and the pen.

King Owen, concerned about the political turmoil, pushed through an order to demote his brother to the status of commoner. Then, he revived the extinct aristocratic family of Southmark, and ennobled his brother Duke Ethelbald Rex Southmark. In other words, he appointed him in charge of the entire expansion effort to Southmark.

Once Duke Ethel received his title, he gathered together a group of vassals of both military and non-military prowess, finished making the necessary arrangements, and immediately crossed the sea to the south. As the turmoil on the continent continued—

"That all the necessary functions of government are somehow still operating around Whitesails is the result of His Excellency's excellent governance."

The situation seemed to be pretty dramatic.

As we talked about all these things, we walked up a road with fields on either side. The ears of wheat rustled in the wind. The air was cold; we were still in winter, but I could detect a hint of spring.

When we reached the top of the hill, the faint salty scent of the sea tickled my nose. Spread out before us was a horizon of ocean.

It was the bay.

Long stretches of land spread out on both sides, as if it were hugging the sea. The blue sea was busy with boats with white sails coming and going, and right in the inlet was a large town. My eyes caught the vivid red and brown tiled roofs, then the rows of white houses lining the slope toward the sea, the steeples, and the bell tower. And was that beautiful series of arches running along the outer edge of the city an aqueduct?

This was a city—an actual, living city. Several thousand people were probably living here—maybe even close to ten thousand. There were city streets filled with people. There was activity, the busyness of people going about their daily lives. Even though I was looking at it all from a great distance, I could feel the city's vibrancy like I was there in the middle of it all.

A *city*. An assemblage of human activity. It was a symbol of what Blood, Mary, and Gus had risked their lives to see protected.

As sunlight glittered on the surface of the sea, I remained gazing at the bustle of that dazzling city until Menel and Bee called my name.

Chapter Four

Whitesails was a wealthy city. The people walking through the streets were wearing clothes dyed in all kinds of colors, and I could see certain tendencies in their hairstyles and accessories.

In short—get this—*trends* existed here! They had the time and money to think about *fashion*! Just that fact alone was shocking to me.

In fact, my first shock had come before that, when I entered the city. There was no kind of check required, and no toll to pay to pass through the city gate. I'd subconsciously been assuming that there would be that kind of thing based on what I knew about medieval cities, and I'd been prepared to be kept waiting, but they just let us right in.

"That's one of His Excellency Ethel's policies. He's the one governing this city," Tonio explained to me.

A huge volume of goods was being sent into this city via the sea route to the north, and spreading to the rest of Southmark via the land routes and waterways as if they were blood vessels. Because there was such an overwhelming amount passing through, stopping it all at the city gate would be a recipe for chaos, and in fact would create a hotbed of smuggling.

So His Excellency Ethel brought in the money needed to run the city by imposing fees for the ships to dock at the wharves, rental fees for space at the market, taxes upon the companies setting up

Chapter Four

shop within the city, and avoided interfering with the movements of people, goods, and money as much as possible. That was the direction he'd taken, at least for Whitesails, Tonio told me.

I hmm'ed, somewhat impressed. I wasn't that well versed in economics, but I got the impression that this was quite a progressive, open-minded, and liberal policy.

The way people speak about Duke Ethelbald seems well deserved, I thought as I walked around the city. "Hm? What are those?"

Some kind of pillar-like objects were lined up along the road. Each had something like an... umbrella at the top...?

"Uh, those are streetlights."

"Streetlights?!"

What?!

"You didn't know what those were? Oh my God, Will, get with the times! They have the Word of Light engraved on them. Apprentices at the Academy of Sages come around in the evening and light them up. The apprentices get to practice binding mana to Signs, and the city people get to have light during the night as well, so that's pretty useful."

"Exactly. It is good training for apprentice sorcerers, and an avenue to earning a little bit of pocket money as well. Similarly," Tonio said, pointing at a large building ahead of us, "that is another large source of income for sorcerers-in-training. It makes frequent use of the Words of Heat and Purification, after all."

"Is that—"

"Hehe..." Bee gave me another mischievous laugh. "I bet even you know what that one is," she said, spinning around on the spot just to be funny. "You guessed it, it's the balnea!"

Balnea?

"Hm? Something up, Will?"

"Is something the matter?"

Wait, I knew that word! Wasn't that a public bathhouse?! I could take a *bath* there?!

"Let's go!" I announced without a second thought. The other three looked surprised.

◆

To cut a long story short, my first bath in some time was a wonderful experience.

After all, considering the time period, I'd honestly been considering the possibility that the water would be dirty, unhygienic, and carry all kinds of diseases, but the Word of Purification was doing its job, and the water was crystal clear. The problem of needing an immense amount of fuel to maintain the temperature had been solved by the Word of Heat. Wonderful. I'm repeating myself, but it was wonderful.

It wasn't like the Japanese-style bathhouses I was familiar with—instead, there was a sauna-like hot bath and a cold-water pool—but even so, it was amazing. The travel fatigue that had accumulated in all the muscles throughout my body melted away in the heat and disappeared as I relaxed. It was a moment of bliss.

After exiting the public bath, I felt like a whole layer had slipped clean off my body like the shell off a boiled egg. My body felt toasty warm, and the breeze felt good against it. Even while on the road, I'd been keeping clean with the Word of Purification, but a proper bath was something else.

The three of us men killed time in the open area outside the bathhouse, and after a little while...

Chapter Four

"LA LA LA... ♪" Bee came out holding the things she'd left with the bathhouse owners. She was singing a tune to herself and was clearly in a very good mood. "It's really nice to have a bath every once in a while," she said.

"Absolutely."

"Won't deny it, but I don't like packed places like that very much." Menel had attracted an awful lot of attention because of his beauty and the fact that it was rare to see a half-elf in the first place. Normally he could get around this by wearing a hood or something, but there was just no way for him to conceal himself like that at a bathhouse.

At this very moment, he had his hood firmly down over his eyes with a sour look on his face, so we decided to hurry up and change locations. "Lessee," Bee said, "how about we get something to eat at a tavern, and then..."

"What next?"

"I suggest we head to a temple," said Tonio. "Will is a priest, so I imagine he will want to pay them a visit."

"Oh!" I said. I'd had my attention pulled in so many different directions that I'd almost forgotten. I had to make contact with an established temple. I was technically a proper priest bestowed with a god's protection, so I was hoping they'd make time for me, but I had my doubts.

The four of us walked together to a tavern and had something to eat. I was very surprised when I saw their cooking used rice. It seemed to be what I had once known as Indica rice, probably grown in a dry field. They first stir-fried vegetables in a flat-bottomed, shallow pan with oil and (fittingly for a port) a selection of seafood, including shrimp, shellfish, and whitefish, then added the rice and water and cooked it all together.

The rice had absorbed the flavors of the fish well, and the dish was salted to perfection. I could have eaten this stuff all day. The diluted wine it was served with tasted good too.

This was civilization. That was the only thing I could come up with to describe it. This was the taste of civilization.

Tonio and Bee were debating the meal.

"This tastes quite good, wouldn't you say?"

"Hmm." She didn't sound entirely convinced. "I could have done with it not being boiled down so much."

For these two, a traveling hawker and a troubadour, this city was a base of operations. They were probably relatively used to it.

As for Menel and me, conversation was just not what we cared about right then, so we skipped that entirely in favor of gorging ourselves on what was in front of us. And when we were done, we both ordered seconds.

Civilization really was such a wonderful, marvelous thing!

◆

And so we reached the temple in Whitesails. It was a majestic building made of smooth white stone, with big wide columns, column-lined walkways, statues of the gods, and a front garden full of carefully pruned plants and trees. It all looked brand new, but still it had a kind of artistic character. Menel commented under his breath that they must have spent a hell of a lot on this place.

I asked Menel, Tonio, and Bee to wait in the front garden for the time being, and I walked into the temple proper. Once inside, I thought I'd find a priest and ask to be shown to someone high ranking.

However, the first reaction that came from the young male deacon who stood before me wearing loose white robes was an uninformative "mmm." It sounded like I was giving him problems.

Chapter Four

"You say you've been blessed with the protection of Gracefeel, god of the flame?" he asked.

"Yes, that's right."

The young deacon mmm'ed again. "That is a deity not often seen... By our rules, we like to make use of the prayer of Detect Faith in this instance..."

"That's perfectly fine."

Just imagine if a priest of an evil god, not caring about the consequences of his actions, nonchalantly walked in and said, "I would like to greet the high-ranking priests." Not all priests were trained in combat as I was, so I could see the need for a security step to check that someone suspicious stopping by—like me, the priest of a minor god—wasn't working for an evil god and trying to conceal their identity.

"Yes," he said, "but most unfortunately, I'm afraid that everyone sufficiently blessed to determine the faith of others is out at the moment..."

"Out?" In a large temple like this? I was surprised that was even possible.

"Yes. Attacks from beasts big and small have been on a significant rise everywhere recently. Everyone from the vice-bishop down is being kept very busy."

From the vice-bishop down... Did he say *vice*-bishop?

"What are you doing that requires taking up the walkway?" someone said from behind me in a grave voice that seemed to echo. I turned around to see an incredibly fat middle-aged man, dressed in loosely fitting priest's robes embroidered with gold and silver thread. They did nothing to hide his noticeable potbelly, nor did his big, puffy cheeks compensate for the sternness in his expression. He was wearing several gold and silver rings on his sausage-like fingers.

"B-Bishop Bagley!" The deacon twitched in surprise and visibly straightened his posture.

"I asked you what you were doing," Bishop Bagley repeated. He looked irritated.

The deacon seemed very uneasy and didn't look like he was going to be able to give a proper answer. Although it was slightly bad form, I decided to interject.

"It's a pleasure to make your acquaintance. My name is William G. Maryblood. I was blessed with the protection of the god of the flame, Gracefeel, and have come to this Whitesails temple to introduce myself." I put my right hand over the left side of my chest, brought my left leg back a little, and bowed. Mary had taught me this.

"Hmm. Bart Bagley. I am in charge of this temple." Bishop Bagley bowed to me roughly in return, and then glowered at me. "Gracefeel... God of the flame. Practically a lost god. The possibility remains, of course, that what we have here is a suspicious character misusing Gracefeel's name to carry out some nefarious plot..."

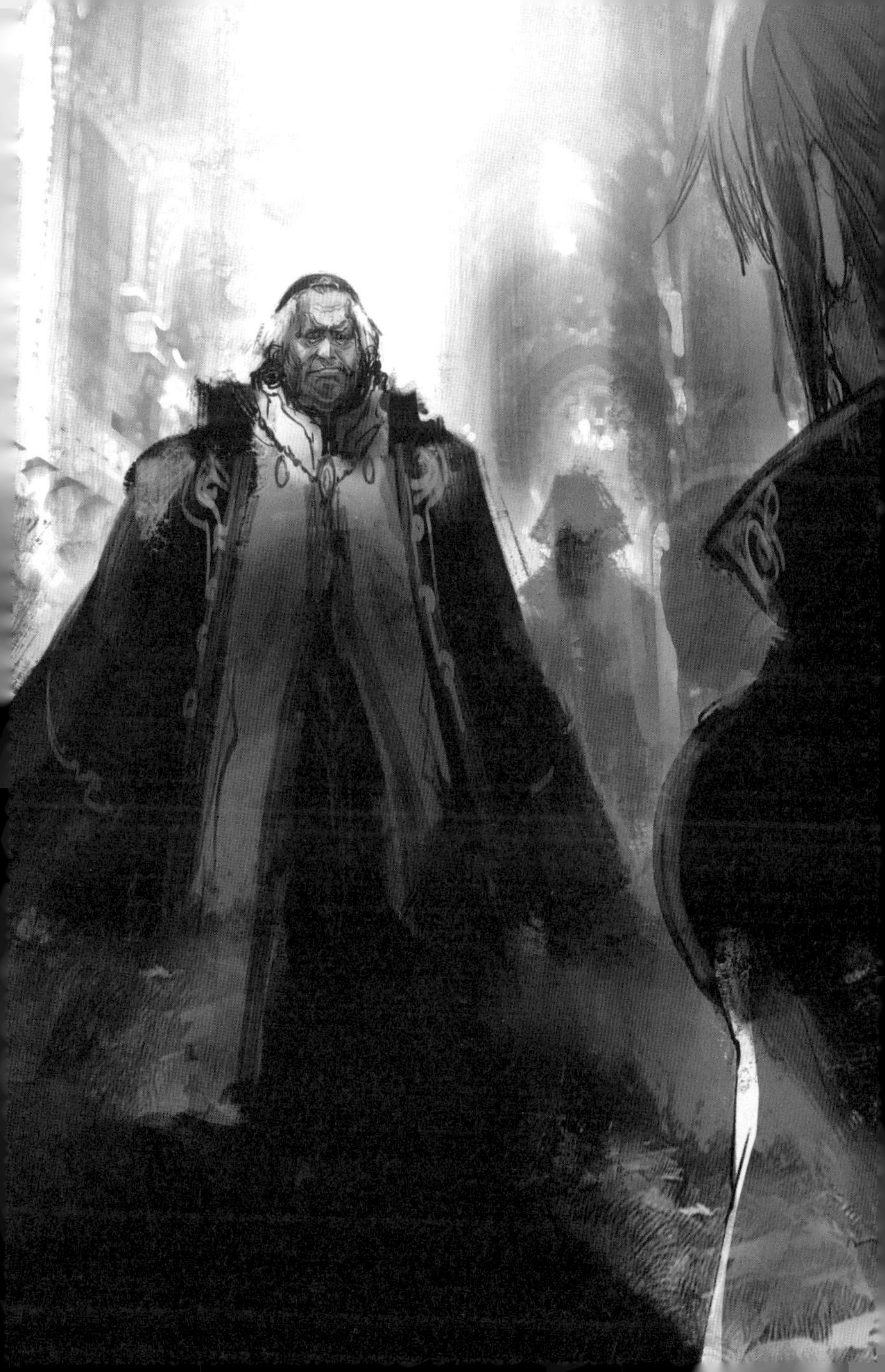

"That is a reasonable suspicion. Would you like me to perform a blessing as proof?"

Bishop Bagley snorted. "Neophytes are quick to turn to divine protection when in trouble. The protection received from a god is not to be brandished lightly and *certainly* not to be vaunted."

Wow. I hadn't expected that response, but now that I thought about it, he made a good point. Gus had said the same thing about magic. Blessings didn't carry much risk, so I'd been using them more casually, but he was definitely right.

"You're absolutely right. Thank you very much for making me aware of my naivete."

The bishop snorted again. "What do you understand to be the teachings of the god of the flame?"

"Light is the existence of dark. Words are the existence of silence. And living is the existence of death."

The bishop breathed out through his nose once more. "You," he said to the deacon. "Add him to the register and show him around the temple."

"Huh? But... We still have the prayers of Detect Faith and Detect Lie to—"

"*Idiot!*" It was a thunderclap. "Did all of that simply miss your ears, you cretin?!" His voice echoed throughout the temple, lingering in the air like static in a thunderstorm. Other people were looking at us now.

"I have to put in an appearance at the Weavers' Guild banquet— spend your time here as you please, do not cause any problems, and donate a little," Bishop Bagley told me without pausing for breath, then clomped away to somewhere else in the temple. The deacon still had his head ducked into his shoulders.

Chapter Four

Once the bishop had disappeared completely, the deacon finally started talking to me, in a voice that showed he was still a little shaken. "What are the odds we'd run into Bishop Bagley?" he said. "He gave us a hard time, didn't he? I was impressed by how well you handled it."

Then he talked about how the bishop was now a hedonist who spent a large amount of his time at banquets, never performed a single blessing, was quick to anger, and constantly complained; on the other hand, the vice-bishop was noble and wonderful and there were only good things to say about him.

Not wanting to take sides, I gave some vague hums in response as we completed my registration. Then, after meeting back up with Menel, Bee, and Tonio, I had the deacon show us all around the temple and assign us a guest room. It was quite plain, but we'd at least been given more than just a bale of hay or something to sleep on; there were actually beds with sheets.

"Say," I said, "about the bishop here, um…"

"Mmm, I don't hear much good about him, I guess?" Bee said. "Like how he's kinda snooty. And materialistic."

"He also appears to have behind-the-scenes influence in the city's commerce and industrial guilds," added Tonio.

Huh. That was the reputation he had? As I tried to put this information together with my own impression of him, I realized I was finding it hard to concentrate. What was all that noise going on outside? It sounded like incessant clanging, maybe a bell.

Bee started, and I looked at her in confusion.

"That's… not the bell for the hour…" she said. "They're *hammering* it… Is there a fire or something?!"

"That sounds like the emergency bell, yes," Tonio said.

Unrest started to spread around the temple. We rushed to our equipment and other stuff we'd stashed in the corner of the room. We heard the sound of footsteps rushing down the hallway, and then screaming.

"Wyvern! Wyvern! Everyone, RUUUUN!"

Beyond the walls of the room and above the roof, a low rush of wind and a vast shadow passed overhead. The next instant, the force of an impact echoed throughout the temple.

◆

"Hnnngggggggg!"

"Ow, oww, owwww!"

"Someone! Someone help! There are people being crushed under here!"

"What's happening?!"

"Don't shove, don't shove!"

"My child, has anyone seen my child?!"

"Oh God!"

The inside of the temple was in a state of panic. Still putting on my armor, I went out into the courtyard surrounded by walkways. Using the temple's architectural decorations and pillars for traction, I jumped up the side of the building and, after only a few leaps, I made it to the roof.

The temple was comprised of numerous buildings, like the living quarters, assembly halls, and so on, and as I looked around I noticed that the roof of the main hall had fallen in.

I looked down inside. It was chaos down there—I guessed there were probably people under all that rubble. It was a disaster that the high-ranking priests were out right now; it looked like it was going

Chapter Four

to take some time to bring this situation under control. I furrowed my brow unconsciously.

But I couldn't go down there to help them.

I turned my eyes away, and saw the gray silhouette circling the sky over Whitesails. It had a long tail and enormous wings made of stretched sheets of skin. Running down the spine of its back was a series of bladelike spikes, and it had a neck so thick it looked like you could only just barely get your arms around it. I could see occasional glimpses of fire from its mouth.

The circling, twisting movements of its slender silhouette were full of power and energy, and I was certain that the sight would send a shiver up the spine of anyone who witnessed it.

It was a wyvern.

It flew at one of the city's steeples and grabbed hold of it with its legs. The force of the landing smashed the structure apart. As the stone walls of the steeple crumbled, the wyvern kicked off again, launching back into flight and circling the sky over the city once more.

Figures on the ground that seemed to be soldiers were firing occasional crossbow shots at it, but it didn't seem to care. It was moving around too much. Those few soldiers holding crossbows could chase after the wyvern all they liked; they wouldn't even be able to keep it within range. And if they did manage to get close enough, they would never land a single shot on a wyvern flying at such speeds; their quarrels would fly straight past.

Flames erupted from the wyvern's mouth—it was breathing fire. From the area licked by those flames came screams and cries so loud I could hear them from the temple. Houses caught fire. People ran, pushing and shoving each other in the scramble to escape. And the wyvern cried out in excitement and dived straight in.

Roof tiles, blown off by the wind pressure, fell randomly and smashed on the streets. Some houses had collapsed. The panic was escalating. Several people fell over. I was sure there were others being trampled. I could hear buildings collapsing. The wyvern destroyed another one.

I had no idea what was going on. Why on earth was the wyvern doing this? But it didn't change reality: the city was being destroyed before my eyes. Civilization—what those three had fought to protect—a place where people still lived like people should—was being destroyed.

The blood rushed to my head.

"*Verba volant...*" This was a slightly long incantation—not something I normally used. In parallel with my verbal incantation, I added another Word with a single movement of my finger to extend the range, and then—

"*Tonitrus!*"

At that moment, there was an ear-splitting sound, like the sound of a broken bell being struck as hard as possible, or maybe the sound of a cannon. I smelled the air burning as a single bolt of lightning flew from where I stood on the temple roof directly toward the wyvern flying so proudly over the city.

But it didn't connect! The distance was too great. Not only that, but a straight-line attack was far too inaccurate against the wyvern when it had total freedom to move around three-dimensional space. The range of ancient magic was not that great to begin with; that probably wasn't helping, either. Words being Words, they attenuated with distance, having a smaller effect on farther targets.

I prepared for a second shot. Of the Words I could use with a reasonable amount of stability, the Word of Lightning boasted the longest range. I could fire it as many times as necessary until I hit. That was the thought going through my head, and it came from a place of desperation, and anger, and zero composure—

Chapter Four

"What the hell are you doing, you fig idiot?!" The back of my head suddenly stung. I turned around, and Menel was behind me. He must have followed me up onto the roof. "Don't cast magic over and over again out of anger! You're gonna blow yourself apart!" He looked angry. "And high-level magic like that?! Are you nuts?!"

"But—"

"But nothing!" Menel grabbed my collar. "You're up against a wyvern! Do it efficiently is what I'm saying! For a guy with a brilliant brain, you're as thick as pig shit, you know that?! You were given that brain, fecking use it first!"

Pierced by his jade eyes, I suddenly came to my senses.

— *Just learn to use small amounts of magic, sensibly and precisely.*

Gus's teachings revived inside my mind. I could feel my head clearing. Gus wouldn't lose his head in a situation like this. Be efficient. Be precise. Only use magic when needed, and only as much as needed.

"Got it."

"Good."

I started thinking. With what I had available to me, how could I do something about that wyvern? Countless thoughts flashed through the circuitry of my mind like sparks, each being considered for a moment before fading away. "Okay." I nodded. "Menel, I need your help and the help of your elementals."

"Gotcha." Menel nodded, too.

"And Bee, Tonio!" I called in the direction of the courtyard, where I could see those two standing. Thanks to that Word of Lightning, a lot of people's attention was currently focused on us on the roof. "Get everybody around to help get people out of the temple's front garden!" I waved my arm dramatically and shouted. "That's where we're gonna bring down the wyvern!"

"Here goes. *'Sylphs, sylphs, maidens of wind. Your steps are the wind's steps, your songs are the wind's songs.'*"

His voice rang out clearly as he recited the words. The elementals gathered and danced.

"*'Sing in chorus, sing in rounds, cheer and shout applause. Thine harmonic tones spread the primordial Words in the ten directions—'*"

Ever since Menel started casting his spell, I'd started to see glimpses of tiny white maidens all over my vision, blurred by the flow of the wind.

Sylphs—wind elementals. Once I was sure of it, I started incanting Words.

"*Verba volant...*"

It was the same invocation as before, the Word of Lightning, but I expanded upon it with the Words that Gus had used to destroy the splinter of the god of undeath.

"*...conciliat, sequitur...*"

I put my fingers to work as well, drawing several complex Words in the air. Like a crest or a magic circle, the intricate glyphs spread through the air. And finally, I spread my arms solemnly and shouted—

"*Tonitrus... Araneum!*"

The Words echoed instantly. The gathered sylphs sang them out in rounds, their harmony ever-increasing, and lightning forked again and again, darting and spreading through the air. The web of bolts expanded outwards, and though it weakened as it traveled, still it descended and fell like a net upon the wyvern flying far overhead.

The monster cried out in pain. It was convulsing, its flight posture broken. But it had only been struck by a single fork of many, weakened over a great distance; it wasn't enough to bring it down. It quickly recovered its balance.

Chapter Four

To the wyvern, the lightning strike had probably been a matter of "that really hurt," and that was all—but that was more than enough. It looked in our direction. It looked at us, who had caused it pain—and then it circled around and began to fly toward us. The wyvern had recognized us as enemies.

These kinds of monsters were generally aggressive. Gus had told me that in situations where normal wild creatures would flee, monsters like wyverns would instead opt for aggressive behavior.

"Here it comes."

There was only one issue, one question left—and that was how who I was now measured up to the way those three had once been.

As the wyvern drew closer, I rapidly placed spells and benedictions on myself and Menel to enhance our physical abilities. Menel also called to some elementals, and strengthened us both in the same way. With every passing moment, the almost birdlike figure grew larger and larger as it approached.

Gracefeel, I thought, *I will now fight for my oath: to drive away evil and bring salvation to those in sorrow. Please, bless me with your protection!*

"On the flame of Gracefeel!" I held my spear, Pale Moon, in both hands and offered a prayer. A huge wall of light rose around the temple. It was the blessing Sanctuary.

There was some buzz from the people watching, but I ignored them for now. I didn't have the time to worry about it.

The wyvern headed straight toward us and collided with the luminous wall. There was a violent crash.

I prayed. I prayed.

Be unbreakable as adamantine. Be eternal. Be everlasting. Reject all that is evil!

But I heard a sharp intake of breath followed by the resonating sound of cracking, and then the stunned, hollow voices of Menel and others.

"What—"

Even I, for a moment, forgot all about praying, and my eyes opened wide. What was I seeing?! The wyvern was fighting against the glowing wall, and the veins across its whole body were turning black, noxious air pouring from each and every one. The black miasma was encroaching on the sacred walls, breaking them down, and then—

With the spur on its foot, the wyvern kicked the wall of light. There was a sound like glass shattering, and as the wyvern descended, now black with miasma, I saw its emotionless, reptilian eyes capture me in their sights.

By reflex, I dropped into a roll, and the thick claws on its legs just barely missed me. The wind pressure blasted roof tiles everywhere. I lost my balance and almost fell straight off the roof, barely managing to stay on the edge.

"*'Sylphs! Elegant maidens of the wind, princesses who dance in the gale!'*" It was Menel's voice. He had skillfully kept his balance and still had both feet firmly on the roof.

The wyvern blew past and then spun around, leaving a trail of miasma behind as it flew, and once again closed in on the roof where Menel stood—

"*'Those foolish enough to fancy themselves better dancers—'*" It was another incantation. "*'Show them the bitter taste of earth!'*"

At that moment, there was a rush of air, a powerful downburst. No matter how strange the wyvern's appearance and behavior, there was nothing it could physically do about an intense air current hitting its wings. Its flight posture broke down, and—

Chapter Four

"Will!!"

"*Ligatur, nodus, obligatio!*" I cast the Word of Knotting over and over. The wyvern's wings stiffened.

It plummeted through the air, struggling all the way down, and impacted the ground. There was a deep *boom*, and the earth shook. I looked down and saw that the wyvern had fallen on the fountain in the front garden.

I leaped down from the roof, landed safely, and sprang upon the wyvern.

◆

Inside my head, I could feel chains straining, fissures forming in a ring of steel. The wyvern was fighting against the Word of Knotting. Given enough time, it would break free of it and take to the sky again. I had no intention of allowing it to do so.

The fountain was broken, and water was spouting out over the temple's front garden.

Wielding my spear, I sprinted toward the wyvern planted there. My aim was simple: a spear charge directly into its heart or windpipe. Just like Blood, who had finished off a wyvern in a single swipe of his sword, I was going to finish this with a single strike through its weak spot.

The wyvern sensed my approach and turned its head.

"*Acceleratio!*" I shot forward like a bullet. I aimed for the wyvern's heart, Pale Moon glinting in my hands. The landscape soared past with furious momentum, the wyvern's body quickly grew enormous in my vision—and the next moment, there was a furious howl, and the wyvern charged at me as well.

We crossed—and then—impact. I pushed my spear into its miasma-spewing chest, and with a gasp of panic, I immediately let go before my wrist and elbow were crushed by the monster's momentum, and I rolled to the side. The spear had stuck. There was no doubt.

A cheer rose around me.

However—

"No way..." I heard Bee's voice from somewhere.

I turned, a terrible feeling building inside me. The wyvern was slowly turning its head to me as well. Had I been hindered by its rubbery skin? Its tough muscles? Or had I simply missed my target? The fact was—I hadn't managed to impale its heart.

More miasma poured out. The wyvern looked at me, red flames burning inside its mouth.

"Run! It's going to breathe!"

There were still people behind me who hadn't gotten away yet. I couldn't let it breathe fire. But I had no time, I had no plan. I had to act. Act! But how?!

And then—in my heart—Blood laughed. He laughed loud. And he said:

Wreck him.

"*Acceleratio!*" With the Word, I charged right up to the wyvern, too close for it to release its breath. To keep from hurting itself, the monster let its flames pour out the sides of its mouth, snapping its jaws at me instead. I narrowly dodged, and threw both my arms around its enormous neck.

Can't think of a good solution? Nature of your enemy is unknown? In my mind, Blood raised a fist and yelled at the top of his voice. *Then MUSCLE! Violence! Wreck him!!*

Chapter Four

The miasma spouting out of the wyvern started to slowly attack my arms, but the burns I had there—my stigmata—flared white and held it back.

I grunted as I strained my muscles. The wyvern resisted. I held its neck tight, choking off its airway and blood flow. I spread my legs wide apart and dropped my hips, making sure I had good footing. With all my strength, I twisted my body to hold on tight as the wyvern resisted.

The wyvern's entire bulk lifted into the air.

I brought it crashing back down onto the fountain, long since broken and spraying water in all directions. The earth shook again, but I kept my arms firmly clutched around its neck. I wasn't going to let go.

"A... A headlock throw?!" someone asked.

Yes a headlock throw, I thought. *I'm grabbing it by its head and throwing it, of course it's a headlock throw. Isn't it obvious?*

I threw myself on top of the downed wyvern, continuing to throttle it as hard as I could. Behind me, the monster's body struggled wildly, kicking and convulsing. It was desperately trying to stop me from strangling it. I roared and put all my strength into my muscles. This was now a contest of physical strength against a wyvern, with all the power I had. I kept it from resisting and getting up—in fact, I pressed the wyvern down, shoving it hard into the ground.

You're not getting away, pal. I won't let you run. I won't let you breathe any more fire from that throat.

I won't let you use those wings to fly anymore. I won't let you use those fangs or those claws to hurt anyone anymore!

As the crowd watched, hardly breathing, there was a snap as finally, the wyvern's neck made a sound it was never meant to make.

Chapter Four

♦

The wyvern's neck went limp in my arms. To be extra cautious and make absolutely certain it was dead, I continued to strangle it for a little while longer, and then I noticed that silence had fallen all around me.

The people who had been in the temple to begin with, the people who had evacuated here from elsewhere in the city—so many people were looking at me. The emotions in their eyes were complex, and I suddenly realized I was in trouble.

I had broken the neck of what must have been a two-ton wyvern (I seemed to remember that six-meter-long saltwater crocodiles weighed about a ton), and I'd done it in front of them. I had been only moments away from the wyvern's fire breath burning me and everyone else nearby to a crisp, so in order to win without anyone getting killed, I'd had no choice but to choke the monster to death. That said, even I recognized that what I'd done had been completely crazy. If they decided I was someone to be feared—

"Spectacular! Marvelous!" The sound of applause rang out. Confused, I turned and... there was Tonio. "Thank the gods that they sent a hero like you to this place!"

Clapping in an exaggerated fashion, Tonio stepped toward me like he didn't know who I was. Then, he flashed me a little smile and a mischievous wink that the people couldn't see from where they stood. I let go of the wyvern's neck and got to my feet. Tonio held both my hands together and shook them while telling me how grateful he was.

It was only then that I finally realized what he was trying to do.

"No problem," I said with a smile, and shook his hands up and down.

Bee must have guessed his intention as well. Strumming her instrument, she shouted, "The Wyvern Killer! Today, a new hero has been born!" Her voice carried well. "Let's have a round of applause for our hero!"

She led, and a few odd claps followed her cue—then the clapping got louder. It was joined by cheering, and soon enough I was being mobbed by people. They touched my arms and asked to shake my hand, saying "Thank you" over and over.

I got the feeling that I'd just survived a pretty dangerous situation. Menel and I probably wouldn't have been able to figure a way out of it on our own. Only the savvy Tonio and Bee, with all their experience in navigating society, could have defused that so well. I felt very grateful.

After the accolades had died down, I raised my voice and called out to the crowd. "There must be people still buried under the rubble, and others with injuries! Let's all do our part to help and rescue everyone!"

A cheer of assent rose from the crowd. As one, they headed to the hall and worked together to remove the rubble and care for and treat the injured. A strange sense of solidarity had formed among all these disparate people.

While everyone was busy, I found a moment to quietly thank Bee and Tonio.

"Oh, not at all," Tonio replied. "I look at it as an investment."

"Hehe." Bee laughed teasingly. "I'm going to make a song about this later, okay?"

While helping lever away some boulders, I also exchanged a few words with Menel.

"Seriously, is there anything you can't do, you freak of nature?" he said.

"Surprised?" I asked.

Chapter Four

"I've gotten used to you being ridiculous."

"Well, for me, it was a painful reminder of how far I still have to go."

"The hell?"

That wyvern had black veins covering its whole body and spewed eerie, noxious gas. I didn't know what had happened to it. Perhaps it had mutated somehow, or been cursed after activating a trap in some ruin, or someone had subjected it to some evil procedure. But in any case, I couldn't help speculating that its abnormal appearance and the reason it had attacked might have been related.

Of course, I couldn't deny the possibility that it was completely unrelated, and the wyvern's actions had been purely instinctual in some way. However, as violent as wyverns were said to be, I couldn't see attacking a human city of this size as anything but suicidal. The wyvern had been overpowering to begin with, but that was simply because taking the city by surprise had given it an advantage. It hadn't gotten to that point, but once the city had started to plan instead of panic, and sent out legions of proper soldiers, sorcerers, and priests, the wyvern would have been done for.

So it had been an abnormal, and most likely *stronger* wyvern than usual, but even so, it had been far too messy a battle. If Menel hadn't been there, I could well have died. Furthermore, if not for Tonio and Bee, I couldn't deny that I might have suffered *social* death.

A roundtable of criticism was in progress in my head, scrutinizing all the ways I'd been naive, all the mistakes I'd made, and all the ways I didn't measure up.

"Will. Brother." Menel called to me. I snapped out of my thoughts and looked at him. "I don't know how high a bar you're setting for yourself, but come on. You just brought down a monster. It's good to be self-critical, but give yourself some credit. I'm trying to be happy for you here."

I hadn't thought about it that way. And although there were a lot of things I wish I'd done differently, I *was* now a "Wyvern Killer," just as those three had once been.

"Yeah…" He was right. I *was* happy about that. "Yeah… Yeah. Thanks, Menel! I couldn't have done it without you!"

"Ya. Good job. And you were the one who did most of it, dummy!" He gave me a fist bump. That simple gesture really made me feel like we'd connected with one another in a lot of ways.

How many hours did we work after that?

We had left the corpse of the wyvern to the soldiers who came running to the scene afterwards. My greater concern was whether we'd managed to get all the injured people out of the rubble. I was just at the point of thinking we might have gotten everyone we could find, when I heard a lot of commotion around the temple's front gate.

Several priests came running up to us. "Wyvern Killer! Is the Wyvern Killer here?!"

"Oh! That's me, what is it?!" I waved my hand to them.

They looked like they were in a real hurry. They told me between short breaths that they would take care of the rest of the work and it was urgent that I followed them.

"H-His Excellency…"

"His Excellency, brother to the king, wishes to speak with you!"

I blinked.

◆

The room was full of vibrant colors. Woven fabric in various hues adorned the walls, and the decor could be summed up in a single word: grandeur. It suggested power without being in poor taste. The room had probably been specifically designed with that intention.

Chapter Four

Menel and I had been invited to the mansion that belonged to the Lord of Whitesails, and we had just now been shown into the room where he received guests.

"Welcome to my mansion, hero." Standing on the other side of a big ebony desk, Duke Ethelbald Rex Fertile welcomed us with arms spread wide. Brother to the King of the Fertile Kingdom, he was the feudal lord of Whitesails and the ruler of Southmark.

He has piercing eyes, I thought. They were dark gray, and seemed to penetrate to my very soul. They reminded me of the keen eyes of a bird of prey.

His hair was thin, gray, and cut short, his gaze was stern, and he looked like he had done a good amount of physical training. He was wearing high-quality, tailor-made clothes, a sword on his hip. The scabbard wasn't highly ornamented, and looked quick to unsheath, which told me that the weapon wasn't just for decoration.

Behind him stood two serious-looking guards in full armor.

"It is an honor more than I deserve to be in the presence of your glory. My name is William G. Maryblood, here at Your Excellency's request." I placed my right hand on the left side of my chest, brought my left leg back slightly, and bowed.

"Oh?" the Duke of Southmark said quietly. Had I messed something up? "I am surprised you are familiar with such old ceremony. Am I correct in assuming you are a man of blue blood?" he asked, then responded to me with an identical gesture.

It seemed as though I had done okay, but he'd gotten slightly the wrong impression. "Not quite, um… I would appreciate it if Your Excellency would avoid questions about my birth."

Well, it couldn't be helped. It was my fault for not explaining.

"Ha ha ha. So you have some circumstances. Very well, then. Please, sit."

He offered me a chair and sat down in his own. I bowed slightly and sat.

I quickly realized without looking that Menel hadn't taken a chair himself, but had remained standing behind me and a little to my right. That took me by surprise. Why was he acting as if he was my servant?

Wait... Did he just leave me to handle this entire conversation with the big cheese?!

I turned my head slightly and sent him a death glare. I saw the corner of his mouth curling upwards. *Ass*, I thought, and returned my eyes to the duke. Looking around too much in front of the host who invited me would be rude.

"I am surprised to see that only a representative is here..." he said. "My orders were to bring all of you."

"Huh?" I said, shocked. Was I supposed to have brought Bee and Tonio with me? Bee had actually been interested in seeing the inside of a feudal lord's mansion, but she hadn't played any part in the battle against the wyvern, so we'd asked her and Tonio to wait at the temple.

"William, you were traveling in a party of four or perhaps five, I'm assuming."

"Ah, yes. There's four of us." How did he know that?

"A sorcerer, a priest, an elementalist, and a warrior then. Yes, that's quite a nice balance."

"Huh?"

"Hmm?"

Okay, uh... "We're a priest, a hunter, a merchant, and a poet..."

"Hmm...?"

Was one of us... misunderstanding something?

Chapter Four

"One who cast lightning at the wyvern, one who erected a wall of light around the temple, one who manipulated the wind, and lastly, the man I've heard so much about, the warrior who engaged a wyvern bare-handed and broke its neck. Four. Yes?"

"O-Oh." Now I understood. "Your Excellency, I am terribly sorry for the confusion, but if that is what you mean, I am certain that there has been no mistake in simply the two of us coming here."

"Hm? You mean—"

I nodded. "My friend Meneldor called to the elementals, dispersed the Words, and made the wyvern plummet to earth by manipulating the wind."

"Then he is the elementalist. I see. What about the others?"

"They were me."

"Sorry, could you explain in detail what exactly you did?"

"First, I attempted an independent lightning strike against the wyvern. This failed. With the help of Meneldor's powers, I attempted a second strike. This succeeded in provoking the wyvern and luring it to us. After that, I attempted to use the Sanctuary prayer to prevent it from swooping in and managed to kill its momentum, but unfortunately, after the wyvern emitted a mysterious corrupting gas, I ultimately allowed it to break through…"

Describing my own failures out loud was making me feel a little pathetic. Mary would have been able to stave off the attack for sure.

"Things were looking precarious for a moment, but with Meneldor's elementals helping by providing a burst of downward air, I forced the wyvern down into the front garden with the Word of Knotting. A crowd was still assembled in the area, so I aimed to finish the wyvern off not with highly destructive magic, but by stabbing my spear into its heart. However, I failed at this."

Blood would have given me a strange look for making a mistake like that. I seriously needed to go back and train again from the ground up.

"The wyvern was on the verge of breathing fire and causing casualties in the crowd, so I had no choice but to take the offensive once more, this time with my bare hands. It tried to bite me. I dodged. I grabbed its neck and threw it against the ground, held it down, and throttled it to prevent it from breathing fire. I had magically enhanced my strength beforehand, so I remained in that position and let my muscles do the rest, the battle concluding with me breaking the wyvern's neck."

What a mucky fight. After I finished outlining the battle—a battle which, for me, left a lot of regrets—the duke's mouth twisted into a crooked smile. "So you killed a wyvern and aren't even proud. It pleases me to see that truly brave warriors exist not just in legend." And he chuckled.

◆

"If Your Excellency doesn't mind me saying, are you sure you can afford to spend time talking to me like this?" I asked. "Don't you need to be helping the city handle the damage done by the wyvern?" With many civil servants and people who seemed to be military officers busily moving around, things had looked pretty hectic outside the mansion.

"Of course. I have seen to a number of things already, and I have much more to do after you leave as well. Reports, instructions, visiting the sites personally and offering reassurance, hearing petitions..." The duke humorously counted them off on his fingers. "But there are matters of higher priority." He looked at me.

Chapter Four

"For example... giving my thanks to the hero who solved the root problem." He gave me a roguish smile.

"Oh, no, you don't need to..."

"Do not humble yourself. I do not wish for my people to speak ill of me and call me a man who doesn't know gratitude." The duke sat up straight and faced me and Menel. "On behalf of Whitesails, I would like to express my gratitude to the both of you. Thank you for greatly limiting the damage that could have been caused by that sudden wyvern attack." He even bowed slightly.

Even I realized that a person with this much power bowing their head was not a normal occurrence. Some people may think that it doesn't cost a person anything to bow and is of little consequence, but when you become someone this powerful, bowing to others will cause you to lose your authority.

"Your words are wasted on me. I am honored." I bowed back.

But... Oh gods. Thinking of what was about to unfold was giving me a serious knot in my stomach. But I couldn't let this opportunity go to waste.

"I would very much like it if you would accept a reward," he said. "Do you have anything in mind?"

"I do." This was probably going to cause me big problems, but I had to commit to it. *Okay*, I thought. *Here goes nothing.* "I came here today through Beast Woods, to the south. The villages of said region are currently being menaced by demons in command of ferocious beasts."

"I see."

"Firstly, I would like to confirm—does Your Excellency have the power to mobilize soldiers to hunt demons? Is that possible?"

A serious look came over his face. "Speaking purely in terms of capability, it would not be impossible. Not impossible, but certainly difficult. You saw that wyvern," he said, massaging his temple in little circles. "We never foresaw a monster that great coming directly to Whitesails, but we have been experiencing similar monster incidents frequently within the areas of Southmark governed by the Fertile Kingdom."

I was almost afraid to ask. "When you say similar incidents..."

"Yes, I mean that strange, toxic miasma. Those touched by it are corrupted by the poison and go berserk." He explained that beasts with that stuff flowing through their body were rampant right now. "What about you, William? You had your arms around the neck of that wyvern as the gas flowed from it. Has it not affected you?"

"I don't poison easily, Your Excellency."

"I am glad to hear it. Soldiers often collapse after a fight with those beasts, you see."

Thinking back on what had happened with the god of undeath, it looked like these kinds of poisons didn't affect my body, which had been raised on holy bread. So that was what happened when an ordinary person came in contact with that miasma... And there were many monsters like that...? This was probably, no, definitely the demons' doing.

"We are spread too thin as a result of the previous king's expansion policies. We are unable to even provide adequate protection to all of the villages that *are* under our governance. I hope you can understand what I'm saying."

I could, and what he had left unsaid, as well. Under such circumstances, he couldn't spare troops for independent settlements on the frontier, which neither paid taxes to the Fertile Kingdom nor were under its aegis. If he did, he would face backlash from the villages that *were* a part of it. He couldn't pull his forces from those paying their way and give them to those not paying

Chapter Four

a penny. In terms of capability, it was technically possible, but practically speaking, impossible without a doubt.

"In that case—" I'd found out what I needed to. Now for the real talk. "Could Your Excellency grant me permission to organize adventurers and hire mercenaries at private expense to hunt the demons?"

I'd been thinking about it for some time. There was no way I could go out on my own and hunt down the huge number of demons running rampant in Beast Woods. And if I couldn't do it alone, I was going to have to spend money to hire people and increase my numbers.

But the moment I asked, I saw the Duke of Southmark's temple twitch. He silently brought his hands up to his eyes and rubbed his temples again and then, slowly, he returned his gaze to me.

"William, do you understand the meaning of what you have just asked me?" He stared at me hard. The mood inside the room slowly began to change.

◆

"I do understand the magnitude of what I am asking for."

"And still you request it?"

"Yes."

The duke stared at me for a long time. I felt like I'd just learned the true meaning of the phrase "powerful eyes." That stare alone would be more than enough to make a person of weak temperament quake in their boots and withdraw their opinions. But I had my oath to fulfill.

"I beg you to consider," I said carefully, "just how many villages will otherwise be put to the torch, how many people will end their lives amid hunger and suffering and violence."

"But to save them all would be a feat so great that not even the gods could accomplish it."

We stared at each other, neither backing down.

The duke was the first to look away. Then he shrugged. "What rotten luck," he muttered. "This would have been far easier had you simply been a man of no repute."

"I sympathize fully, Your Excellency. That said, had I not killed the wyvern, I may not have been granted an audience."

The duke put his hands up to his eyes and rubbed his temples again. It was probably his tic. "Quite. However..." He fell silent.

The accomplished Wyvern Killer was already starting to act undesirably.

It was just as he had said: if I were just an ordinary man who couldn't bear to see the border areas in such a state and wanted to gather a few people at private expense and do a little bit of demon hunting, that would have been fine. He would probably have been able to overlook that. The reality was that this world was full of evil races, and hiring adventurers because the lord couldn't respond fast enough wasn't uncommon at all, so that would have been within the limits of acceptability.

But I was none other than the hero known as the Wyvern Killer, who was furthermore being mistaken as having some noble background—and I was declaring my intent to assemble forces that could potentially serve as a private army, and operate in Beast Woods, an area to which the lord's power didn't currently extend.

What's dangerous about that, you ask? Only that there are *so many* potential risks stacked on top of one another in that scenario that it's impossible to list them all. For example, I could become the leader of a rebel movement. I might be acting in another country's interest. I could overdo it and end up provoking the forest beasts and evil races instead.

Chapter Four

So the prudent course of action was obvious.

"I must give consideration to having you killed."

The duke suddenly looked a lot more intimidating.

"That's frightful. How will you say I died?"

"I will leave you with your dignity, that at least I promise. How about this: you suddenly started coughing up blood, presumably poisoned from your battle with the wyvern. We tried to treat you, but alas."

The solemn guards standing behind the king's brother shifted slightly. The moment he gave them the order, I was sure those two would kick over the desk and lunge at me.

I could probably dispatch those two, but I thought I sensed soldiers concealed in hidden rooms on the left and right, who would probably try to hack me to pieces. I would also have to worry about projectiles. The duke himself looked quite skilled too. And if he ordered them to, the guards would go on the defense while he retreated, so it would be difficult to take him hostage...

Just in case this developed into a battle, I found myself thinking about how it would play out, but the truth was that there was really no point thinking about it. Even if I could kill everyone in this mansion, it would be the end of me socially. It was never an option.

"Oh?" The duke's eyes flickered toward Menel. "Oh my... How frightening." He made a big show of shrugging his shoulders. Wondering if something had happened, I turned to look behind me, but only saw Menel standing there, expressionless.

"What?" he said.

"I thought... Never mind."

Hm. What was that? I couldn't keep looking at Menel, so I turned back to the duke.

I may have brought this on myself, but even so, things were not headed in a good direction. I had to get through this situation. My hands were getting clammy under the table. I had no confidence that this was going to work...

"Your Excellency."

"What?"

"If the salt of the earth loses its flavor, with what will it be salted?"

◆

"Hmm?" The duke regarded my sudden question with suspicion.

I continued. "If all the world's torch bearers remain under the light of day, on what will their torches shine?"

He said nothing. I looked into his keen eyes. I met his gaze. I didn't look away, I didn't flinch. I looked straight at him.

"I have been gifted with a portion of the light of Gracefeel, god of the flame."

Look into his eyes, I kept telling myself.

"I believe that those who carry the torch of Gracefeel must take the first step into darkness, ahead of all others. They must shine a light on people suffering in the dark, and show the way to those that would follow them. I believe that to be my mission."

Face what's in front of you. Appeal to him with words from the heart. That was the only way, and the *right* way. Affectation and trickery were clearly going to be counterproductive against this man.

"So I beg you. Can you grant me some form of permission for my activities?" I got up from my chair, kneeled down, and lowered my head in a deep bow. I wasn't being clever or wily. I was just being completely straight with him. It might have been naive, but I thought that if you were going to make an unreasonable request of someone, you owed it to them to be honest.

Chapter Four

The duke was silent.

"William," he said, after a long pause. "In almost all cases, that road leads to despair. It will rarely lead to the result you desired, and even if it does, you will be paying a hefty price for it."

Hearing those words, I slowly raised my head, and smiled at His Excellency. *I know that*, I thought. *But all the same—*

"The thing is, I have some business with despair," I commented.

"Oh? What kind of business is that?"

"Well, I just don't like the looks of it, so I was planning on kicking its ass until it gets the message," I said, shrugging.

The duke looked a little stunned at my answer for a moment... and then he burst out laughing. "Hahahah! Kicking its ass, huh. I like that. Hah hah hah!"

It had gone over well. The duke was holding his sides and slapping the table. There were even tears in his eyes.

"Haha. Yes... That was a good reminder. You are, after all, a high priest, who even wields the prayer of Sanctuary. Not to mention the good friend you have!"

"Huh? Uhh..."

"Hm? You didn't notice? The instant I mentioned killing you, that half-elf behind you had the nerve to shoot me a murderous glare. Those were the eyes of a soldier ready to die for his cause. He was prepared to kill everyone here and go down fighting to protect you! Most impressive, most impressive..." The duke laughed.

I slowly turned back to look at Menel.

"Th-That's bull! I was just... steeling myself, figured he'd kill me as well, that's all... Dammit, quit grinning like an idiot!"

I didn't realize I was, but it made Menel's mood even worse.

Suddenly, from somewhere down the corridor, I heard a rush of stomping footsteps and a great deal of shouting.

"B-Bishop, I beg you to stop, His Excellency is engaged in conversation—"

"Wait! Papa, wait!"

"Let go of me! I said let go!"

I could hear all kinds of voices.

"Cease your meddling, you witless fools!"

The door flew open with a bang.

It was Bishop Bagley. He was followed by a train of the mansion's servants, a young woman who I assumed was a deacon, and more besides. Breathing heavily, he tromped into the room, dragging people along as they clung to him in protest, and without any reservation, he stood before the duke.

The bishop's eyes glinted in a different way than Ethelbald's, and he took a moment to glare at him before opening his mouth. "I would greatly appreciate it if Your Excellency would refrain from this sort of bullheaded behavior."

"Oh? Bullheaded behavior? To what do you refer, Bishop Bagley?" He shrugged as he asked, looking almost amused.

"Do not take me for a fool!" The bishop stomped loudly on the floor. "*This young man*," he shouted, pointing at me, "is registered at *my* temple! Temporary arrangement or otherwise, he is a *member* of the temple! Yet you beckon him here without a single word of notice! What is the meaning of this?! Does Your Excellency mean to completely disregard the temple's authority?!" He was so incensed he hardly paused for breath.

"Oh, I see... I had no idea. Is that true?"

"Um... yes." I did write my name in the register. But that had clearly not been anything very important... It was more like a guest book or something...

Chapter Four

"Ignorance is no excuse! Just because I was absent does not give you license to forgo the process of running it by the temple!"

"That may be so, but the people at your temple seemed quite happy to send him here."

"A simple lack of training! I will give them a good scolding later!" he said, and slammed his bloated hand, covered in gold and silver rings, on the table. The way the fat wobbled from the impact looked somehow ridiculous. "In any case, he belongs to my temple! It is not acceptable for Your Excellency to freely—"

"That is where you are mistaken, Bishop. He is more than that."

"What…?"

"He asked me to let him form a private army. He says he wants to save the poor people of Beast Woods."

"What?!" The bishop's head snapped toward me this time. "Y-Y-You…" he sputtered, his eyes wide.

"To be honest, I would be lying if I said the thought of killing him didn't cross my mind."

The bishop was speechless now, and his mouth was flapping open and closed like that of a goldfish.

"But he spoke his mind so openly," the duke continued, "that I found myself intrigued."

"Wh—?!"

"I am thinking of appointing him as a knight. What would you say, Bishop, about the temple giving its blessing?"

"Wh-What?!"

"You know, a holy knight. A paladin. Both I and the temple would take equal share of the responsibility and the profits… Well?"

"WHAAAAT?!"

He was *so loud*. The entire room was trembling.

"He would fall under our joint authority, and if it came to it, you could always have him excommunicated."

"That is not the issue!"

"The temple can attest to his good character, and with him being the Wyvern Killer... Yes, I'm sure it will work out."

"That is *not* the issue!"

"Then what is?"

"This is too sudden!" He slammed a fist against the desk again. "I will take him back with me and we will discuss this! Will you settle for that?"

"Hmm, that will do fine. Discuss all you wish. But I would be truly happy to see this a reality, Bagley. I have taken a liking to this man."

"You played these ridiculous games when you so graciously hauled me off. I'll thank you to keep me out of them!" he said at the top of his voice, then scowled at me and Menel. "You! Neophyte! We are leaving! Come along!"

"Y-Yes!" I hurriedly stood from my chair.

Hurricane Bagley was gone as quickly as it had come, and with that, my meeting with His Excellency Ethelbald, Lord of Whitesails, came to a close.

◆

"Menaces causing me trouble, the lot of them..."

Bishop Bagley griped constantly on our way back. Menel pretended to listen, but I could tell the clergyman was getting on his nerves. Yeah, these two were not going to get along.

"Um—" I was about to step in and say something, but...

"Especially you, neophyte! Did you not think to consult me before going off on your own?!"

Chapter Four

As Bishop Bagley's complaints became increasingly vehement, Menel finally started talking back. "Consult? Fig to that. We aren't your pawns."

"What did you say to me?! I am the head of the temple!"

"So what?!" They started quarreling, and after that, it was impossible for me to intervene. Gods, these two were like oil and water...

As I watched them argue, the deacon who had been attempting to stop the bishop back at the lord's mansion spoke to me. "I'm sorry about Papa. There are a lot of things troubling him recently, and he seems to be a little frustrated..." She had her flaxen hair loosely braided and was smartly dressed in a jacket, waistcoat, and long skirt.

"That's all right. I apologize on behalf of my companion. So, are you Bishop Bagley's daughter, then?" I'd been wondering about that. True, as far as I was aware, there was no restriction on marriage for members of the clergy in this world, but was the bishop really married?

"Yes, I'm his daughter. We're not related by blood though."

"So..."

"Before being appointed here, my father was in the capital. He was in charge of running a temple with a large orphanage."

"Ah, I see."

Exactly how he'd gotten the duke's attention I had no idea, but somehow he had, and the duke plucked him from the capital and brought him here. I hadn't known Bishop Bagley for long, but the incident at the mansion had taught me that he was capable of being pushy. Maybe the duke had judged that he would be well suited to running a temple in a remote region like this.

"Many of my seniors and friends who left the orphanage found jobs back on the mainland. Papa helped them get into a lot of different places, but I and a dozen or so others followed him over here."

Not only did he have quite a few connections, he had some very loyal people under him as well. Although I'd been keeping an open mind about the man for a while, it was probably time that I formed a definite opinion.

Outwardly, he looked corrupt, was terribly grumpy, and gave a ridiculous first impression—but despite all that, Bishop Bagley was probably quite competent.

"Bishop Bagley." I called out to the bishop, who was still arguing with Menel about something or other. "Thank you very much. You intervening really helped me."

"You think I did it for you?! I merely defended the temple's authority from His Excellency's self-centered actions. *You* come second!" Then he went back to grumbling about the duke and how he did outrageous things when something captured his interest.

Bishop Bagley really did complain a lot. Even though getting all this off his chest was probably his way of staying sane, I felt like I understood why he didn't seem well-liked within the temple.

"But still, all that aside," he said to me, "the authority of the secular world must be respected. Please remain in the chapel after Evening Prayer. We will discuss His Excellency's proposal."

"All right, understood. Ah, but... umm..."

"What now?!"

"Sorry... What's Evening Prayer?"

A noticeable vein bulged on the bishop's temple. There was a pause, and then he let loose a furious volley of insults.

Yes, I'm really ignorant, I'm sorry...

Chapter Four

♦

Apparently, religious services had undergone a lot of reformation over the last two hundred years. All the daily cycle's observances, which in Mary's time had included Vespers, Compline, and several others, were now combined into something called Evening Prayer.

Considering how multiple services had been combined into one and the language used during it had also been simplified, it seemed likely that the collapse of the Union Age had meant that some places hadn't been able to maintain that complicated system of rituals. Also, the bishop and deacon both looked shocked when I told them that I knew about Vespers and Compline, so it looked like even those terms weren't heard much anymore.

"Were you studying with people who were familiar with the old liturgy?" he asked me. "A tribe of long-lived monks or something?"

"Umm, yes. That's more or less correct." I wasn't sure if becoming undead counted as being "long-lived," but there was no doubt that Mary had been very familiar with the old ways of worship.

"So you're not completely ignorant, then." Bishop Bagley hummed in thought. "Anna, there should be a book or two in the library that cover the revisions to the liturgy. Get them for me, and while you're at it, see if you can arrange for a suitable teacher for him. Not only is this man a neophyte, he's a relic of two centuries ago. This is going to take some effort."

I got the feeling he was deliberately bad-mouthing me again, but I couldn't complain—he'd pretty much hit the bullseye. Behind the bishop, the deacon called Anna bowed her head repeatedly to me, looking really apologetic.

After that, I returned to the temple, joined back up with Bee and Tonio, was subjected to a barrage of questions (mainly from Bee), and after dealing with a lot of other random tasks that needed to be done, I took part in Evening Prayer.

Even though the people of the temple were still very busy clearing debris and treating the injured, it looked like none of them intended to neglect their daily prayer. They clearly felt that times of hardship were when it was *most* important to pray. I thought that was a very laudable attitude.

The service was very solemn and impressive, but I felt a little uncomfortable. Everyone suggested good seats to me, and eyes flicked toward me from all directions. I wasn't used to receiving hospitality like this or being the center of attention, so I never felt settled throughout the service.

Once it was over, everyone left the chapel, and I waited there for a while in prayer. Soon enough, the bishop arrived. He'd apparently had an appointment to keep and had cut out on the scheduled prayer.

"One moment," he said. Then he got down on his knees, put his hands together, and prayed.

In an instant, the atmosphere in the chapel—empty except for me and the bishop—completely changed.

The bishop's praying looked astonishingly natural. It was a beautiful sight, even though the bishop himself was far from so. I had never seen anyone look so in their element while praying before—no one, that is, except Mary. I found myself with my hands together as well.

"Now then." The bishop prayed for a far shorter time than I thought he would.

"U-Um..."

"What?"

Chapter Four

"Bishop Bagley, this has been on my mind for a while, uh..." I paused for a moment to choose my words. "You have definitely been blessed with a high level of protection from the gods, I can see that."

I had no doubt about that after what I just felt. I'd had a kind of sense of it ever since I first met the bishop, but now I felt confident saying it: the protection he'd been blessed with probably equaled mine, or even *exceeded* it.

"But I heard from the people at the temple that you don't use blessings. But if that's what your prayers are like, then I think you either don't let people see them, or you deliberately tone it down in front of them. Why is that?"

"Hah. Stupid neophyte."

He insulted me...

"What do you understand benediction to be, boy?"

"Protection received from the gods."

"Then tell me, why did the gods bless you with protection? To give you special treatment? I hardly think so, do you?"

I was silent.

"It is because *through* you—do you understand this? *Through* you, the god has something they want accomplished. And we must constantly think of how to use our blessings in a way that is consistent with the desires of the gods who gave us our protection. Those who treat them like a tool to be used whenever convenient merely take away from the majesty of the gods; they do not add to it. The protection such fools receive only declines over time. Many of those nitwits fail to understand that. Because they do not understand, they remain forever novices, and eventually lose their protection."

The bishop was really sounding off about this.

"I am the head of this temple. It is in a rough area that has only just started to be developed. To secure money and rights, we must shout and intimidate; to build consensus, we must do favors and use bribes. Imagine what it would do for me to parade around high-level blessings under those circumstances. The populace would think, 'What are the gods thinking, giving protection to a man like that?'"

He glared at me. "Let me ask you, boy, do you think that is consistent with what my guardian deity desires? Do you think that would be useful in raising the prestige of Volt, god of lightning and judgment?"

"No."

"Precisely. No. In which case, the correct conduct for both blessings and prayer is to keep them stored away inside. I have left the spectacle of blessings and the promotion of the gods' prestige in the very talented hands of the vice-bishop. He is also good at winning over the hearts and minds of the people. I can leave the bothersome and stressful task of being the pretty face of the temple to him."

Then, Bishop Bagley turned the conversation on me. "And what about you, greenhorn? Do you think yourself a 'hero' just because you killed a wyvern?"

I couldn't come up with a response.

"A paladin," he said, snorting derisively. "A paladin?! Here we have a stripling who still does not even understand what it means to be blessed, and he is to be called a paladin?! His Excellency does enjoy his jokes!"

The bishop displayed his astonishment through exaggerated gestures, and because I honestly didn't know how to respond, I just listened.

Chapter Four

"Boy. I can even tell him for you, if you like. If I refuse firmly, even His Excellency will surely let this go. Well?" he asked, his tone overbearing.

His stare and his large body worked together to give an intimidating impression that was no less than what I'd felt from the Duke of Southmark.

"Put the idea to rest, greenhorn," he said. "Nothing good will come of it."

"Even so…" I didn't look away. I looked right back into the bishop's eyes. "Even so, *through me*, my god is trying to accomplish something."

The bishop frowned and looked at me, his expression stern.

"You will not budge?"

"I will not."

"Fool."

"Probably."

"What did you swear to the god of flux?"

"To dedicate my life to her, to drive away evil, and to bring salvation to those in sorrow."

"Rejoice. I have met many nitwits over the years, and you have exceeded them all." He gave a massive sigh. "I will find a few people for you. You do the rest yourself."

I bowed my head very deeply and thanked him. No matter what anyone else said about this man, I decided that he had won my respect.

◆

After that, the brakes seemed to come off, and everything became frenetic.

Out of the corner of my eye, I could see the bishop contacting the duke to inform him of our intention to accept his offer, while the solemn-looking priest that Anna had found lectured me on matters of etiquette and current ceremonial procedure for priests.

The wheels had already been set in motion for me to receive my decoration. It was all happening terrifyingly fast. Was it really supposed to be this easy to receive a knighthood? I wondered what on earth had driven them to act with such unprecedented speed.

That said, the damage the wyvern had done was not to be taken lightly; there were people who had lost their homes and jobs, and I'd heard whispers that they wanted a celebration that might create some temporary work. Ah, come to think of it, even in the ancient and medieval histories of my former world, new temples and shrines were erected whenever disasters occurred. There must have been aspects of wealth redistribution to that too.

In any case, if I was knighted, things would move a lot more quickly. People, money, and things—all would be easier to manage with authority and the power underlying it. When I thought about it that way, it didn't feel terribly important that I'd be collared by the duke and the bishop. I didn't think that those two would treat me too badly, anyway... probably.

"Whence came he? And where trained, and where studied? Of him we know little, but that he is the disciple of the lost god of flux, and carrieth within him the divine torch."

This was probably a necessary step.

"The depth of his faith equal to that of a bishop, the depth of his study to that of a sage. And dwelling in his arms, a strength without peer that crushed a wyvern. Through this man's body, Souls of the Three Heroes, do you intend your names of great renown to boom forth once more?!"

Chapter Four

Th-This was... necessary.

"The Disciple of the Torch, the Wyvern Killer, the Peerless Powerhouse—the Faraway Paladin, William G. Maryblood. One and all, learn the names of the new hero who appeared in the city of white sails! Hmm, that feels about right!"

Okay, even if it *was* necessary, c'mon!

"Bee, would you mind not practicing your story right in front of me?!"

"Come onnnn. Don't be such a sourpuss."

"It's ridiculously embarrassing!"

"That's the level of what you *did*, so it's your own fig fault! What's she supposed to say?"

"That doesn't make it *not* embarrassing!"

We were in our room at the temple. As the three of us talked and argued, Tonio quietly fiddled with an abacus. "Hmm."

"What's wrong, Tonio?"

"I am unfortunately coming to the conclusion that a large number of draft animals will be quite pricey, no matter what I do."

"Ah, about that..."

Things had gotten really messy with all this knight business that came from me killing the wyvern, but I hadn't forgotten my main objective. My goal was the same as ever: to hunt the demons of Beast Woods, and at the same time, do something about the economic issues of that area and promote the good name of the god of the flame.

And to that end, I had a plan.

"Oh? And what might that be?"

"Could you look around for any animals that are sick or injured, and do a bit of negotiating to buy them at a low price?"

"Huh?"

"Then I'll heal them all."

"Oh!" Tonio's eyes opened wide.

Yeah, I have been thinking about this, Tonio. This and all kinds of other things.

The livestock merchant would be happy for the chance to sell off their sick and injured animals, and we would be happy because we'd get the animals we needed. As for the potential impact on the merchant's future sales, the villages of Beast Woods were very poor and had extremely low purchasing power, so they wouldn't have been big customers for the merchant in the first place.

I'd also get to save the animals that were suffering. They would continue to be draft animals and be put to hard work, so I couldn't say if that was something to be happy about—but at least in theory, everyone would end up satisfied.

In practice, the merchant would probably not feel too great that he'd sold off his injured stock only to have them healed right after, so we'd need to tread carefully there, but that was only a slight problem.

"Also... it would be really helpful if I could keep relying on you for trading between Beast Woods and Whitesails... How much money do I need to put in?"

Tonio put his hand on his chin and hummed in thought. "Will," he said, "I think we need to sit down and talk business for a moment."

"B-Be gentle with me..."

My to-do list was getting longer and longer. But I had only one objective, and I was ever progressing toward it. *Gracefeel*, I whispered in my mind, *I'm doing okay. And I'll do my best.*

I felt the quiet and expressionless goddess give the slightest of smiles.

Chapter Four

◆

It looked like a reasonably large inn. It had two floors: the bottom level was a bar, and upstairs, there were rooms for travelers. They were on the second floor, of course, to prevent sleep-and-runs. *Some things are the same in every world*, I mused.

The sign hanging out front said *Steel Sword Inn*, and below it was a small banner with a weapons motif. That was apparently the symbol of an "adventurers' lodge"—a gathering spot that also served to bring adventurers and jobs together.

Adventurers were outlaws, making their livings as mercenary-like hired muscle, bodyguards, Union Age ruin-hunters, beast exterminators, and anything else that paid reward money. In terms of my previous world's history, the professional gladiators of ancient Rome may have been closest, or perhaps the gunslingers in westerns. Their social status wasn't high, yet at the same time, it was a class that produced both heroes and fortunes in a heartbeat.

It was evening, and the streets were full of laborers on their way back from work. Menel and I reached the inn, whose door had been left wide open, and we peered inside. There was already a din inside, despite the hour. We saw people wearing warm clothes—we were, after all, still in winter—clacking together horns filled with ale. But there was something a little strange about it.

"Those are... beast horns. And leather." The drinking horns they were casually using had come from horned beasts, and some of the cloaks and waistcoats they were wearing had been made from beast hide. Menel whispered to me that those were their battle trophies, an easy way for them to flaunt their power.

We stepped inside. Heads turned, there was a moment of silence, and then chatter.

"A young'un with chestnut-brown hair and a silver-'aired mixed elf with 'im."

"He's done a hell of a lot of training. You can tell..."

"That's him. No doubt."

The first voice that called out to me was a clearly agile-looking man who was pleasantly drunk. "It's the man of the hour himself! Wyvern Killer! What d'you want with a bar all the way out here?"

"I have a job that needs doing."

"Then you should talk to the owner and pay a bit to use the board."

"Thank you." I looked over to the wall of the inn and saw that there was a large wooden board hanging there, onto which numerous pieces of paper and leather had been pinned. I called out to the owner, bought several pins (that was how they charged the listing fee), and pinned up my sheet beside all the others.

That attracted a lot of interest, and everyone gathered around to see what my job was.

ADVENTURERS WANTED

For search of demon-infested Beast Woods.
Months of complete darkness.
Constant danger.
Safe return doubtful.
Meager reward.
Honor and recognition in case of success.

— William G. Maryblood

And the place fell silent.

Chapter Four

◆

"Hey. Mister Hero." The first reaction I got was a drunken and taunting voice. "We ain't a charity. Ain't none of us gonna go in on that."

The person talking to me was a thick-armed, red-faced man who looked about thirty. He was wearing a sparkling steel breastplate and had a sword on his hip in a vibrant red sheath that didn't have a single scratch. "Right, guys?" he said, and a few people who I guessed were his party hooted back their agreement and called me stingy.

Menel started to ball his hands into fists. I had a moment of panic, and then—

A scruffy-looking man sluggishly wandered over.

"Shut it, blowhards."

His few words silenced them.

The man had a beard, and I couldn't guess his age. He seemed to be in good shape physically, but looked pretty spiritless. The cloak he was wearing was scorched, worn down, and covered in scratches. The sword sheath on his hip looked beaten up and like it had some alterations made to it. But more than any of that, what I paid the most attention to was his fingers.

They were covered in scars and dirt, and all his nails were clipped short. Once, while relating one of his former exploits, Blood had said to me:

— *When you see a swordsman, look at his fingertips. Whenever there's something inside you making you doubt, saying drawing your weapon is a bad idea, and you wanna know, do you listen to that voice or do you shut it up? You just look at his hands.*

"It looks to me..." He spoke slowly. I guessed he wasn't good with words. "Like you're looking for madmen. You're not interested in blowhards, who have manners and patience and a business smile, but not much skill. You want a bunch of crude shitheads who fear nothing. You want scum-of-the-earth madmen who will dice with death for a dumb idea."

I nodded. I wasn't planning on giving them poor compensation on purpose, but the fact remained that exterminating demons in a poor area like this was a dangerous and not very lucrative job. There were still some untouched ruins still remaining, but even those came with dangers, and I didn't want people working for me under false pretenses.

Menel and I had both agreed that we should look for adventurers who were after honor, glory, and risk rather than adventurers who were only doing it for the money. And I'd heard that this "Steel Sword Inn" was where those kinds of people were based. So I replied:

"That's exactly right. That's why I chose this place."

"You hear him? That's what he wants! Mister Hero's looking for madmen!" After he yelled this, a number of people who had been watching us from their tables rose to their feet.

"Tch. You Strider bastards," one of the blowhards said. "If you strike it rich out there, toss us a coin or two for once!"

All the people with attractive equipment, like the one who had first called out to me, lightly clicked their tongues and returned to their tables. I guessed they'd been hoping for something they could profit from, and if that's not what this was, they were clearly not interested. It was only natural that some people would put their livelihoods first and foremost.

Chapter Four

Those who now approached me, on the other hand, were largely uncouth people with dirty gear and a prickly manner. Most of their equipment was covered in beast hide, and they had been drinking their booze out of beast horns. These were people who would hardly give a second's consideration to safe and secure jobs, like being a merchant's bodyguard. They were ruffians to the core who liked the flames of their lives to burn hot, stoked with fighting, risk, and adventure.

Yes—they were people like Blood!

"What're you looking for in Beast Woods?" one asked.

"Ruins or open air?" asked another.

"I don't do small shit."

I deliberately gave them all a fearless grin. "The boss of the demons."

When I said that, some of the adventurers went silent for a moment. I cast my eyes over them all. "The leader of the demons that are running wild in the western part of Beast Woods. He's thought to have beasts under him. He is our target."

"Big one..." the bearded man who had first spoken to me said, thinking aloud.

"Yes, it is," I replied.

"Location's unclear... It'd take some work to even find him."

"You're absolutely right."

"And if we get ambushed while we're searching, they'll kill us in a blink."

"I imagine so."

"Long story short—this sounds like a stupid, full-of-risk, fun-as-hell adventure." He laughed, as if at death. "If there's a spot for me, I'm in. Just need food and a place to sleep and I'm good. If there's some pocket change in it for me, even better."

"Me too."

"And me."

Other voices quickly followed, saying the same thing.

"Of course. You will have them. And payment as well."

A cheer rose from the group.

"But before that," I said.

"What?"

I smiled and extended my hand to the man.

"Would you all tell me your names? I'm Will. William G. Maryblood."

"Reystov."

Something that Bee had once said resurfaced in my mind.

— Oh right, have to pick something. Of the recent songs... Reystov the Penetrator is overplayed right now...

"The Penetrator?"

"Get called that," the bearded adventurer replied gruffly.

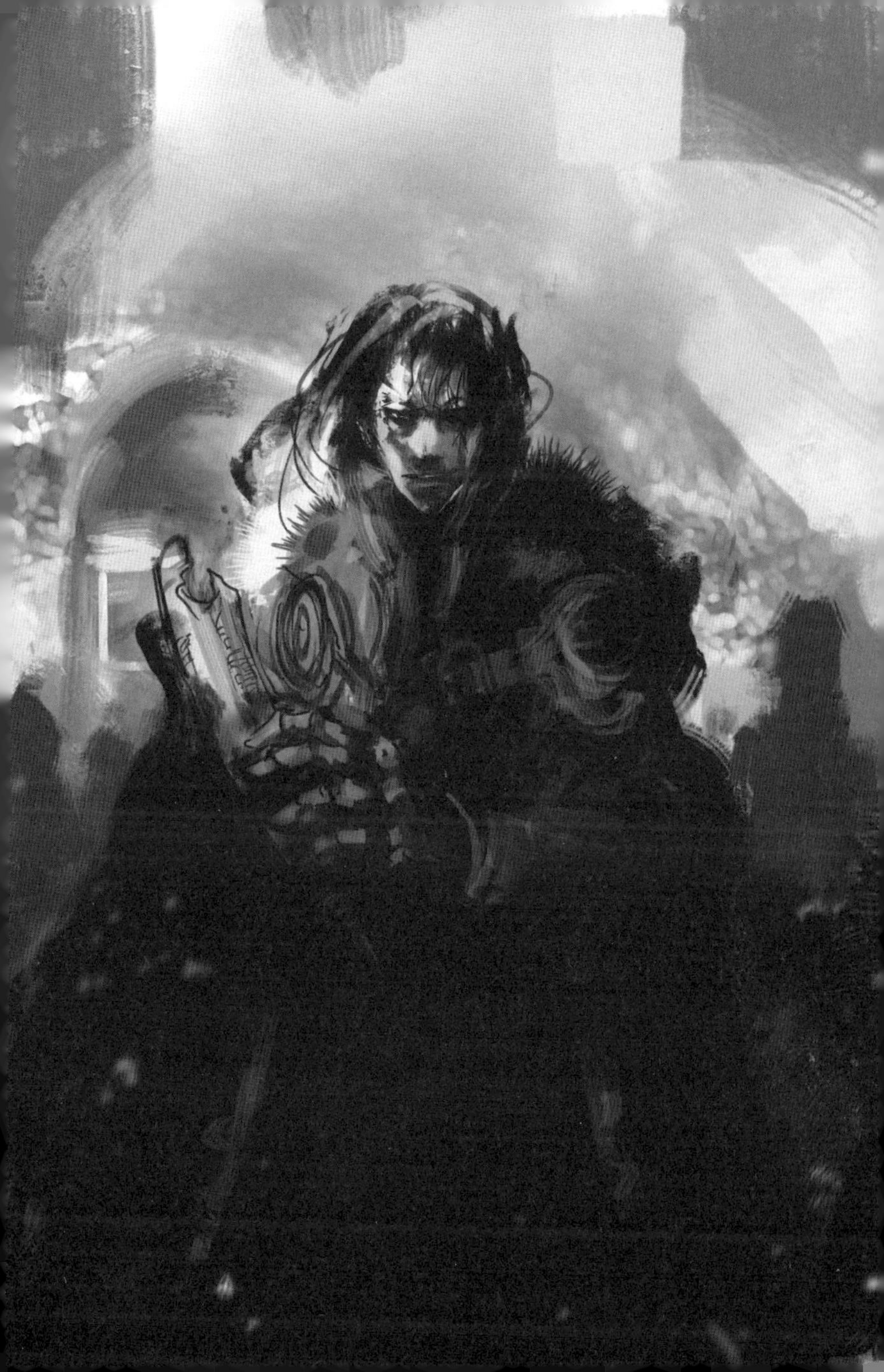

The sword was handed to the vice-bishop, then passed to me. I put the sword into the sheath that had been arranged for me beforehand, and then, following the ceremony as I had been instructed, I drew and re-sheathed it three times. The clear sound of the sword's motion against the sheath echoed around the church.

The duke continued his speech. "To you, the one who will now become a knight: you must defend the teachings of the good gods and protect the temple, the needy, and all those who pray and work in earnest."

I dropped to one knee, adjusted my hold on the sword so I was holding the sheath with both hands, and presented him the handle. His Excellency drew the sword, and with the side of the blade, he lightly tapped my shoulders three times.

The sword was then returned to me. I accepted it, stood, and placed it back in its sheath, the sound once more filling the church.

The vice-bishop used the blessing of Sanctification, and a holy aura filled the air. "I beseech thee, my guardian deity Enlight, god of knowledge, that through thee our voices may be heard! May the blessing of Gracefeel, god of the flame, be with this man always and forever!"

The god of knowledge, Enlight—he was the aged god with one eye, the god of learning, who could perceive both what could be seen as well as what could not.

"Hold fast to your oath, respect your god's teachings, and protect the vulnerable. May you be a light unto the world!"

He shouted the end with arms spread wide, and cheers and applause erupted from the crowd.

"May you be a light unto the world!"

"God bless the birth of our new knight!"

"May the light shine on the frontier!"

Chapter Four

"Blessed be the knight of the torch!"

"Long live the Paladin!"

And very quickly after that, the place was taken over by festivities. To loud cheers, all the influential, powerful people present gave generous donations to the crowds. This decoration ceremony had provided an excuse for a big handout to those who had suffered damage from the wyvern. That alone had made it worth it, I felt.

An enormous feast was held. It was a whole-city event. Wrestling matches were arranged as entertainment. After I won by fall against five people in a row, my satisfied grin was the last straw for a whole group of knights who surrounded me and made me suffer the same defeat.

"We beat the Wyvern Killer!" they shouted out gleefully, laughing their heads off.

"You cheaters!" I laughed with them. "Menel, Menel! Come on, you fight me too!"

"What?! No, feck off!"

As usual, Menel didn't want to join in on party stuff. I dragged him out.

"Oh! You're the Paladin's servant, uh…"

"He's not my servant, he's my friend!"

"We're not *friends*!" Menel shot back.

"R-Right…"

Bee was cheerfully singing my story. She said something about how much money she was raking in. I was too embarrassed to listen.

Tonio and Reystov seemed to be taking advantage of the feast to make connections with all kinds of new people. They never missed a trick.

The festivities continued into the night.

And that was how I became the paladin of this faraway land.

Chapter Five

All kinds of things continued moving forward at an incredible pace. After all the merrymaking was over, I put in a formal request to Ethel and the vice-bishop and received permission to go demon-hunting. Ostensibly, I was a single priest doing some independent charity work, but I had the backing of proper authority and power. The scale of what I was now involved in was incredible, but this was the smoothest way to get things done. If there was any trouble from now on, it would probably be necessary to demonstrate my allegiance to the bishop and the duke, but that was the price to pay for my new authority. I couldn't imagine that anything would develop that quickly, so I decided to think about that later.

Bishop Bagley supplied me with a number of priests, including Anna, who could use benediction and was versed in all kinds of ceremonies, from celebrations to funerals. The priests all had a wealth of experience, reliably making up for the areas where I was lacking. I felt so indebted to Bishop Bagley that I didn't know if I'd ever be able to fully pay him back.

Tonio seemed to have used the festivities surrounding the knighting ceremony to collect donations and contributions for my work. He'd gathered together lots of carts and wagons, agricultural and workshop tools, textiles, consumables, seeds for commercial crops, and animals cured of their injuries and diseases. And he'd found workers to manage them all.

Tonio laughed and said, "I might be able to start up my own trading company soon with all of this." I nodded enthusiastically, thinking that I would very much like him to do that, and he said with a mischievous smile, "I can look forward to receiving your business then."

I put the ruffian adventurers I'd contracted to work as convoys guarding our purchases, and we all returned to Beast Woods. That was the start of yet another hectic period.

I dropped by each of the villages we'd visited on the way to Whitesails, giving them a further round of medical treatment and having Anna help me organize religious festivals. With help from Tonio, I lent out draft animals and various kinds of tools in exchange for providing us shelter; I also allowed the villagers to buy them from us and pay in installments.

When there were reports of demons or beasts, I had Reystov and some of the other adventurers form a party and go out to hunt them. Reystov in particular was incredibly skilled; by and large, the corpses of the beasts he brought back had been penetrated straight through their most vulnerable spots, just as his nickname boasted.

Just out of curiosity, I asked him, "Can you do that to a wyvern?" and he replied gruffly, "If it's within sword's reach."

That wasn't all. When there were disputes between the villages, I mediated them. When there were crimes in a village, I asked for the help of the priests and we held trials for those involved, so the matters would be solved as fairly as possible. I hadn't originally been planning to do so much, but Tom, the elder of the village I'd first helped when a dispute arose, asked me if I'd help him out again since I'd done it once before. I couldn't say no. And as my reputation spread, other villages also started to request my help to handle

Chapter Five

disputes that were getting out of hand, and I found myself with more and more to do. That's how I ended up traveling all over the place, doing all kinds of work.

When I heard about a village I hadn't come into contact with, I got someone from the village we were currently in to introduce us and forge a connection, and then I'd do the same thing there. Bee really came in handy for making friendly first contact with unknown villages and whenever we had some message we needed spread around. I got the feeling I was paying for that with all the embellished stories she was also spreading about me. Maybe I needed to think of it as the cost of doing business.

Of course, if I kept on doing this kind of thing, I'd quickly find myself in debt in the literal sense. But while that was true, the livestock and agricultural tools that I'd lent out and sold off to the villages hadn't gone anywhere; they remained in the village as valuable community property, and were visibly accelerating the villages' development and production. These villages were essentially nothing more than places where vagrants had gathered together, so for many of them, just a plow, an iron axe, and a hoe would be tremendously valuable additions. And if we made that a plow *and* a horse to go with it, and threw in a ten-piece set of metal farming implements and other tools, work efficiency would jump up dramatically. If that improved, there would be more fields giving greater yields. With greater yields, the people would be able to repay their debts to us, and they'd become able to afford to purchase goods.

In parallel, the adventurers and I would be clearing Beast Woods of the dangerous demons and beasts, making the area safer. As the area became safer, merchants would be able to go to and from the villages without the need for heavy escorting, which would lead to a burst of commercial activity. The Fertile Kingdom's authority didn't extend here anyway, so it wasn't like there was going to be a toll for them to pay. They could do business here freely. And with more merchants coming in and out, the villagers could buy things with currency. Their improved production capacity should lead to them obtaining all kinds of things with money. Before long, an increasing number of those places would start dabbling in commercial crops in their desire for cash, anticipating demand for them from the city. And once money and goods started changing hands, neighboring areas would naturally become more interconnected for the sake of commerce. Access and transportation would improve. This was what Gus lovingly called "living money," money that moved around and made itself useful.

"And then one day, perhaps we can climb back out of the red," Tonio said, while doing some estimates on his abacus. "That is, if you and I are both still alive." That was definitely something I was aiming for, living at least long enough to get back out of the red.

Of course, we had only just gotten the ball rolling, and not everything was going according to plan. Often, people would try to engineer things so they'd keep all the profit for themselves, or intentionally default on everything they'd borrowed. I tried to contain situations like that as much as I could. Usually, this was by getting help from Anna and the other priests, who knew about law and how to persuade people, but some of the scarier-looking adventurers were also effective deterrents. Fortunately, in the short span of time that we were involved, there wasn't anyone dangerous enough to try something too disruptive. Even if a person like that was lurking somewhere, it was probably natural that they hadn't tried, in a way. If you did something like that in a place like this, you'd find yourself surrounded and beaten until you became tree food.

Chapter Five

Mary had once told me, "The greatest trap one can fall into when trying to do something good is to make the mistake of thinking that because you are acting with a good goal in mind, you are bound to get results." Even if you decide to do something good, the people around you won't lend you their help unconditionally, nor will the gods bless you with protection. Results come only by setting a reasonable goal and using appropriate methods to achieve it. And so, Mary had told me, the most important thing is to be practical and realistic. I took advice from everything Gus had taught me about money and regularly consulted with Menel, Bee, Tonio, Reystov, Anna, and the elders of villages all over, all of whom were very familiar with this world and its customs.

And together, we moved things forward. We went all over Beast Woods, back and forth, and as the winter transitioned into spring, I started to get the feeling that I was seeing more smiles in the villages. I felt as if there were now slightly fewer people who had no idea what tomorrow would even bring, who would wear gloomy or expressionless faces, or who would lose it completely and go off the rails. Perhaps that was what triggered the memory of something that Gus had once lectured me on.

— If you want something done, you don't have to use magic. You just buy the tools you need or hire some people. Reshaping the terrain is a powerful piece of magic, but if you've got money, you can just hire laborers and workmen to do construction for you instead. Make no mistake, the ability to earn money and make it work for you is just as important as magic!

"Yeah..." I finally understood what Gus had been getting at— and he was right. Even when he said something that made you twist your head, Gus's lessons were always right. Making people smile and giving them hope... It felt like magic greater than magic itself.

◆

Under a canopy set up in a vacant lot I'd rented from one of the villages, I was giving Pale Moon an inspection, checking that the neck of the blade and the metal collar were in good shape. As I idly wondered whether summer might start to make itself felt soon, a gruff voice called out to catch my attention. I looked up as Reystov came over.

"Pip's party's not come back," he said. "They were the ones searching the west."

Pip... If I remembered correctly, he was a young lad who'd come from some farm. He'd been in a party with two other men, Harvey and Brennan. "How long have they been gone?"

"They said they'd take ten days at the longest. They're over by two already. And those guys have skills." He was obviously implying that something must have happened for them to be this late.

"All right. We'll go out and search for them." I thought for a moment about who should go. It was possible that there had been some kind of accident, or they'd been attacked by wild beasts. But there was also the remote possibility that Pip's party had been spotted by the demons' lookouts. In which case, we'd need party members with combat skills. Also, to be absolutely sure we could follow their trail, we'd need a hunter or ranger skilled in tracking.

"Me, Menel, and you are definites. Also, whichever two parties you think are most skilled at forest exploration, I'd like to merge those into our search party as well. Are you okay with that?"

Reystov nodded to say he was happy with my suggestion. "I'll get everyone together right away."

Chapter Five

Our party members gathered quickly in the village square. I explained the situation to them simply. I could talk about the details once we were on the move.

"Pip and the others are two days past their return date. We're going to go searching for them, but there's a possibility that there's been more than just an accident. They may have been spotted by the demons' lookouts. If that turns out to be the case, we may also end up in a battle against demons." When I said that, I noticed everyone's faces visibly tense up.

"It'll get a bit more peaceful around here if we take them out." Menel nodded in response.

It wasn't a certainty that there'd be demons—it might just have been a simple accident that had befallen them—but the tension in the air was palpable as we all got ready and headed out.

◆

"Hey, uh." Menel called to me as we were walking. We had followed the trail of Pip's party and were just about to enter where they had been planning to search. "I gotta… thank you."

We were hanging back from the group. Ahead of us, Reystov and the other adventurers were deep in discussion about the trampled leaves dotted about the forest floor.

"Umm… For what?"

"A bunch of stuff." Menel's jade eyes weren't looking at me. In fact, he was practically facing the other way as he talked. "Without you, I would've hit rock bottom. And now I'm living for something good, and that's 'cause of you. So… Uh… Yeah." He paused awkwardly for a moment, trying to get the words out. "Thanks, brother," he said, still looking in the other direction.

I felt something warm filling my chest. "I'm the one who should thank you. Thanks for helping me out when I was so ignorant about the world." I smiled and nodded at him. "But..."

"What?"

"Say it again while looking at me."

"Feck off!" He stormed away, still refusing to look me in the eye or even turn his face toward me. The other adventurers gave a collective "ooh" in our direction.

The search for Pip's party continued.

It took several days before we found their bodies.

◆

Several days after we left the village in search of Pip's party, the dense greenery of the forest which had been around us for so long disappeared, and a blue sky came into view. What lay ahead of us after we exited the forest of green was a valley of craggy rocks. Beyond the valley was more forest, and beyond that, I could see a reddish-brown mountain range: the Rust Mountains. It was probably safe to assume this valley had been created by a flow of water pouring down the mountainside. The flow had either changed or dried up, and only the valley and rocks had been left behind. The valley wasn't that deep, but it ran for a good distance, and where the riverbed must once have been, there were a lot of round stones lying around.

Pip and the others had been *scattered* around that area. It looked like the kind of mess left behind after a young child's playtime— as if a child had gotten their hands on something insubstantial, like a paper doll, and clumsily pulled it apart, ripped it into many randomly sized pieces, thrown them everywhere, and then moved on to something else.

Chapter Five

Menel and the others chased away the birds and other animals that had gathered around. Crows took off, their black wings flapping noisily, and other carrion feeders large and small darted away in all directions.

"Look at this." Menel's eyes stopped on some tracks. They were the footprints of a beast, stained with blood, each about as large as the shield I had over my back… "Extremely large. What kind of beast is this?" Menel asked, and the other adventurers also gathered around and stared hard at the tracks.

"Hm… Not sure."

"It's big. Bigger than a manticore."

"A wild creature living in the valley? Or…"

Was the demons' stronghold somewhere deep in this valley? I got that far in my thinking when one of the adventurers said in a chipper voice, "Well, they got to fight a monster. Good way to go. I'll bet Pip, Harvey, and Brennan are pretty damn satisfied with that, and kicking themselves, too."

"Yeah. Bet they're saying, 'How awesome would it have been if we could have killed that?!'"

"They died good deaths. Adventurers' deaths!"

"O gods of good virtue, please grant their souls repose!"

"Have a last drink on me, lads," one of the adventurers said, and took a bottle out of his inside pocket and poured its contents over the scattered body parts. I did my part too, using the blessing Divine Torch to make extra sure that their corpses wouldn't turn undead. Menel and a number of the others talked and kept an eye over the area while Reystov went around the bodies collecting clippings of hair, which were often kept as mementos.

"Hmm?" Reystov sounded confused. "There's only two heads. They've been damaged so badly it's hard to tell, but…"

I looked around. Now that he'd mentioned it, I *was* kind of getting the feeling there should have been *more* here. "Probably just got eaten, right?"

"Plausible."

"No... wait," Menel said, raising his voice. He'd noticed something. I looked in the direction he was pointing and saw that there was a sword, a shield, and gauntlets scattered on the ground along a line that seemed to be heading into the valley.

"Did he... run away shedding his equipment?"

"Why into the valley?"

"If it blocked him from going into the forest, he probably wouldn't have had another choice."

"Good point." We all nodded to each other and went down into the valley to check.

◆

We walked down into the valley.

Helmet, breastplate...

After following the trail of dropped items that far, something suddenly occurred to me, and it seemed to have occurred to Menel and Reystov at the same time. "That's weird..." I muttered. Menel and Reystov both nodded in agreement.

"Yeah. This is strange."

"What's strange?" one of the others asked.

"The ground in this valley is pretty bad..."

There were loose rocks scattered everywhere. It certainly wasn't suited to sprinting. And as for useful obstacles to hide behind, there was only the occasional large boulder; the view we had down the valley was actually pretty clear.

Chapter Five

Let's assume that the large, unknown beast had been preoccupied with slaughtering the other two people. Even *if* that were the case—in a place like this, over this distance, there was no way a human could get away from a beast of that size.

I gasped. I'd seen it now, but far too late. As if to prove my fears correct, placed on the top of a large boulder in the middle of the path ahead was a decomposing human head.

"It's a trap! Retreat—" I had barely started to speak before my words were drowned out by a deafeningly loud roar that echoed through the valley. It was coming from the forest we'd just left. No, *they* were coming from the forest, toward us. Several beasts— a giant, two-headed serpent, a huge deer with bloodshot eyes, a wildcat that could have been mistaken for a leopard... Everywhere I looked, there were beasts, beasts, beasts. Every one of them was *spewing miasma from its body.* Someone gasped out a terrified scream.

"Don't panic!"

"Keep calm! Wall of shields!"

The adventurers who had shields all stepped forward and lined up in a row, protecting each other, and Reystov and I stood on either side to protect the line. Now that we'd fallen for the trap, we'd just have to push through it.

No sweat, I told myself. *We should be able to deal with guys like these.*

The beasts and their miasma closed in.

Right... That gas was poisonous. I quickly used a number of spells and blessings, and cast Vitality and Anti-Poison on everyone. From the looks of it, Menel had also called to the fae and given everyone some protections of his own.

"You have my gratitude."

"Thanks, guys!"

"Real help!" They shouted their thanks one after another.

"Here we go. Those brutes think they caught us in a trap. We better remind them who's the hunter, and who's the prey." It was rare to hear banter like that from Reystov.

I could feel Menel calling to the fae and readying his bow behind me. The other adventurers were also holding their weapons and shields up and trying to steady their breathing. The group of monsters approached slowly, slowly, as if to strike terror into us.

Still holding up my shield, I took some stones from a bag hanging from my belt, then pulled out my sling. I put a stone inside and spun it around with one hand, faster and faster—

"Now! Fire!" The distance carefully judged, Reystov shouted the command and arrows flew, inflicting serious wounds on several of the beasts. I let my stone fly as well, blowing off one of the beasts' heads. The attack set the rest off, and they charged. Even as they did, more arrows were fired, and I smashed two more heads with my stones.

"Braaace!"

Everyone bellowed in unison. We dropped our center of gravity, ducked behind our shields, and prepared for impact.

That was the moment an enormous shadow was cast over our heads.

The winged shadow effortlessly leaped over our frontal defense, attempting to attack from the rear. I wanted to go deal with it, but I told myself no. I had to keep the beasts from advancing.

"Menel!" I continued facing forward and shouted out the name of the person I trusted the most. *I want you to buy us time somehow—*

"Gahackk—"

I heard a sound like… a slab of meat being punched.

Chapter Five

I couldn't bear not knowing. I turned to see.

As if he were nothing, Menel, the person I trusted more than any other, had been smacked by the giant beast and sent flying.

◆

The beast was enormous.

Extending upward from the soles of its feet, which were as big as shields, were great, thick legs that looked like barbed wire had been twisted and coiled together. The typical farmhouses I saw in the poor villages around here were far tinier than this monster, even if it curled itself up as small as possible. Even the wyvern would have looked slimly built next to this thing. Standing in front of its lion-like body felt overwhelming, like standing directly in front of a towering cliff face.

The beast had three heads: a goat, a lion, and a demidragon. Each of those heads was filled with contempt, ridicule, and malice for everything smaller than itself. It was a chimera—an extremely savage, dangerous beast created by crossing other beasts in a blasphemous ritual.

"Oh—"

It looked like Menel had called to the earth elementals in an attempt to protect himself and those of us behind him. The wall of stone and earth jutting out of the ground, a huge chunk taken out of it by the chimera's elephantine front foot, was proof.

Menel's body slammed against a sheer wall of rock.

The chimera looked at him—

"Stop—"

—and, with a gloating grin—

"Stop!"

—from its demidragon head—

"Nooooo!"

—it breathed fire.

Menel's body flailed within the flames, burning. He was going to die—he was dying before my eyes—

I heard something snap inside my head.

"AHHHHHHHHHHHHH!"

My boiling blood dyed my vision red. I'd never felt this much anger, even when the wyvern attacked the city. Filled with that boiling emotion, I incanted the Word of Lightning.

"*Tonit—*"

At that instant, there was a heavy impact on my shield.

Oh, right, the beasts... were charging...

The Word... died in my throat...

Misfire. *Backfire.*

Those fragmented thoughts flashed through my head, and not an instant later, the lightning I'd failed to activate ran through me. I shook. My body convulsed. I collapsed.

Wh-What was I doing? Why was I being so pathetic? I had to fight. I had to protect everyone. Why was I letting myself get destroyed—

As I fell to the ground and my vision clouded, I saw the other adventurers trying to somehow endure. Reystov was fighting for his life, swinging his sword fiercely, but I doubted he would last long.

A despair colder than arctic ice washed over me and extinguished the flames of my anger. Why? What did I get wrong? I'd been doing pretty good, hadn't I? Where—Where did I go—

A serpent head closed in on me while I lay on the ground. It opened its mouth to swallow me whole. It lunged at me, and I—no, my body, trained by Blood... drew Overeater as if by instinct.

Chapter Five

Slash. The serpent's head flew off. Crimson thorns shot through the air. My wounds disappeared. Life force filled me. I roared, even louder than before.

Everything began to fade, began to grow cold. All thought disappeared from my mind. Everything emptied to white, until only the positional relationships of me and the beasts occupied my head.

A slaughter began.

◆

Fangs came from the right. I slashed.

Claws swung at my left leg. I let them hit me, then slashed. The pain was excruciating.

I slashed. My wounds healed. The excruciating pain was gone.

I slashed the next foe. Deep red thorns filled the air.

I punched with my shield and slashed. Let them stab me and slashed. Let them bite me and slashed. Held them close and slashed.

Slashed. Slashed. Slashed.

Thorns. Thorns. My vision bled red.

I roared.

It was shameful, blind desperation. My trained muscles, my polished technique, my fortified spirit—none of that was there. I was just leaving everything to the abilities of my demonblade, and slashing and cutting my way through without any strategy or grace. It was an incredibly, hopelessly pitiful, embarrassing, and saddening battle. I felt like I'd failed them all. I felt pathetic.

I slashed and cut the beasts down like a madman, tears spilling from my eyes. Drenched in blood and guts, I'd lost count of how many I'd slain so far. But I had to kill more. More. More—

"Stop! That's enough!" A voice shook my eardrums. Someone had forced my arms behind my back.

It was Reystov.

"Huh—Ah—"

I realized that nothing was moving. The chimera had run off somewhere. The area around me was a literal sea of blood and guts. Reystov and the other adventurers weren't uninjured, either—

"Heal Menel! He's going to die!"

I snapped back to reality. "M-Menel!" I sprinted, almost tripped my way over to him.

He was charred black, and his beautiful face was burned beyond recognition. His arms were twisted, and he was missing several of his fingers.

I started hyperventilating.

I prayed and prayed.

The miracles of the god of the flame began to heal his body.

"P-Please—Please—" Tears filled my eyes. "Wake up... You can't... You can't die..."

He was so gravely injured. The healing was progressing slowly, but he wasn't opening his eyes. I prayed, prayed, prayed...

I was feeling very faint. I'd swung that demonblade so much and indulged in its power for so long. Maybe that was taking its toll on me.

But I... have to heal... Menel...

And while I was still mid-thought, the ground suddenly tilted at a strange angle, and I blacked out.

◆

Chapter Five

When I woke up, Reystov was there to explain the situation to me.

I was in a village close to the valley, and this was an empty house that they had allowed us to rent after being filled in on what had happened. After the battle, Reystov and the others had retreated here, carrying Menel and me over their shoulders. Fortunately, I had cut down the entire horde of beasts, and after the chimera's retreat, there had been no sign of it attempting another attack.

Menel had escaped death.

It was probably thanks to the number of spells and blessings I'd cast on him beforehand. It had also majorly paid off that Menel hadn't foolishly attempted to hold his ground when the chimera struck him, but had rolled with the blow and willingly been knocked away. The collision with the rock wall and the chimera's fire breath had both nearly killed him, but the magic I had bestowed upon him had somehow kept him breathing, and my blessings had made it in time.

However, because I overused my demonblade, I had passed out halfway through treating Menel, so he hadn't come to yet.

"For now, just rest a little more," Reystov said.

"But—"

"Meneldor's condition is stable. You've exerted yourself too much. *Rest*," he said emphatically, giving me a hard look. Then he left the room.

He'd looked exhausted as well. There must have been other victims besides Menel and me in that chaotic battle, but he hadn't mentioned anything, probably deliberately.

And so, in this unoccupied house with its simple mud walls, I sat under a faint ray of light that shone through a gap in the roof, my head lowered in thought.

Where on earth had I screwed up?

Was it when I trusted Menel with defending against the rear attack? No, given the situation, that had been unavoidable. The choice ultimately resulted in our suffering a near-total defeat and having to flee with our lives, but nevertheless, from where I stood at the time the decision to leave the chimera to Menel wasn't an obviously bad move. I was pretty sure of that. If I'd gone to handle the chimera myself, there was a chance that everyone else might have been trampled by the charging demons.

The worst moment for us was most likely when we fell for the trap that used the dead body. We had a good number of people, we'd been very successful up until that point, and we were acting a little braver than we should have to insulate ourselves from the shock of having seen the corpses of people we knew. All those factors combined must have resulted in each of us being a little bit careless.

We should have been on alert from the moment we discovered the bodies. We should have been patient and thorough, and sent out scouts in every direction. If we'd done that, we wouldn't have aimlessly wandered into a wide-open valley and gotten lured into a battle where we were at such a disadvantage.

So the cause of this failure was a very, very simple lack of caution. We got our comeuppance for allowing ourselves to get distracted in enemy territory and take careless actions. End of story.

And yet—

There was something... something that didn't feel quite right about this explanation. I was overlooking something critical. I could feel it. What was it? What hadn't I realized?

I was lying on my back with my head full of this feeling I couldn't place when I heard voices through the thin walls.

"Forced to retreat, huh..."

Chapter Five

"Unbelievable, right? It's the Wyvern Killer and the Penetrator we're talking about here."

"There was some unearthly big chimera thing there, I heard. A horrible mix of different beasts."

"What's the plan to deal with *that*?"

"Beats me."

"That mixed elf guy got injured badly too, you hear about that?"

"Yeah, he's got it rough. He shouldn't let himself get roped into the kinda battles the Wyvern Killer fights, it's just suicidal. The guy's a monster."

The two of them—adventurers, I thought—passed by outside, probably completely unaware that I'd been able to hear their conversation.

A black realization flickered into my mind. Now I saw it. It wasn't the *strategy*. It was the *strength of our forces*.

In my mind, someone talked in a sticky voice.

I trusted Menel to have my back. I thought that even if we were faced with a powerful enemy, Menel would be able to stave it off for a little while if I left it to him. And when the chimera appeared, I thought the same, as if it were a totally natural expectation.

However, what was the reality? Menel couldn't put up any resistance against the chimera at all. He wasn't as strong as I'd been casually expecting. I'd assigned him more danger than he could handle, innocently, without thinking twice about it. I treated him like a friend, and I just thought he could handle that much—

"Oh…"

It was all fitting together now. Something came crawling out of the very darkest part of my heart. It was probably something I'd been unconsciously trying to avoid confronting. I'd been putting it out of my mind, but I wasn't going to avert my eyes from it anymore.

By this world's standards, my level of strength was completely insane.

I had been told this countless times since leaving the city of the dead, both explicitly and not so explicitly. And every time, I'd smiled humbly and politely, and let those words pass me by.

Why hadn't I thought about this until now? I'd probably unconsciously been avoiding thinking too deeply about it. No matter how much everyone around me praised my abilities, I kept on being modest. I elevated all the other skilled people I met, and felt shame at my immaturity. Because otherwise, it would have meant admitting it.

No matter how pitiable the people I met were, no matter how horrible the sights I saw were, I avoided feeling sorry for anyone. I just tried to be a good problem solver. Because otherwise, it would have meant admitting it.

That *we weren't equal.*

And once I admitted that—

Once I recognized that I was above them, and everyone else was far, far below me—

Once I started to realize that asking someone to fight alongside me might be forcing a terrible burden upon them—

I could never be like them. Not like the three who raised me. Having each other's back, supporting each other, respecting each other. I'd never have friends like that. Because I would be alone.

So I refused to acknowledge that there was a difference in our strength.

But what was the reality like? I wanted Menel to fight alongside me, but he was weak. I'd beaten him effortlessly when we first met. Even in my battle against the wyvern, all he did was spread out my Word and help me to drop the wyvern to earth. That was all. I'd been unconsciously averting my eyes from the simple truth that, compared to me, he was very weak. It was like it was something disgusting I didn't want to look at.

Chapter Five

Why? Why was being alone something to be afraid of?

The instant I thought that, a scene flashed into my mind, with a flash not of bright light, but of pitch-black darkness.

It was my old room, in my past life. It was an empty room with no one there, a house without parents, a place as silent as the grave. I was scared. I was afraid. I was lonely. I hurt inside. I couldn't take it—

"Oh…"

Oh.

So that was it. It was so simple. I didn't want to be alone. I was afraid of not having anyone by my side.

So even though he was someone I should have been protecting, someone who I should have been saving, I'd tried to see him as an equal against all reason. I made excuse after excuse to not think about the clear and obvious facts. I coaxed him into standing alongside me, and as a result, I nearly destroyed him. And it was all for the single, most despicable reason that I didn't want to be lonely.

I finally understood… what I'd been doing wrong.

I got to my feet. I wobbled a little, but a prayer sorted that out with no trouble at all. There was no need to worry. I was very strong.

I started walking. First of all, I had to go see Menel. I had to heal him.

It had started drizzling at some point, but it didn't bother me in the slightest. I felt like all my cares had been blown away.

And I laughed, from the bottom of my heart.

◆

It was drizzling outside.

Menel had been laid on a bed, in a farmhouse that looked like it had wealthy owners. His wounds hadn't fully healed, and fluids were seeping from the burns all over his body and soaking into his bandages. He looked like he was having difficulty breathing. His cheeks looked somehow sunken, and his silver hair looked dull.

This was my sin.

I was vaguely aware that I was overwhelmingly powerful, and at the same time, I tried to remain unaware of it. I feared being better. I shied from solitude. I ran away from being responsible for my power.

I caused this, I told myself. *I'll do it alone.*

Do it alone.

I couldn't force other people to bear the burden of standing by my side, especially not in battle. What did it matter if I couldn't become like my parents, anyway?

I offered a prayer to my god. *Gracefeel, please heal poor Menel, who lies before me.* God healed Menel right away, just as she always did. His gruesome burns, his partially-healed claw scars—all of them started to disappear.

My vision suddenly warped disorientingly, taking me by surprise. I was experiencing a revelation.

I saw my black-haired goddess, who always wore a hood over her head and rarely spoke or showed expression. But she had her hood down now, and her lips were pressed sorrowfully into a thin line.

Oh, Gracefeel... Thank you for worrying about me, I thought. *But it's okay. I've been a fool. Just watch me. I'll stop your sadness. So I beg you—put your mind at ease. I'll save everyone, everyone within my reach, as your blade, and as your hands.*

Chapter Five

"It's okay," I whispered. "I'll solve everything, everything, all by myself…"

I walked unsteadily out of the room, and returned to the house where I'd been sleeping.

There was my equipment. I gave it a quick check. There wasn't much of a need. All I *really* needed was myself, a sword, and a spear. I could heal both disease and injury. I could receive gifts of food from my god. And if I felt like it, as long as I had nothing by my side to protect and nothing else to consider… I could kill anything.

Yes—it was time to admit it. My strength was not normal for a person of this world. I'd killed a splinter of an evil god; I could kill wyverns with my bare hands. I was like a video game character who'd maxed out the level counter—or even a hacked character, created by using cheat codes to mess with the data. I was far and away stronger than anything else in this world.

So there was no need to worry. I would kill the chimera. I would kill the demons. I would bring peace to this area. And I would make a bloodbath of any enemies who got in my way. That was the shortest, fastest, most efficient way to do good, to see justice done. It was the best path to making my goddess's wishes become a reality.

I left the house through its gate and into the pelting rain, and headed for the outskirts of the village and the woods beyond—

"Hey!" A figure stood in my way. He had silver hair, sharp facial features, tightened lips, and jade eyes burning with anger.

I had no idea when he had gotten up, or when he had circled ahead of me, but one way or another—Meneldor was there.

◆

In a field near the edge of the village, Menel and I faced each other in the pouring rain.

"Where do you think you're going?" he asked me, his voice sharp.

"What?" I tilted my head. "To kill beasts, Meneldor."

Meneldor narrowed his eyes and pressed his lips together. "Alone."

"Yes?" *Of course alone.* "You can't keep up with me. Right?" So I had to protect him. Wasn't that obvious?

Meneldor's expression twisted.

Feeling cold and empty, I slowly put on a smile. "Don't worry. It's going to be okay. I'll go solve everything myself. I'll kill the chimera and the hordes of beasts. If there's demons behind it all, I'll kill them, too."

And then everything would be resolved. Why had I been overcomplicating this? This was what I should have—

"The hell you will!" With quick movements, Menel closed the distance between us.

He never swung his fist back. It was simply thrust at my face at close range. The motion was beautiful.

His fist collided with my cheek. "Wake up, you stupid shit!"

But all I felt was... disappointment. I was right. This was all he had. I hadn't moved an inch. It just stung a little. That was all.

"Is that it, Meneldor?" I said quietly, his fist still pressed against my cheek. Even I thought my eyes must have looked terribly cold.

As I started to turn away, planning on ignoring him entirely and leaving, he lashed out with more punches and kicks. I made slight movements to change where the blows landed, and they barely hurt at all.

Chapter Five

"Dammit! Why are you acting like this?!" He still wasn't giving up.

At this point, I was starting to get a little irritated. I couldn't have him following me. What could I do about this?

Maybe just one arm wouldn't be too bad.

As he lunged out with his fist, I grabbed his arm.

"Wh—?!"

Then, I pressed it with all my body weight and dislocated it. The feeling of his shoulder popping out of its socket was horribly recognizable. Meneldor seemed to jerk, and then he let out a long, indistinct groan and fell to the ground, squirming in pain.

I'm sorry, I thought. *It's for your own good…*

"Get someone to treat that for you."

Figuring that now he wouldn't be able to fight me, I started to walk off.

"I'm… not done with you yet…" From behind me, there was the sound of clawing at grass. I turned to see Meneldor with tears in his eyes, clutching his arm, and yet, staggering to his feet.

I sighed. What was I supposed to do now? I'd been the one trying to think of him as a friend; really, we'd only paired up because it was easiest, so I'd thought this would have been enough to get him to let this go. But for some reason, he was still keeping at it.

What could I do?

Maybe I could seal him from moving by using a Word. But Words were a little bit unreliable… Aha. I could choke him out by compressing his carotid artery. I took a step toward him.

"'*Gnomes, gnomes, form a fist! Clench your hands and strike the foe!*'"

The ground behind me ruptured, and a great many small stones came flying toward me. It was the spell Stone Fist.

Apparently the pain was causing Meneldor to make bad decisions. That surprise attack from behind was something I'd already seen when I first fought him, and although this was certainly a powerful spell, it gave me a lot of advance warning. It was the kind of spell best used as part of a team. I could simply dodge it.

But as I started moving my feet, I realized. *The spell was headed for Meneldor.*

In that instant, I was pressed to make a decision. If I avoided it, Meneldor would take serious damage. So without even thinking, I stopped in my tracks and hardened my defense—and an endless onslaught of pebbles battered my body.

◆

I groaned. My body was throbbing all over. I lost control of my legs, and they gave out.

"Hah! 'I'll go solve it myself.' What a load of pig shit!" Menel approached me while I was still in terrible pain from Stone Fist. "You're just being a goddamn coward!" He kicked me in the stomach as hard as he could.

I was wearing mail, but even so, he'd kicked me in a spot where his spell had also hit moments ago. It hurt like hell. I crumpled to the ground, trying not to shout out in pain.

However, Menel wasn't entirely unharmed himself. His shoulder was dislocated, and as I looked up at him, I saw that Stone Fist had hit him too. That wasn't surprising; he'd been asking for it with the way he used that spell. He was covered in mud, he looked unsteady on his feet, there was foam at the corners of his mouth, and his eyes were bloodshot. His usual handsome features were nowhere to be seen. It was painful to look at.

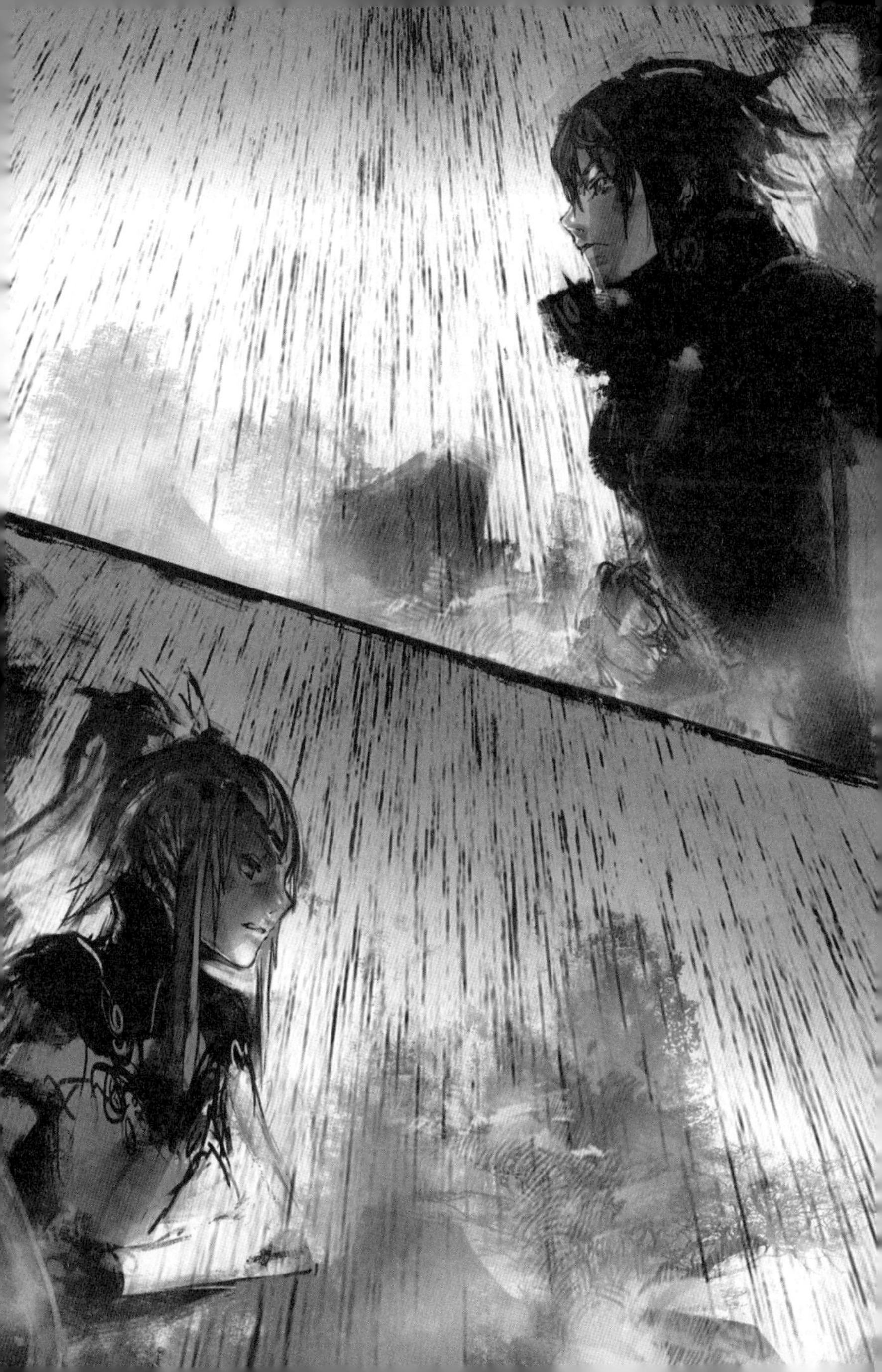

I shakily got to my feet. "What's the point of you doing all this?" I suddenly found myself asking. "If you keep going like this, you'll be putting your own life in danger. We were just together because it turned out that way. There's no reason for you to go this far."

"Hah. Maybe, yeah." He smirked. "You're right. I've got no reason to follow you anymore, and no reason to go out of my way to try to stop an emotionally unstable wimp who'd take things to this extreme and go running off just because he got horribly beaten one time."

"Then why—"

Menel's smile softened, and he cut me off. "See... We're friends," he said, with a mud-covered smile.

I almost doubted my ears.

"Friends stick together. When my friend goes nuts in the head, I feel like doing something about it."

"Oh..." Those few words hit me much harder than any fist or spell.

"Where you came from is a mystery, you don't know half the things you should, and I've sometimes thought you might be a bit suspect. But you're a kind person, and you're always trying your best to do things right. I know that."

I didn't know what to say.

"You saved my life, you saved the villages... And all this time we've spent traveling and fighting together was fun. And I'm really grateful for you sending off the people back at the village."

Like holding my hands over a warm campfire on a freezing night, those words quietly warmed the cold and dark parts inside me.

"Will, you're my friend," Menel said, standing unsteadily in my way. "Friends don't abandon each other."

Chapter Five

No words would come. Tears welled in my eyes.

"So... We still fighting?" He stood defensively.

I slowly shook my head. "You win." My despair, my sense of being all alone, all of it had vanished without a trace. I didn't think I was this temperamental. "Sorry. I was... I dunno. I lost control."

Menel laughed dryly. "Happens." He winced, clutched his shoulder, and glared at me. "You're a real pain in the ass." Then, his tone completely changed, and he said brightly, "A win's a win though. One to me, I guess!"

I grumbled. "I only said that so you'd quit bugging me!"

"Hah! Yeah, you just keep telling yourself that."

I suddenly realized that the rain had lifted. We joked with each other and laughed together. It seemed that we'd had our first ever argument, and I had lost.

◆

There was a bit of a commotion going on in the village when we got back. After all, I, my equipment, and Menel had all disappeared. Reystov and the other adventurers had been just about to go looking for us.

"What happened?" Reystov asked.

I may have healed Menel's wounds, but both he and I had come back covered in mud. It was no wonder Reystov had such a scowl on his face.

"I'm sorry for making you worry. I lost my head thinking I didn't want anyone else to get hurt, and tried to do everything myself. And then Menel beat the stuffing out of me."

"No no no. You don't get to just skip over what you did to me. Feckin' ruthless..."

"I'm really, truly sorry." I abjectly apologized.

Yeah, simply speaking, that was what it came down to. I tried to do everything myself and got punched. That summed the whole thing up. It sounded ridiculous, even to me.

"Tough-guy disease," Reystov said, shaking his head.

Maybe he was right. This might have been the kind of idea that only strong people were susceptible to.

"Sometimes it kills the tough guy."

That might actually have happened, had I just gone running off like that. I was so glad Menel had been there for me.

"I'm really sorry for all the trouble I caused. I'm okay now."

"We won't screw up next time."

"Are you planning to take on that thing again?"

"Yes."

Even now, I could remember exactly what that chimera had looked like. I remembered that huge body, bigger than a wyvern's; the horde of beasts it had following it; the way it was charged with contempt, ridicule, and malice toward the small. I could remember vividly the wickedness dwelling in its glinting black eyes. That thing had to be hunted down and killed. And besides...

"Chimeras don't come about naturally. That was definitely the product of a demonic ritual."

There were definitely demons behind that, and more than likely, they still had their sights on that city of the dead and were intending on reviving the High King.

"Let's bring them all down before they run off someplace else."

The adventurers laughed when I said that.

"So we're going right back up against the enemy we just lost to?"

"This is a dumb and fun-as-hell adventure, all right."

"Right, I'm gonna go hunt down some reinforcements."

Chapter Five

"Let's go big! We gotta show that thing who's boss."

The powerful enemy made them laugh all the more ferociously. They looked happy, like they were really enjoying themselves.

"Yeah, it'd bug me to let that beast have the last laugh. I'm gonna crack all three of its heads open." Menel laughed too.

"Yeah... Let's get our honor back." I grinned too, as if everyone's smiles were contagious. And then, to raise everyone's fighting spirit even more, I used one of Gus's special tricks.

"One silver coin for every demon's head! And for the head of the boss, I'll pay ten in gold!"

The adventurers immediately broke into a jubilant uproar.

◆

After that, we spent a few days making preparations, sending out scouts (multiple times), and readying our forces—and then I, Menel, Reystov, and a large number of other adventurers made our way into the valley once more.

We weren't going to be using any tricks in particular. The plan was simple: get enough people together, prepare properly beforehand, and overcome our enemies head-on. I had Pale Moon, Overeater, my circular shield, and my mithril mail. Menel had his bow, a knife, and leather armor. That was us fully equipped.

The trees were sparse. The river that had formed the valley had long since dried up, and where once there had been a riverbed, there were now only rocks scattered on the ground.

We made our way deeper and deeper into that barren place, and soon the long howls of beasts echoed around. I could sense their presence deep in the valley. It looked like the demons' base really was down here.

"How many do they *have*?" Menel said quietly. "I think things might be pretty peaceful around here if we wiped out all of them."

"Yeah. Let's kill them all."

"You come out with the most heavy shit sometimes, you know that?"

The adventurers chuckled slightly at our back-and-forth.

We had provided all the support we could by magic, benediction, and the use of the fae before we even stepped into the valley. All that was left was to fight.

"Here they come," Reystov said.

All kinds of beasts started appearing ahead of us. Every one of them was gushing miasma and had eyes possessed by madness. Their numbers didn't look as hopeless as before. Maybe I'd cut most of them down a few days ago.

"Hey. Will. I've got your back."

"Thanks. I'm counting on you, Menel."

Menel and I nodded at each other. Then, I raised Pale Moon, and shouted.

"We'll storm them from the front!"

War cries came back, one after another.

"Readyyy!"

Swords were raised.

"For the glory of the Beast Killers!"

Spears were raised.

"By Volt's lightning sword!"

"Burn hot, fire of Blaze's valor!"

"Whirl! Grant us winds that blow in our favor!"

We beat our weapons against our shields, a warrior's gesture to gather the attention of the gods and intimidate our enemies. Everyone cried out the name of their guardian deity and wished for protection.

Chapter Five

"May the good gods bless us all!"

"Kill! Kill! Kill! Kill!"

Everyone's mouths were curved into wild smiles brought on by the tension and excitement of battle. They were sweating; their arms and legs were trembling. Then, as one, we drew a deep breath and roared. The war cry reverberated all around us, and everyone broke into a forward sprint, vying to be the first into battle.

"Fire!" Arrows from Menel and the others flew from behind me and into the beasts' ranks.

"*Sagitta Flammeum!*" Several magic wielders cast a spell for flaming arrows.

The victory and glory-seeking adventurers sprang hungrily at the beasts, whose order had been thrown into chaos. Swords glinted. Shields were battered with violent sounds. Blood boiled. Hearts beat faster and harder, and muscles heated up.

This was battle. Blood had talked fondly about this sight many times. This was *battle*!

It was meant to be a terrible thing to witness, but for some reason, I was laughing. I felt like I'd arrived in the world of Blood's epic stories, which I'd only been able to imagine while living in the city of the dead.

I chuckled. Now I was on the battlefield, I appreciated how small I really was. What had I been thinking, saying I'd solve everything myself? In the end, I was only a single element of this battle. A large element, perhaps, or a powerful piece, but not enough to decide its entire course.

For some reason, I was happy that the battlefield no longer looked like a place trivial enough that a single man of exceptional power could do something about it on his own.

I gripped Pale Moon. I could tell that my goddess wasn't looking sorrowful anymore.

"On the flame of Gracefeel!"

I steeled myself, I shouted my god's name loud... and I ran straight at the horde.

◆

I swung my spear around and forcibly cut down a pack of small beasts in front. A bull-beast bubbling blood from the edges of its mouth charged at me. I used its momentum and threw it. It smashed into several beasts that weren't quick enough to get out of the way. A pack of our enemies had been disrupted. Other adventurers rushed in, weapons in hand, and added to the damage.

On the battlefield, it is often more effective to simply overwhelm your opponents with muscular strength instead of trying to add stupid little tricks. I incanted a number of Words as well, and restricted the movements of the enemy group.

While protecting my allies from side attacks, I pushed forward and through, letting nothing stand in my way. Swinging my spear in all directions and yelling, I impaled and struck beasts one after the other, their blood splashing over me, and pressed directly forwards. From behind me, countless arrows and wind and earth elementals helped to clear my way. I could feel that Menel was keeping up behind me and providing me support.

And after running all the way through and past the horde, I found the ruins I'd been looking for hidden between trees and rocks.

It was quite a large structure, made of stone and surrounded by stone walls. The entrance was large, as were the corridors and rooms. From its construction, I guessed that this had once been a secluded monastery where priests had trained; now, it was probably one of the bases of the demons running rampant around here.

Chapter Five

The moment I sighted it, my senses, sharpened by magic, picked up a subtle presence. But I couldn't see anything around that matched it.

"*Omnia Vanitas... Erasus.*" I quietly incanted a Word of Negation, aiming it forwards, and a large beast showed itself in the shade of a rock in front of the monastery. It had been hiding under the Word of Invisibility.

It had a goat, a lion, and a demidragon's heads, huge wings, and a tail that was a venomous snake. And all of its heads, and all of its eyes, were filled to bursting with contempt, ridicule, and malice for everything small. It was the same disordered, blasphemous amalgamation of beasts I'd seen before: the chimera.

"Hello," I said.

I'd considered the possibility that our second meeting would be like our first—that it would fly above us and try to attack us from the rear as the other enemies charged. We'd even prepared a means of shooting it down and made sure everyone knew in advance, but apparently the beast was intelligent enough to know not to use the same trick twice.

If it had been generous enough to fly, I'd been thinking about taking away its wings and sight, slamming it into the ground, and thereafter having everyone beat it up at once. Unfortunately... this was a foe to be reckoned with. After the aerial back attack, it had chosen to lie low, hide itself, and aim for an attack from the side. This really didn't seem like the intelligence of a beast to me.

"Do you have a bit of... demon in you as well?"

When I asked that question, the chimera's three mouths all curved upwards into closed-mouth, crescent moon-like smiles.

Multiple beasts and intelligent demons had been crossed together to create an even stronger beast. It wasn't hard for me to imagine how much blasphemy and bloodshed it must have taken to achieve such a feat. "Are you after the High King...?"

"Ohh...?"

The beast slowly emitted the common language from its vocal cords.

"You know of the High King's seal. Are you a warrior sent by some god or other?"

I nodded, a little surprised at its lucid question. And if that was its answer to me, then I could be virtually certain: the demons' objective was neither deep nor far from here.

The demons taking over this base had all been part of the greater plan.

That city of the dead, the ground of the High King's seal, still wasn't under the control of any power. If the demons could take the city, they could break the seal, and calamity would once again sweep across this continent. Conversely, if people could take the city, and came to learn about the seal, the seal would be strengthened further.

So, for the demons, Beast Woods was a place that had to remain ravaged. It had to be a crucible of conflict, poverty, and disorder.

They couldn't allow mankind to advance any further south.

They couldn't allow people to set their sights on the south.

They couldn't allow people to think there was any hope to be found in the south.

Once you considered the existence of the demons' king, their goal in subjugating beasts, attacking cities, and constantly applying pressure was incredibly easy to understand, and blatantly incompatible with the happiness of people.

"In the name of Gracefeel, I will destroy you all."

"Ohh? But wait. It seems there has been a little misunderstanding. A false impression."

The chimera's enormous body slowly walked toward me.

"A false impression."

"Yes. You see—"

Chapter Five

It flowed from its slow walk into a horizontal swipe at me with one of its massive front legs. If it hit me, it would smash my head clean off in a single strike. I leaned back and avoided it, and as I did, I gave the beast a quick spike to send it a message.

"Ghh—!"

It leaped back and put distance between us.

"I'm surprised that demons still use those antiquated classics."

My mild provocation enraged it. The chimera let out a loud roar and began to charge at me. Real battles rarely began with a clear "ready, set, go"; usually, they started just like this.

I wasn't going to use any clever schemes this time. There was only one main aspect to my strategy, and it was very ordinary: *to make full use of all the power at my disposal.* This wasn't like my battle against the god of undeath, where there had been an overwhelming difference in power between us. This time, I had properly prepared, discussed, taken all measures that could be taken, and now, I was going to win—because that was perfectly possible, as long as I didn't lose my cool.

"Menel!"

"Gotcha!"

Shouting out a signal to my partner behind, I faced the chimera rushing at me.

◆

The chimera's huge body came toward me. As I faced it, its demidragon head was on the left, the middle was the lion, and on the right, the goat.

From behind, Menel ran around to the right in a wide arc. The goat's mouth spoke in a muddy and indistinct voice, and *Sagitta Flammeum* came flying at Menel.

"You're not getting me with that!"

The sylphs changed the arrow's direction, offering him their Protection From Arrows.

Keeping Menel in the corner of my eye, I faced the rushing chimera head-on. I was staring down a frontal assault by a beast of greater mass than a wyvern. I may have been strong, but with my small body, it was going to be impossible to physically block or throw this thing.

So I prayed for protection with the blessing Sacred Shield. Drawing from my experience with the wyvern, I set up the shield at a diagonal.

The wall of light rose in front of me. The chimera collided with it, its momentum was redirected by the diagonal wall, and it glanced off to my right. Instantly, I erased the shield, and with a shout, I stabbed Pale Moon deep into the chimera's right side.

"*'Gnomes, gnomes, take his feet! Harden, bind, and nail him down!'*"

It was the spell Hold, sent out just at the moment when the wall of light and my spear together had slowed the chimera's charge. Menel's spells wouldn't have been powerful enough to do anything about a chimera in peak condition, but his timing was exquisite. Forced to devote most of its attention to me as the closest attacker, the chimera got its feet caught in Menel's trap.

Menel sprinted nimbly over the craggy ground. It was hard to run in this place, but the fairies were making sure the path was clear for his feet.

Chapter Five

With a proper frontline attacker in front of him, Menel's skills at mid-range were more impressive than I imagined. It was true that I'd overestimated him, but apparently I had been underestimating him as well. People are so complicated and multifaceted. I realized that coming to a quick conclusion about someone and thinking you had them fully understood was a very foolish thing to do.

As the chimera fought to shake off the earth and stone clinging to it, I took my chance. Screaming a war cry, I relentlessly gouged into it with the blade of my spear. The chimera finally gave out a roar of agony. Its demidragon head attempted to bite me, but stopped abruptly an instant later. On the other side of it, Menel had shot an arrow toward one of its goat eyes.

Being a multi-headed beast meant it had multiple brains, and if each issued a different command for a different reflex action, it was obvious that the body receiving them would become confused. This beast was simply unnatural as a living creature.

As the chimera fought and screeched wildly, I ran to the other side, where Menel was. The chimera's enormous body was causing it problems. It couldn't fully keep track of my movements. Having a huge body made it strong, and fast by the same token, but that body was obstructing its field of view, and there was nothing it could do about it. Having something dance about in close proximity to it was probably the behavior the chimera found the most unpleasant.

I stabbed it repeatedly with my spear, twisting it in the wounds and making it bleed. I avoided it when it tried to bite me, and deflected its heads with my shield.

There was no need to win cleanly in a single strike. I just needed to fight normally, and win by being better. I didn't have any spectacular tricks up my sleeve, or any ultimate moves.

I just had what I'd been taught by my parents, which had raised all my abilities to an equally high standard. So I would put them all together, and press forward to victory. Through experience, I was finally beginning to understand that that was the way of fighting that suited me best.

With the help of the wind elementals, Menel fired off an arrow accelerated to terrific speeds. I didn't miss the chimera switching its attention for an instant. I swung down Pale Moon with all my might.

The goat head was crushed. Its teeth smashed together and flew everywhere, and blood squirted out of its broken skull. The chimera screamed in obvious agony.

"One down!"

There was just the demidragon and lion heads left, plus the venomous snake tail—no, that was already gone. Menel had found an opening to sever it with a spell. He was quick.

While Menel was using Stone Fist to crush the head of the snake that had fallen to the ground, I decided to do something about either the lion or the demidragon head. But before I could, the two heads let out a terrible howl, and I sensed something dreadful coming. Menel and I both leaped back and kept our distance.

"It is an accursed dragon power, but you leave me no choice!"

Dragon? I thought, but had no more time to think about it. The chimera's veins turned black. Its muscles swelled, becoming misshapen and even thicker than before, and miasma gushed from its entire body.

"This guy too?!" Menel spat out, infuriated.

"Menel, keep just a little more distance."

"Got it."

Poison didn't work on me. I'd been raised on Mary's holy bread, and I had the stigmata of Mater on my arms. So—

Chapter Five

"I'll beat him down now."

Although I'd used this magic spear, Pale Moon, for a long time and felt very comfortable with it, I hadn't had great results with it against stronger enemies. I thought that it would probably like some glory of its own soon. I held my spear tight by my side and ran toward the chimera once more.

◆

It struck at me with a ferocious swing of its front leg. I ducked under it and swung my spear upwards. The lion neck bent and avoided it. Its right foreleg swiped toward me, trailing miasma. I'd seen it coming; I dodged with a back step. As its right foreleg completed its swing, its demidragon neck stretched toward me. It was about to breathe fire.

Back when I fought the wyvern, I'd avoided this by choking it just before it got the chance. But this time, I'd only moments ago leaped backwards. With my center of gravity tilted back, I couldn't just leap forward like I had before. Moreover, its lion head was still alive. If I attempted a strangulation move, I would be snapped up in its jaws.

So I held my shield firm and pressed my feet into the ground. As the fire belched out, I prepared myself for what was coming. It was possible that I would be burned all over in an instant or that my eyeballs would boil. Yeah, it was possible—but surely just an instant of fire would be fine! I was using defensive blessings! That fire was probably only just a little warm anyway, appearances can be deceiving! *Don't hesitate*, I told myself, *charge in!*

Telling myself anything that came to mind to muster up my courage, I held my shield up in front of my face and charged forward. I closed the distance in less than a second and slammed my shield into the demidragon head's wide-open mouth.

I felt the all-too-real sensation of slamming into flesh. Several fangs broke off in different directions, and the fire breath stopped. The chimera stiffened for a moment. Maybe it hadn't expected me to come straight at it through the flames.

"*'Gnomes, gnomes, form a fist! Clench your hands and strike the foe!'*" Menel cast Stone Fist. There were a lot of small stones scattered all over the ground. They leaped up like a rising fist, and pounded into the chimera's vast belly.

The chimera let out a cry of intense anguish. As it writhed in agony, I thrust my spear through its demidragon neck, finishing off its second head. As soon as I felt the spear sink in, I immediately pulled it back into my hands. I stepped in closer, spinning the spear as I did, and flicked the heavy metal end upward, cracking it into the lion head's jaw.

The chimera flailed and threw its front legs around me, trying to grab me. My way forward was completely blocked by the lion head, and left and right were closed off by the wide reach of its front legs as they closed in. There was nowhere for me to escape.

"*Acceleratio!*"

Except *up*.

I leaped almost directly upwards. The Word of Acceleration was one of my favorites, but I hadn't used it even once in this chimera battle until now. The ground was just too unsuited for it. If I tripped on one of those stones after speeding myself up, it was very possible the momentum would carry me face-first into rock.

Unlike Menel, who had completely ignored the problem by using his elemental powers to run everywhere, I hadn't been using any particularly fast maneuvers this entire time. So this move was one the chimera had no knowledge of.

Chapter Five

It lost sight of me for an instant and then, realizing what had happened, it looked up—and was momentarily blinded by the light of the sun.

"*Gnomes, gnomes, take his feet! Harden, bind, and nail him down!*" Simultaneously, Menel cast Hold with perfect timing.

I roared, and with the sun at my back and Pale Moon in my hands, I let my fall give me momentum, and drove the spear down into its lion head.

I felt it sink through skin, muscle, and bone, and then the impact of my landing. I immediately tried to pull the spear out and leap away, but it was stuck. I had an instant of panic, and I released the spear and leaped back without it. Then I realized. The chimera had already expired.

It was no wonder I couldn't pull out Pale Moon; it had sunk all the way through the chimera's lion head, and was stuck in the ground on the other side.

◆

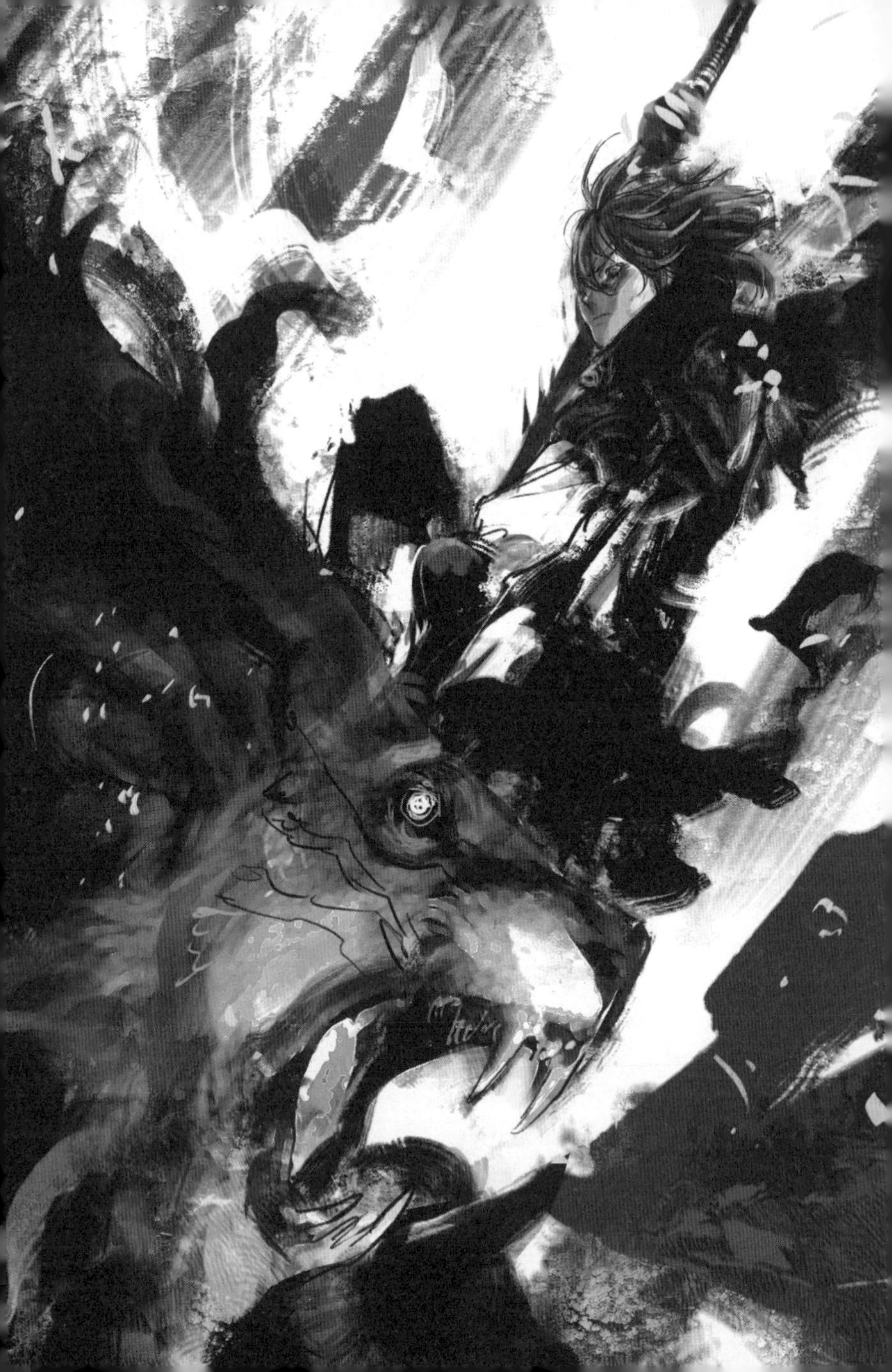

Chapter Five

I turned around to see that the beast extermination was almost over as well. Most of the beasts were already sprawled on the ground, and even those that were still running about looked badly wounded. It didn't look like the others needed any help.

"We won!"

"Nice!"

Menel and I high-fived. It made a satisfying sound.

This hadn't been the kind of magnificent victory I'd scored against the god of undeath. It wasn't a triumph of the underdog against the obvious favorite; it was an ordinary, routine win. But even so, I thought that was fine. If grueling battles like the one I'd fought against the god of undeath were a regular occurrence, that would be unbearable. And besides—we still had enemies ahead of us.

"Moving on!"

"Ya!"

Wary of traps, we stepped inside the ruins of the monastery.

The inside was being kept illuminated by magic, which had probably come from the demons. The place had been stripped of its former stillness and holiness and transformed into a place of hideous rituals and research. We ran down long corridors, passing room after wide-open room, taking side glances at their contents: blood, meat, guts, beastlings preserved in strange fluid, magic circles in ghastly colors of paint.

They had to already know about our assault. It was possible that the demons who were controlling this base would choose to flee, and if that happened, the same thing might repeat somewhere else. We had to finish them off here, and both I and Menel were determined to do whatever it took to make it happen.

We burst out of the corridor. Our view opened up.

We were in the monastery's chapel.

It was a very spacious place where sculptures of the gods were enshrined, and it reminded me of the temple in the city of the dead that had once been my home.

But the several statues of the gods lined up at the back of the chapel had the details of their faces scraped off, just like the ones I'd seen previously in that village. The text honoring the gods, which should have been on the wall, had been scraped away. In its place were Words of praise for the god of dimensions, written large in darkened blood in a unearthly style that was nauseating to look at. And there was Dyrhygma's crest, featuring an arm grasping the eternal cycle.

It was a demonic ritual site.

"Took you long enough."

A quiet voice echoed about the chapel.

When Menel and I heard that voice, our eyes bulged. There was a bearded man there looking at us, wearing a scratched-up cloak and holding a sword. And on his face he was wearing a grin the likes of which I'd never seen.

No way...

"Rey...stov...?"

"Yeah."

Unbelievable.

How on *earth*—

How—

His grin widened as he watched me try to make sense of this.

"You owe me ten gold coins," he said cheerily, and pointed to the body of a large demon lying dead on the ground.

The demon, which was turning slowly to dust before my eyes, looked like a cross between a bat, a wolf, and a person. I had a memory of learning from Gus that these demons, called belalgors,

Chapter Five

were Commander demons considered to be extremely powerful for their rank. And this belalgor's chest had been penetrated with a single, beautifully clean strike.

Yeah... so... in short... what had happened here was...

"You *beat us to it*?!"

"No way! How the *hell* did you do that?!"

"Went around. You guys were fighting the chimera. Thanks for that, by the way. Made it nice and easy."

Reystov had made his way inside the monastery while we were desperately fighting the chimera. He'd hunted down every last demon here and stuck them all with his sword; and then, here in the chapel, he'd confronted the belalgor who had been the unifying force for this base, and stuck him too.

Of course, it couldn't have been as simple as he'd made it sound.

"Reystov the Penetrator, my god... You live up to your name."

He clearly hadn't been given it for nothing.

"No wonder you get all the glory... You are way too good at getting the jump on people."

"You need to be to land the real tough ones," Reystov answered, sounding for once like he was in a good mood.

From the entrance to the monastery, I heard a jumble of noise and voices.

"Okay, now watch yourselves! Who knows what traps are in there!"

"We'll be first in! Hope you're all ready!"

"For honor and glory! And ten gold coins!"

They sounded pretty pumped up. I laughed weakly.

It was a pretty unsatisfying conclusion, but for some reason, I felt that was fitting.

Final Chapter

Under the brightness of the summer sun, long grass swayed in a pleasant breeze.

"Yeeeaaahhh!"

"Here's to victory!"

The field was full of adventurers clapping each other on the shoulder and raising their horns in toast.

There had been a lot to deal with in the immediate aftermath of the battle, but we'd sorted most of it out, and were attempting to head back to Whitesails. However, the enormous number of beast heads and the immense amount of demon dust we were carrying with us caused roars of celebration in each village that we passed through. Casks were brought out, and parties started in the middle of the day. The ale poured into the horns tasted refreshing under the early summer sunshine.

All the villages had that same kind of party mood. The adventurers, too, were enjoying the feeling of release after their life-or-death battle, and raising a racket in every place they went. The trip back was very lively.

We were soon able to join back up with Bee and Tonio, whom we'd unfortunately left behind some time ago.

With his usual soft expression, Tonio congratulated me on a job well done. It was thanks to his help that I was able to provide dozens of adventurers with the supplies they needed, and get them all working together. He was always lending me his subtle and modest support when things began to look shaky, the time after I beat the wyvern being the perfect example. I wanted to find some way to thank him sometime soon.

Bee jumped at me and Menel with her usual brightness. She pestered us repeatedly to talk more about our adventure, and ran ideas for her tales by us. And then, clenching a fist, she declared, "Looks like I need to get Menel included in this one!"

"Oh, shit! No!" The look on Menel's face completely changed as he suddenly realized that he should have been paying attention to this conversation as well.

"Awww, why not?!"

"This weirdo might be happy to grin like a goofball while everyone gawks at him, but I'm not!"

"Meanie pants! I can tell you're planning to follow your darling Will down the path of heroes anyway, so put up with it, mister grouchy!"

"Shut up! And he's not my darling!"

"He so is! Oh! I know! I'll make your title Meneldor the Beautiful!"

"Then all the poets are gonna add some twist, like turning me into a woman!"

"And then you can be Will's girlfriend!"

"Dammit, if you agree with me, don't do it!"

Everyone burst out laughing watching the two of them running around. I laughed too. As usual, Bee was cheerful, spoke her mind, and had a way of making all my worries seem completely stupid. Watching her really made me think: *Yeah, there* are *other ways to go through life! You can be pretty carefree, if you want!*

Final Chapter

Incidentally, let me add that as a result of Menel's fierce objections, his nickname was revised from "Meneldor the Beautiful" to "Meneldor of Swift Wings."

The excitement of taking down a powerful enemy seemed to have worn off for Reystov; he had returned to his normal, lethargic self, taking tiny sips of his drink with a sullen, dull look on his face. He was the kind of guy who didn't make a big thing of himself. He had a kind of subdued coolness.

The finesse he had with that sword was very impressive too. He'd killed that demon in a single thrust. I asked him if we could train together sometime, and he gave me a silent nod. I hoped my eyes would be good enough to spot the secret to his stabbing technique. I badly wanted to steal it.

I looked around at the villagers. Now that the threat from demons and beasts had eased off, their faces were looking a lot sunnier.

"Everything's gotten so... lively."

Only about half a year had passed since the days when I'd lived in that city of the dead with just me, Blood, Mary, and Gus. What a merry circle of people I'd surrounded myself with in just that short span of time.

"It'll get even livelier," Menel said from beside me. "The beasts and demons are much less of a threat now. More people are gonna come to the south, looking for a new world down here. I bet it'll cause some problems too..." He was looking philosophically into the distance. "Gonna have to live with it, I guess."

"Yeah. You're right. Wonder what I'm going to do now."

Menel tilted his head when he heard that. "Now?"

"Yeah, I mean, what next. Of course, if there are any matters left to sort out on the way to Whitesails, I'll be helping with those... but I wonder what I'll do after that."

I'd reached a good stopping point for this area. I felt confident saying that I'd achieved the task my god had charged me with here. In order to run what looked a lot like a military campaign in Beast Woods, I'd ended up becoming a knight, but I didn't have any land and it wasn't a hereditary knighthood, either. It was pretty much an honorary position. Not only did I have no territory to rule over, I didn't even hold any real official post.

I thought it might be a good idea to get permission from the Duke of Southmark, if I could, and try going on a journey traveling around places like my parents had. Each day an adventure spent searching for ancient ruins and the like. That sounded fun—

"Well, you're gonna be the lord, aren't you?"

...Huh?

◆

"The lord?"

"The lord."

"Of where?"

"The villages of Beast Woods."

"Hahah." I was worried for a moment, but Menel just had the wrong idea. "Come on, Menel. I'm a knight with no land who can't pass on his title. It's kind of like an honor, that's all. In practice, I'm seriously no different from an adventurer!"

When I said that, not just Menel, but everyone around me went silent. Wh-What?

"He doesn't realize..."

Final Chapter

"You can't be serious."

"*Really?*"

"He... hadn't been thinking about it?"

"And here I was, thinking he was doing a pretty good job..."

A small commotion started among the adventurers.

"This guy's smart, but sometimes he's the world's greatest idiot, isn't he?"

"I can't believe he's so good at managing what's under his nose, but he wasn't even thinking about how it'd end up."

"No way..."

"So he's clueless..."

H-Huh?

As I stood there, puzzled, Menel sighed deeply and began to speak. "Even if you aren't given land, you have the freedom to conquer unclaimed areas, don't you?"

"*Conquer?* No, I don't plan on doing anything like that." Maybe back when I fell into that dark place where I was trying to do everything myself, but certainly not now. I didn't want to be a *ruler*...

"Lemme ask you something."

"Okay."

"Say you're someone who wants to start a business in these woods. Who do you go talk to?"

Well... That would be the person who's started dealing with large transactions and is already working industriously to help me with just that sort of thing, namely—

"Tonio."

"And the majority of Tonio's capital is financed by you, right? If you pull your funding, Tonio gets hit hard."

Yep... Hm?

"I don't plan on doing that."

"But you *could*, is the issue, right?"

Everyone else nodded.

"Apart from that, you have the blessing of the god of the flame and you're a paladin sanctioned by the kingdom and the temple. You're authority incarnate! You have the military power, hiring all these adventurers. Oh, and you're also arbitrating village disputes, so this place is literally your jurisdiction for all intents and purposes. And, as I just said, you also have control over goods distribution."

I tried calmly to think of a counterargument. But... Huh? Wait... Wait, what? It was strange... I couldn't think of... anything...

"Basically, in the process of wiping out the demons, you've effectively taken complete control of this region's authority, military power, legal system, and the distribution of all its goods. The position is blatantly about to be yours, and we're all behind you. If you suddenly renege on it with 'I don't want to do it' there's gonna be chaos, brother."

My mouth hung open. Menel and all the others were looking at me with faces of disbelief.

"So you literally hadn't realized?"

I could feel myself going pale as I nodded repeatedly back.

I'd simply been hoping that if I just did a little something about the demons and then improved the poverty situation a bit, the rest would just naturally work itself out, and I hadn't really thought in any detail about what would come after. I'd just been vaguely thinking that I could saunter off into the sunset like my parents had.

"Uhhh..."

"Yeah?"

"Wh-What do I do?!"

In the end, those were the words that came out.

Final Chapter

This wasn't how it was supposed to go... When my parents had solved issues like this, they'd departed the scene dashingly without any problem! Had I somehow screwed up right near the beginning, and I hadn't even noticed?! Where?!

"I... I guess I have to... get some people? Umm... um..."

"You already have merchants and priests who know about law, don't you? If you need anyone else, I'm sure you can get that duke to introduce someone to you."

The bishop had apparently seen this development coming. I could understand the priests who knew about the liturgy and sermons, but now I understood why the bishop had given me people with experience in law and office work as well...

"Oh my God..."

I hadn't realized just how big things had become. As I held my head, the people around me cheered and laughed at my reaction.

"Where did I go wrong for things to turn out this way...? Please, tell me, Gracefeel..."

I felt like I heard faint giggling. Her as well?!

A cool wind carrying the smells of greenery and earth blew by as we laughed together in our merry circle, the dazzling summer sun shining brightly on this faraway land.

— The Faraway Paladin II: The Archer of Beast Woods — *Finis*.

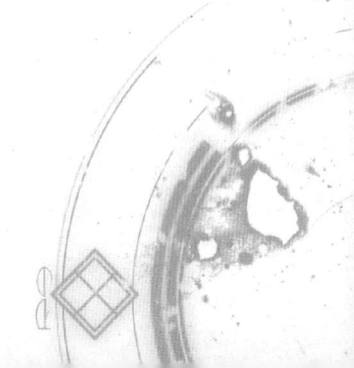

Afterword

To everyone who picked up this book, thank you very much, and to those who have been with me since Volume 1, it's a pleasure to see you again. Kanata Yanagino here.

Four months after the first volume, I've been fortunate enough to be able to publish a second. It's thanks to all of you who pick up my books. Thank you very much.

The text of this second volume is a revised version of what I posted on *Shousetsuka ni Narou* one year ago. In fact, I am finishing my revisions as I write this.

Looking back on myself a year ago, I remember that I was terribly agitated, confused, and frightened. The reason was obvious: it was because my environment was changing so drastically.

The parts corresponding to Volume 1, which I had posted as practice, became the subject of some discussion. I became listed in the site's ranking tables. More and more people started posting their impressions. There was even talk of turning it into a book. The practice work which I simply assumed that people wouldn't take to was treated to a reception far greater than I'd ever been expecting. I was both thrilled and shocked.

Because it was so popular, feelings of self-doubt and a fear of disappointing people welled up in my heart. Would I be able to continue writing stories of similar quality? I had to choose whether to go ahead with the book idea, not go ahead with it, or put the idea

Afterword

on hold; I also had to consider how I could balance it with my current job. I couldn't even have imagined these kinds of worries back when I was writing Volume 1 and overreacting to every little comment.

Of course, at the time, I didn't have the right mentality to deal with a situation like that. I was overthinking everything and getting excited and depressed over the smallest things. Looking back, I'm now aware that I was pretty difficult to deal with.

I am very grateful for my creative associates, who were so patient with me during that period. They lent an ear to my confused and incoherent rambling. They gave me advice on my drafts. They took part in our usual random chats. And above all, they showed me their own works, always created at their own pace. All of us chatting night after night about each other's works was a pleasure with no substitute. By looking at what my friends' creations were like, I was able to continue typing away at my keyboard, even though I still felt very unconfident. This story, which started from a small idea, continues today thanks to the passion and enthusiasm I was able to borrow from them. For that, I am still truly grateful.

However, despite this, my writing was pretty rough due to the psychological state I was in. After I decided to revise the story for publication and looked back over it, I found something I thought I could have done a little better on everywhere I looked, and I had a real headache thinking about how to fix everything and fit it into a single volume. What to leave and in what form, how to change things, how to include new elements… Remaking something once it's already finished is quite difficult. Unlike Volume 1, which came out very well in that sense, the second volume was a real struggle. I did everything in my power to improve it, and now, it's like a completely new work. I sincerely hope you enjoyed it.

Finally, some acknowledgments.

To Kususaga Rin-sensei, who added marvelous illustrations to this book: Thank you, thank you, thank you. I jump for joy every time I lay eyes on one of your beautiful illustrations.

To my fellow creators: I said enough, no more, too embarrassing. Thank you, please keep on being my friends.

To my editor, the editors at Overlap, everyone involved with this book's printing, sales and marketing, and everything else related, and to you, the person who took this book into your hands: I thank you from the bottom of my heart.

The next volume will either be *The Lord of the Rust Mountains*, a journey of adventure about the extermination of an evil dragon, which enjoyed the same kind of good reviews as *The Boy in the City of the Dead* when I published it on the web—or it will be a newly written tale of adventure which I will create specifically for book publication.

Either way, I will do my best to make it something you will all enjoy.

I hope you will read it when the time comes.

Praying that we can meet again,

Kanata Yanagino, June 2016

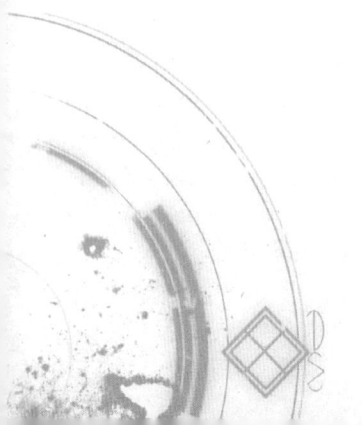

Bonus Interview with Kanata Yanagino

We asked the author your questions and a few of our own!

Q. If you were to be reborn and could only train with Gus, Mary, or Blood, who would you choose?

This question got me thinking... and the next thing I knew, ten whole minutes had passed!

I spent a long while going back and forth between the three of them, thinking things like:

If I was going to be living in a dangerous world of fantasy, surely it would have to be Blood...

Ah, but wait, knowledge is important too, and my intellectual curiosity would be satisfied as well if I went with Gus... But training with either of those two seems like it would be really hard, so maybe Mary...

However, in the end, I think my answer is Blood, because I have a lot of admiration for strong and brave warriors of fantasy like Conan the Barbarian.

I'm extremely far removed from those muscular warriors, but if I were reborn, I think I'd like to try becoming someone like that.

Who would you like to train with?

The Faraway Paladin Volume 2: The Archer of Beast Woods

Q. Which race in *The Faraway Paladin* are you most interested to write about? Are there any plans for entirely unique, never-before-seen races for the fantasy genre? I feel like the genre is in a bit of a rut for racial creativity intrinsic to the fantasy genre. Also, will any character ever be as great as Meneldor!? You've set a super high standard with him!

I like dwarves.

Brawny arms! Thick chests! Bushy beards and bright smiles! Warriors of the mountains, skilled at smithing! And I wrote the heck out of them in Volume 3. I feel very satisfied right now.

I don't have any plans to depict races of my own creation at the moment, but it is something I'd like to try my hand at one day, as long as I'm writing fantasy novels.

The great creations of hobbits, elves, and dwarves left to us by Professor J.R.R. Tolkien are very easy to use, but I think it's important to "fly the nest."

And thank you very much; Meneldor is a character I'm very fond of as well.

I may have set the bar high, but I will jump it, just watch me!

Q. There seems to be a great deal of devotion in this book. Are you spiritually minded or is that part of the characters' motivations strictly fiction?

When I was younger, there was a period when I had a strong interest in spirituality and the teachings of traditional religions.

During that time, I read all kinds of books relating to gods and Buddha, and experienced meditation for myself a number of times.

So the depictions of spirituality and devotion in the book are not strictly fiction, but based on a small amount of actual experience. The things Blood talked about regarding fighting, too, contain some elements of martial arts that I studied a long time ago.

Of course, not everything in there about devotion and martial arts comes from real experience, but knowing even a little about a subject makes it that much easier to write about.

Q. How many hours a day do you write? About how long does it take to finish a volume?

Writing novels is a side job which I have to balance with my main job, so there are some days when I don't write at all and others when I write an awful lot.

As a rough estimate, I'd say about three hours per day. The story itself, I'm constantly thinking about whenever I have a free moment.

The time I spend writing is many times shorter than the time I spend every day dreaming up the story. I bring it to life in my head, and turn it into writing as a finishing touch.

When my imagination is working well, the writing flows easily... and when it isn't, it can be hell!

It takes two to three months in the best case for me to finish up a volume, and sometimes longer.

Some people are fast at this, and those people can be *really* fast. I'm a little envious of them.

Q. If you found yourself transported to the world of *Faraway Paladin*, to which deity would you pledge loyalty and why?

The Earth-Mother Mater, I think. She seems like the god who would show the most compassion to an unfortunate soul thrown into another world!

THE FARAWAY PALADIN

The Lord of Rust Mountains (Primus)

NOVEL HARDBACK 3 ON SALE MAY 2022

Kanata Yanagino
Illustrations by: Kususaga Rin

MANGA OMNIBUS 2 ON SALE NOW

THE FARAWAY PALADIN II

Manga: **MUTSUMI OKUBASHI**
Original Work: **KANATA YANAGINO**
Character Design: **KUSUSAGA RIN**

fifth
5

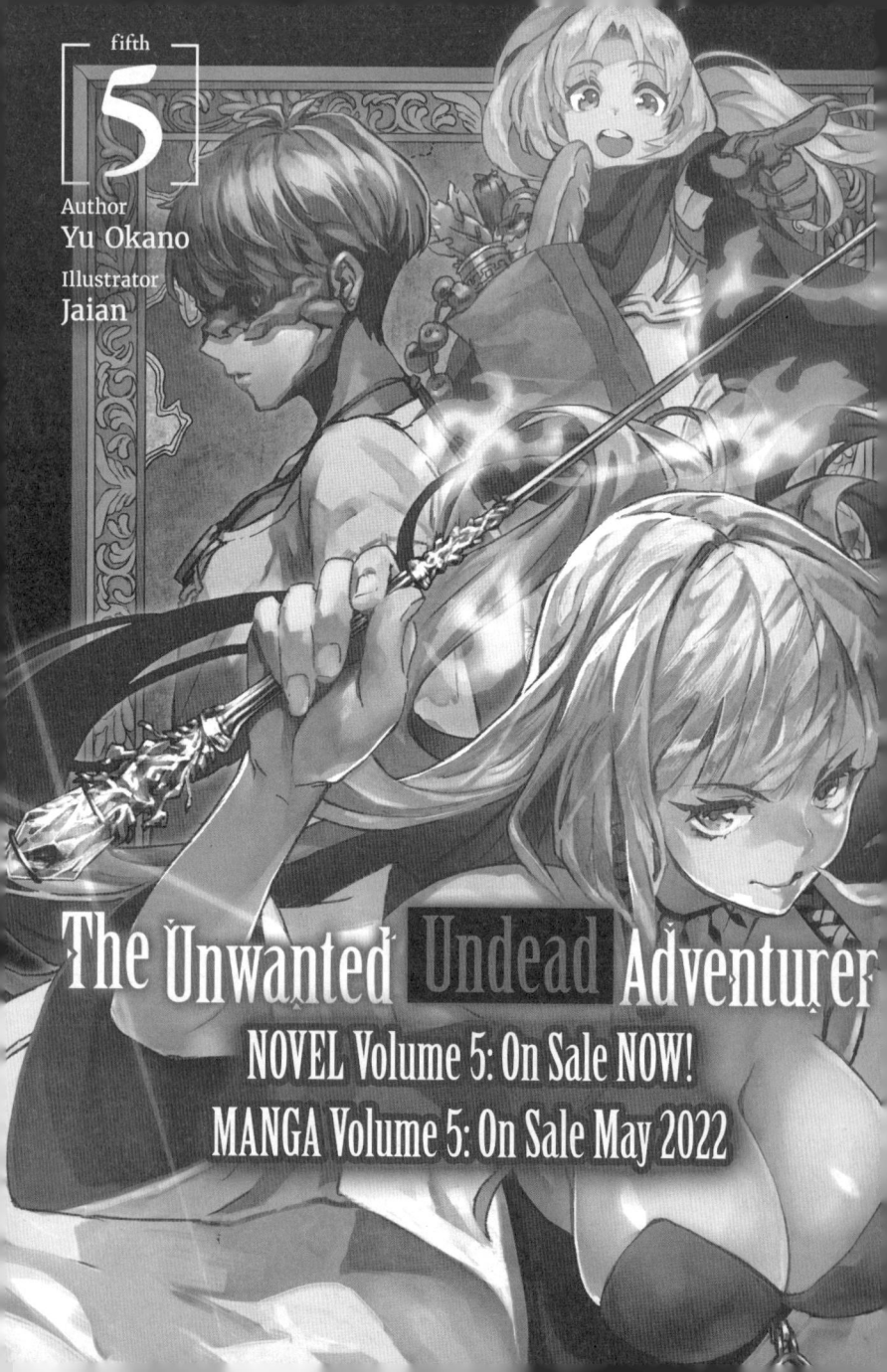

Author
Yu Okano

Illustrator
Jaian

The Unwanted Undead Adventurer
NOVEL Volume 5: On Sale NOW!
MANGA Volume 5: On Sale May 2022

Yuri Kitayama
Ilustrator • Riv

OMNIBUS 5
ON SALE NOW!

Seirei Gensouki:
Spirit Chronicles

SLAYERS
COLLECTOR'S EDITION 2
ON SALE NOW!
BY HAJIME KANZAKA
ILLUSTRATIONS BY RUI ARAIZUMI

ASCENDANCE OF A BOOKWORM

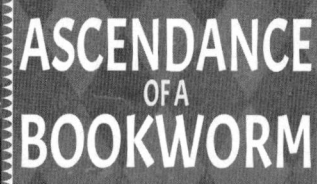

I'll do anything to become a librarian!

Part 3 **Adopted Daughter of an Archduke Vol. 5**

Author: **Miya Kazuki**
Illustrator: **You Shiina**

NOVEL:
PART 3 VOL. 5
ON SALE MAY 2022!

MANGA:
PART 2 VOL. 2
ON SALE NOW!

JOHN SINCLAIR

DEMON HUNTER

THE EUROHORROR LEGEND RETURNS!
AVAILABLE FROM ALL MAJOR
EBOOK STORES!

AUTHOR: JASON DA
COVER ART: NAMCOO

HEY////////
▶ HAVE YOU HEARD OF
J-Novel Club?

It's the digital publishing company that brings you the latest novels and manga from Japan!

Subscribe today at

▶▶▶**j-novel.club**◀◀◀

and read the latest volumes as they're translated, or become a premium member to get a *FREE* ebook every month!

═══ Check Out The Latest Volume Of ═══

The Faraway Paladin

Plus Our Other Hit Series Like:

- Ascendance of a Bookworm
- The Magic in this Other World is Too Far Behind!
- I Shall Survive Using Potions!
- Slayers
- Black Summoner
- Record of Wortenia War
- Seirei Gensouki: Spirit Chronicles

   ...and many more!

- Reborn to Master the Blade: From Hero-King to Extraordinary Squire ♀
- The Unwanted Undead Adventurer
- Marginal Operation
- How a Realist Hero Rebuilt the Kingdom
- Der Werwolf: The Annals of Veight
- An Archdemon's Dilemma: How to Love Your Elf Bride

In Another World With My Smartphone, Illustration © Eiji Usatsuka   *Arifureta: From Commonplace to World's Strongest*, Illustration © Takayaki

J-Novel Club Lineup

Latest Ebook Releases Series List

Altina the Sword Princess
Amagi Brilliant Park
Animeta!**
The Apothecary Diaries
An Archdemon's Dilemma: How to Love Your Elf Bride*
Are You Okay With a Slightly Older Girlfriend?
Arifureta: From Commonplace to World's Strongest
Arifureta Zero
Ascendance of a Bookworm*
Banner of the Stars
Bibliophile Princess*
Black Summoner*
The Bloodline
By the Grace of the Gods
Campfire Cooking in Another World with My Absurd Skill*
Can Someone Please Explain What's Going On?!
Chillin' in Another World with Level 2 Super Cheat Powers
The Combat Baker and Automaton Waitress
Cooking with Wild Game*
Culinary Chronicles of the Court Flower
Dahlia in Bloom: Crafting a Fresh Start with Magical Tools
Deathbound Duke's Daughter
Demon Lord, Retry!*
Der Werwolf: The Annals of Veight*
Dragon Daddy Diaries: A Girl Grows to Greatness
Dungeon Busters
The Emperor's Lady-in-Waiting Is Wanted as a Bride*
Endo and Kobayashi Live! The Latest on Tsundere Villainess Lieselotte
The Faraway Paladin*
Full Metal Panic!
Full Clearing Another World under a Goddess with Zero Believers*
Fushi no Kami: Rebuilding Civilization Starts With a Village
Goodbye Otherworld, See You Tomorrow
The Great Cleric
The Greatest Magicmaster's Retirement Plan

Girls Kingdom
Grimgar of Fantasy and Ash
Hell Mode
Her Majesty's Swarm
Holmes of Kyoto
How a Realist Hero Rebuilt the Kingdom*
How NOT to Summon a Demon Lord
I Shall Survive Using Potions!*
I'll Never Set Foot in That House Again!
The Ideal Sponger Life
If It's for My Daughter, I'd Even Defeat a Demon Lord
In Another World With My Smartphone
Infinite Dendrogram*
Invaders of the Rokujouma!?
Jessica Bannister
JK Haru is a Sex Worker in Another World
John Sinclair: Demon Hunter
A Late-Start Tamer's Laid-Back Life
Lazy Dungeon Master
A Lily Blooms in Another World
Maddrax
The Magic in this Other World is Too Far Behind!*
The Magician Who Rose From Failure
Mapping: The Trash-Tier Skill That Got Me Into a Top-Tier Party*
Marginal Operation**
The Master of Ragnarok & Blesser of Einherjar*
Min-Maxing My TRPG Build in Another World
Monster Tamer
My Daughter Left the Nest and Returned an S-Rank Adventurer
My Friend's Little Sister Has It In for Me!
My Instant Death Ability is So Overpowered, No One in This Other World Stands a Chance Against Me!*
My Next Life as a Villainess: All Routes Lead to Doom!
Otherside Picnic
Outbreak Company
Perry Rhodan NEO

Private Tutor to the Duke's Daughter
Reborn to Master the Blade: From Hero-King to Extraordinary Squire ♀*
Record of Wortenia War*
Reincarnated as the Piggy Duke: This Time I'm Gonna Tell Her How I Feel!
The Reincarnated Princess Spends Another Day Skipping Story Routes
Seirei Gensouki: Spirit Chronicles
Sexiled: My Sexist Party Leader Kicked Me Out, So I Teamed Up With a Mythical Sorceress!
She's the Cutest... But We're Just Friends!
The Sidekick Never Gets the Girl, Let Alone the Protag's Sister!
Slayers
The Sorcerer's Receptionist
Sorcerous Stabber Orphen*
Sweet Reincarnation**
The Tales of Marielle Clarac*
Tearmoon Empire
Teogonia
The Underdog of the Eight Great Tribes
The Unwanted Undead Adventurer*
Villainess: Reloaded! Blowing Away Bad Ends with Modern Weapons*
Welcome to Japan, Ms. Elf!*
The White Cat's Revenge as Plotted from the Dragon King's Lap
A Wild Last Boss Appeared!
The World's Least Interesting Master Swordsman

...and more!
* Novel and Manga Editions
** Manga Only
Keep an eye out at j-novel.club for further new title announcements!